A Fire Devours

Mason Origins Book Three

by

REX HOLLOWAY

ISBN: 979-8-9906572-7-4 (paperback)

979-8-9906572-6-7 (e-book)

Contents

Blow the trumpet in Zion,
And sound an alarm in My holy mountain!
Let all the inhabitants of the land tremble;
For the day of the Lord is coming,

For it is at hand:
A day of darkness and gloominess,
A day of clouds and thick darkness,
Like the morning clouds spread over the mountains.

A people come, great and strong,
The like of whom has never been;
Nor will there ever be any such after them,
Even for many successive generations.

A fire devours before them,
And behind them a flame burns;
The land is like the Garden of Eden before them,
And behind them a desolate wilderness;
Surely nothing shall escape them.

Joel 2:1–3 (NKJV)

1

Chapter 1 – El Huachicolero

December 2014
  Tequila, Jalisco, Mexico

The night breathed fire, even before the screams.

Heat clung to the valley like a wool blanket, and the dry wind carried with it the scent of burned sugarcane and diesel fumes. Crickets chirped from the edges of the agave fields. Somewhere farther up the slope, a lone coyote howled once, then fell silent.

Beneath the soot-black sky, rough men dug a pit.

Armed with shovels and flashlights, their shadows flickered across the field. Half-drunk on stolen tequila, they teased and joked with one another, their voices carrying roughly in the darkness. Five hundred meters away, at the edge of the field, lights shined from the porches and windows of small, one-story homes. The people who worked the agave plantations and tequila plants, called *fábricas*, had lived in those homes for generations. This land, with its rich volcanic soil, was the birthplace of the liquor that carried its name: Tequila. In the heart of Jalisco state, not far from Guadalajara, the famous town spread through the valley around them.

Agave plants marched in neat rows into the darkness, and dogs barked here and there, but no one bothered the men.

Working a shovel in the bottom of the hole, a dark-haired young man in his early twenties, thin but strong, clenched his teeth at the older men leaning on their shovels, slurring their Spanish as they joked and cursed.

There were several pickup trucks and one white van parked near the work site. A rotund man wearing boots, a clean Western button-up, and a bushy moustache ended a call on his mobile phone, then stormed towards the pit. His gut hung over his golden belt buckle, and more gold glittered from chains under his double chin. His name was Guadalupe Ortega, but everyone called him El Tambor—"The Barrel"—mainly because he was shaped like an oil drum, but also because oil theft was his specialty.

"¡No mamen, pinches cabrones! ¿Van a seguir cavando como tortugas pa' que nos quedemos aquí hasta que amanezca?" El Tambor barked. "Don't fuck around, you bastards! Are you gonna keep digging like turtles so we end up stuck here until sunrise?"

The young man put his head down and heaved a shovel-full of dirt from the hole.

The rocky, reddish earth resisted. The land was formed by a volcano, Volcán de Tequila, whose conical crown loomed over them. Dormant for over 200,000 years, the soil beneath their boots was rich in ash, brittle with stone, and jagged with old scars.

They had chosen a spot next to an abandoned, one-story block outbuilding to dig their hole, hoping the structure would block them somewhat from view.

El Tambor's truck sat next to the outbuilding, its cargo bed stacked with gear: coils of plastic pipe, a battery-powered pump, three plastic drums waiting to be filled with stolen crude, and a barrel of tequila stolen from an old fábrica in El Arenal. Beside the barrel, three of the older men passed a jar between them. Their teeth glinted in the torchlight. One of them laughed, sharp and fast, like a dog barking.

A fight had broken out earlier. Over a woman, or money. Maybe both. One man was still bleeding above his eye. No one cared. They'd come to steal oil from PEMEX, the state oil company, on behalf of the Jalisco cartel, and if they failed, they would all die.

The boy kept digging.

With a thud and a cloud of dust, an older man slid into the hole next to him and hacked at the rocky soil with a pick.

"Vas bien, m'ijo," the older man said. "You're doing good, my son."

"Gracias, papá," the younger man said back to his father.

Together, the two men chopped at the ground while the others cackled in the darkness.

"¡Más profundo!" El Tambor shouted. "Deeper!"

They were close now.

The young man's shovel struck something metallic and hollow.

He dropped to his knees and brushed away the dirt. The pipeline was steel, coated with black enamel, and humming faintly with pressure. Running west, parallel to Federal Highway 15, all the way from Guadalajara to the Pacific ports.

"Here!" he called out.

The other men swarmed around. The drunk ones stumbled, while the sober ones crouched. They lowered a man into the hole with a makeshift drill rig, and he started boring into the pipe's skin while the others fitted the hose and pump assembly. As the man drilled, a smell rose.

Sulfur, as thick as rot.

But there was another—a sweet solvent smell, like gasoline or paint thinner.

"Huele mal... no es crudo," one of the older men muttered.

Still, the men continued drilling. There wasn't a constant stream of product through the pipe. Rather, it was sent in batches. The cartel had men inside PEMEX who provided the schedule of runs so they could tap the line when it was empty.

But there were always risks. Combustible fumes lingered in the pipes. Some contained poisonous H_2S gas.

But the most dangerous of all were the pipelines that carried natural gas and condensates. These lighter, more volatile hydrocarbons could be ignited by a single spark, causing massive explosions.

Many had died doing this work.

"Pull us up!" the boy's father insisted, holding up a dirty hand.

Men grabbed their hands and pulled the two men from the hole, their dry callouses like rough stone against the boy's skin. One patted him on the back as he walked away, panting from exertion. He wiped his hands on his jeans as he walked in search of water. He ripped a plastic bottle from a case in the bed of the truck, then wandered over to the outbuilding. There, he leaned against the wall and drank, watching the other men tap the pipeline.

After a moment, his father walked over with a bottled water of his own, slapped his dirty cowboy hat against his leg, and wiped his brow.

"These idiots only know how to drink tequila and steal oil," the older man said in Spanish as he took a long drink. Dirt was caked around his fingernails and in the wrinkles under his eyes.

"At least they're good at doing both," the younger man agreed.

The older man laughed.

"It's the devil's work, Octavio," the older man said. "One a father should not involve his son with."

The boy, Octavio, spit between his worn boots.

"Sometimes, the devil doesn't give you a choice," he said. "And in that case, Jesus forgives us. That's what mama says."

His father cracked a smile.

"Your mama would know," he said. "She knows the Bible. Me, I only know digging."

"And taking care of your family," Octavio protested.

"Yes, I suppose so," his father replied. "Perhaps, Jesus will forgive me for getting you involved."

They both stood in silence for a while, drinking water and catching their breath in the moonlight.

The whine of a power drill and the hushed voices of the other men carried up from the hole. They were just one of numerous crews around Jalisco tapping pipelines. Drug routes weren't enough anymore. Not for men like this. Oil theft had turned into a multi-billion-dollar industry.

This part of the job, the digging and tapping, Octavio could stomach.

It was the next part he could not.

Once the tap was set, the gang helped the last man from the hole. They strolled towards El Tambor's truck and the stolen barrel of tequila, laughing and teasing each other as they walked.

El Tambor whistled and waved at the white van.

Octavio's father spit in the dirt.

"Feeding your family is one thing," he said. "But this...."

His father made the sign of the cross, and Octavio followed his lead.

"Why do they do this?" he asked.

His father sighed.

"Eh," his father responded. "PEMEX sends workers to find the taps and repair them. It only takes them a day or two. The cartel figured out if they leave them a present in the hole, the PEMEX workers are not so eager to dig up the taps and repair them. It buys them time."

With that, the van's front doors opened, and two men wearing baseball caps over black ski masks exited. They wore black tactical vests over t-shirts and jeans, and each carried an AR-15 rifle with rail-mounted sights. One man had a large hunting knife in a sheath on his belt.

They walked to the back of the van, opened the doors, and reached inside.

There was no wind that night to carry away the fumes, and a stench filled the air—

Sulfur.

Sulfur and the sound of whimpering and pleading.

The sicarios pulled two men from the rear of the van. Both had duct tape over their eyes and mouths, and their hands and feet were bound with zip ties. As they dragged them out, the prisoners whined through their gags.

They were forced to kneel in the dust. One masked man held the first prisoner by the shoulder while the other used his hunting knife to cut the zip tie between his ankles.

The sicarios then lifted him up by the arms and half-dragged, half-marched him toward the pit. After a few steps, the prisoner's feet faltered, and his wordless pleads grew louder. One of the hitmen struck him in the face with his rifle butt, and he immediately went silent. His head hung down, and a rope of bloody spit drooled from his mouth.

The masked men dragged the bound man to the edge of the hole where they laid him face down. One man put a foot on his back while the other returned to the truck to retrieve the second prisoner.

Octavio decided he'd seen enough, so he walked around the outbuilding's corner, out of sight of the hole. There he slid down the block wall and sat in the dirt. He could hear the workers arguing around the tequila barrel, and El Tambor shouting into his phone again.

But over it all, he could hear the pleadings of the prisoners.

The young man stared into the distance at the silent silhouette of Volcán de Tequila and wondered if his ancestors, *los Luzcanos*, had ever sacrificed people by throwing them in the volcano, or if that was just Hollywood.

The sicario marched the second prisoner unceremoniously to the pit, drew his hunting knife, yanked the prisoner's head back by the hair, and with a sawing motion, sliced his throat to the bone.

Blood erupted like a waterfall and poured down the condemned man's shirt. The sicario shoved him, sending the dying man twisting into the pit. Octavio heard the hollow, meaty smack of his body as it landed on the steel pipeline.

Next, the cartel henchmen dragged the first prisoner up from the dirt.

As they wrestled him to his feet, a breeze finally picked up.

The smell of paint thinner had increased.

What if when they threw the body in, they knocked the tap loose? What if the pipe was open now? What if the solvent smell is condensate and not crude?

Thoughts raced through Octavio's mind.

At the last moment, the condemned prisoner decided to fight. He shouldered one guard hard, then flailed and thrashed, trying to free himself. The sicarios yelled at him to stop fighting and grabbed at him. Frustrated, one of the masked killers took the man by the arm and spun him off his feet, flinging him into the hole.

In the scuffle, the prisoner's tape slipped from his mouth, and Octavio heard him beg for mercy from the bottom of the pit.

The stench of flammable fumes filled the air, and, for a split second, Octavio saw what was to come.

He heard one of the sicarios rack his rifle.

"*¡Muerte, pinche rata!*" the gunmen growled. "Die, you fucking rat!"

El Tambor's voice rang out.

"*No, todavía no!*" he yelled.

Too late.

Octavio looked to his father.

"Papa!" he shouted.

His father looked back, confused.

At that moment, the sicarios squeezed their triggers, unloading a barrage of rounds into the prisoners at the bottom of the pit, hot steel raining down like brimstone from above. The bright orange flashes of their muzzles sent bursts of flame into the hole—precisely where the fumes were most concentrated.

The resulting blast didn't sound like a firecracker or a gunshot.

It sounded like a volcano detonating. It sounded like the earth coming to an end.

Time slowed.

Then came the heat, and the pressure, and the sound all at once.

The earth split open and erupted. A white-hot concussive roar folded the air in on itself, then blasted it out into the starry sky above.

A geyser of fire erupted from the borehole, throwing two men fifty feet into the air. El Tambor's F150 lifted off the ground, flipped, the stolen tequila evaporating in an instant. The agave field was flattened for hundreds of feet, crops igniting in rows, flames running like cavalry, wild and broken.

Even behind the relative safety of the block wall, Octavio was thrown as the ground reverberated like a trampoline, his ears filled with dust and blood.

He couldn't move, couldn't hear, couldn't breathe.

The only thing that registered was heat. Not on his skin, inside of him. In his lungs. In his teeth. In his bones.

He lost consciousness, then suddenly jerked back awake.

The world was on fire.

The ridgeline to the east had collapsed. Boulders were flung in all directions. The air shimmered with chemical vapor. The ruptured pipeline was now a horizontal volcano. Flame ran underground, a snake of destruction exploding out from the epicenter.

He saw bodies scattered, some whole, most not. One man still clutched a broken bottle, half his torso missing. Another burned silently, curled like a fetus beside a melted toolbox.

Octavio forced himself up.

His shirt was scorched, his hands raw, and the skin on his face felt cooked and blistered.

He turned in a slow circle.

Behind him, through the heat haze, he saw the worker's village aflame.

Windows had blown inward. Roofs had peeled off and walls collapsed.

Liquid fire swept through the alleys and doorways as the flaming condensate spewed from the earth and flowed across the land. It climbed trees, leapt across fences, and torched homes like they were paper.

On shaky legs, Octavio staggered from behind the shattered outbuilding. There, in the light of the towering flames, he saw the body of his father charred and bubbling, his mouth peeled into a toothy grimace.

Octavio's face burned. Eyes streaming and ears ringing, he stumbled away from the flame-spewing crater and staggered toward the village—toward the screams.

As he approached the homes, fires roaring around him, he saw a man crawl from a charred doorway. He opened his mouth to scream, but his jaw hung loose, and all that came out was terrified gurgling. A dog ran past trailing smoke from its singed fur. A man ran down the dirt road, clothes burned away, skin blackened and sloughing away in strips.

The sky filled with smoke, thick with the stink of burning plastic, fuel, and flesh.

Above it all, Volcán de Tequila glowed red in the reflection.

Octavio crawled into a collapsed alley and curled behind a wall.

He didn't know how long he lay there. Minutes. Hours. His skin blistered and his fingernails bled. There, he blacked out, certain he would never wake again.

He was shaken awake by the rough handling of an EMT from Municipal

Servicios Médicos. She wore a surgical mask over her face, and her uniform blouse was covered in black ash. She grabbed him by the chin and waved a penlight in his eyes.

Octavio groaned.

"Hey! This one is alive," she called out. "Bring the stretcher."

He was in and out of consciousness as the medics loaded him onto a gurney and wheeled him quickly to the back of an ambulance. He looked over as they pushed him, at the smoking valley of ash and ruin they had caused.

The agave fields were gone. The *fábrica* was rubble. The village was cinders and bones. Here and there, white sheets covered dead bodies as firefighters fought the flames.

In the distance, the ruptured condensate pipeline they had mistakenly tapped hissed smoke from the chasm where the hand of *El Diablo* himself had reached up from the pits of hell to take his father's soul.

2

Chapter 2 – Rattlesnakes vs. Turtles

November 2025
 Rural Jalisco State, Mexico

The dry desert air smelled like copper and sage. Even at night, the dust clung to Pierce's throat.

He held up a fist, and the squad of CIA tactical operators behind him froze.

They were ghosts in the cacti. Five men in desert camouflage, panoramic night vision goggles over their eyes, suppressed SIG Sauer M7 rifles chambered in 6.8x51mm to their shoulders, drifting like smoke in the moonlight.

Around them, nopal pads leaned out of rocks like green rafts, their purple tunas split open by birds. Farther upslope, tall pitaya columns reached for the moon, thin and ribbed, standing in clusters like watchmen.

"Target's fifty meters," came an operator's voice low in Pierce's earpiece. "Drone thermal shows three targets on perimeter."

Pierce scanned the adobe compound ahead through his night vision. Tall stucco walls with a rusty steel gate surrounded a courtyard strung with incandescent string lights, their orange glow casting harsh shadows. Inside the wall stood a brown two-story hacienda of brick and stucco with a chipped tile roof patched with sheets of corrugated tin. The property was aging and rundown, and the yard around it was filled with junked cars. At first, it looked like any number of farms in the area. But on the far side of the courtyard, parked side-by-side, sat four homemade armored vehicles—hulking pickup trucks with reinforced grills, steel plates welded across the windows, and gun ports cut into the sides. Locals called them *tortugas*—turtles—cartel war wagons built for street battles and ambushes.

This hacienda wasn't a clandestine drug lab or stash house. It was a motor pool, a repair and staging facility for Jalisco cartel armor.

Pierce raised his hand and pointed. Two of his men peeled off, moving in silence through the shadows toward the vehicles. Each operator carried a pair of thermite grenades. They ducked behind a stone wall, pulled the pins, and trotted silently down the row of vehicles, placing a grenade on each tank's hood, directly over the engine blocks.

Within seconds, orange and red sparks hissed from the incendiaries, and soon the metal beneath them glowed red. The men dashed into the shadows, then slipped back into formation.

Pierce tapped his push-to-talk.

"Execute in three, two, one—"

With that, the team stood, rifles up, and quickly strode toward the compound.

Pierce took point.

At the wall, they stacked to the left of the rusty gate.

Under the Christmas lights, Pierce flipped his night vision goggles up. The others followed suit.

The breacher came up from the rear and planted a charge the size of a beer can on the gate's lock.

"Breach, breach, breach!" he called out.

THUMP!

With a flash, a clap, and a puff of smoke, the gate popped inward, and the five-man team slithered in like a serpent.

Instantly, their suppressors whispered death.

The first cartel soldier Pierce saw dropped in the courtyard as a tight group of .277 Fury rounds destroyed his heart and lungs.

Another raised his rifle but never fired, collapsing in a heap of bloody limbs as more suppressed rifles cracked.

A third came running from a side door.

POP! POP!

Two in the head sent him sliding to a halt.

They crossed the courtyard fast, rubber-soled boots silent over the tile. The faint thrum of Mexican music and a generator filled the air.

The hacienda's front door was heavy oak.

"Stack left," Pierce growled.

He knocked his gloved fist twice against his FAST helmet, a signal for the breacher to come forward again. The operator slid in front of him with a short-barreled shotgun. He jammed the muzzle into the door where the deadbolt sat. A single blast blew the lock, and the team surged in.

Inside, a bodyguard crouched in the open with an AK-47 rifle. Vega dropped him with two rounds to the chest.

Someone upstairs shouted in panicked Spanish, then a burst of full-auto fire sprayed from the balcony above, shredding the couches below in a burst of feathers.

The operators barely flinched.

"Frag out!" an operator yelled as he lobbed an M67 fragmentation grenade onto the balcony.

The explosion sent the gunmen flipping over the railing and crashing to the floor below where the squad finished him with a burst of fire.

The team swept the first floor.

"Clear!" someone yelled.

"Found the door to the lower deck, over," came over the radio.

"Rattlesnake 3 and 4, clear the lower deck. The rest on me, main deck, living room," Pierce sent back.

Two operators clicked on their weapon lights and proceeded down the narrow stairway into the basement, while Pierce and two others stormed up the stairs to the second floor.

The upstairs hall was narrow, wood-paneled, and decorated with paintings of Jesus Malverde, the patron saint of narcotics traffickers. The air reeked of cigar smoke and mold.

Pierce edged down the hallway, rifle at the ready. There were two doors on either side of the hall. The three commandos lined up on the left door.

Pierce kicked it open.

The room was set up as an office. A wooden desk held an Iridium satellite phone next to an AKMS rifle. There was a map of Mexico pinned to the wall with pipelines highlighted. A Getac X600—a ruggedized, military-grade laptop—sat atop a pile of papers.

"Grab the map and the phone," Pierce ordered, pointing.

An operator yanked the map from the wall, then stuffed it and the satphone into his assault pack while Pierce powered down the laptop, closed it, and shoved it into his own pack. As he zipped his bag, he noticed an unusual paper on the desk.

A handwritten note with unusual lettering.

Not Spanish.

He lifted the paper between his gloved fingers and looked closer.

Persian.

He folded the paper and slid it into his plate carrier.

"Rattlesnake One, this is Rattlesnake 3," a voice said over comms. "Lower deck is secure. Eye-in-the-sky reports no further heat signatures. One prisoner secured. Adult male. Cuffed and ambulatory. Over."

"Copy," Pierce radioed back. "Secure the perimeter. Prepare the prisoner for exfil. We're out in 5."

He moved to a file drawer and yanked it open. Inside there were more documents: packing slips, schematics, printed reports. Some of them were stamped with unfamiliar seals. He flipped through them. Spanish, English, and again, Persian. Some pages bore diagrams of pipelines. Others featured satellite imagery.

A photo caught his eye.

It was black and white, blurry.

A gaping hole in a desert lined with twisted girders, shattered concrete, and scorched earth like the gaping mouth and rotten teeth of a massive horror creature.

Scrawled across the bottom in Persian script was a single word. He didn't know what it said, but it didn't matter. He recognized the bomb site.

He slid the photo into a sealed pouch and zipped it tight.

Footsteps approached. An operator entered the room, rifle at low ready. "One detainee in the cellar. Claims to be a cartel logistics guy. Says all they do here is steal oil. No drugs. No hostages."

"Did you ask him about foreigners?" Pierce asked.

"Yeah. Unknown foreign nationals he called *'los musulmanes'*—the Muslims. He said they were here a few days ago."

Pierce's jaw tightened.

"I found documents in Persian."

"Damn. Langley was right then. Iranians. But why's Iran stealing oil in Mexico? Don't they have enough in Iran?" the operator asked.

Pierce turned, studying the room, but his mind lingered on the photo he'd pocketed of the bombed-out facility.

"Revenge, maybe" he muttered.

"For what?"

But before he could answer, a call came over the radio.

"Boss, eye-in-the-sky reports three vehicles approaching our location from the northeast. At least one appears armored."

Pierce stepped to a window. He saw headlights approaching in the distance.

"Everyone, out. Rally in the courtyard," Pierce radioed.

They dashed from the office with the captured intel and sprinted down the corridor.

Pierce rushed to the courtyard where the other operators waited with the zip-tied prisoner, a black bag over his head.

Behind them, flames from the thermite grenades danced in the shadows as the sabotaged turtles smoked and popped.

"Contact, contact," Pierce called out. "Turtle coming up. Two other technicals with it."

The breacher shoved the prisoner flat on the tile floor, stuck a boot in the middle of his back, then poked his rifle through a gap in the courtyard wall.

"*Quieto, cabrón,*" he said. "Hold still, asshole."

Pierce took a position at the wall, then paused to listen.

Outside the stone partition, a heavy engine growled. Tires crunched gravel, and men's voices shouted in Spanish.

"Rattlesnake to command. Request Hellfire on advancing hostile column. Grid 9-Bravo-Golf-2-1-7. Say again, Hellfire on the turtle."

"Copy Rattlesnake. Predator is five minutes out. Hold tight."

"Shit," Pierce muttered.

And then—

ZING!

A round whizzed past his face.

"Contact front!" Pierce shouted. "Send it!"

The gunfight started with a trickle—a few shots whining overhead—then quickly built to a roar as rounds impacted the stone walls around them.

With that, the elite team of CIA Ground Branch operators went to work.

Fanned out along the wall, each man found cover and quickly selected targets using their night vision sites.

Rifles snapped in controlled bursts. Brass rang against stone.

One operator, viewing the attacking convoy through his night vision sight, saw two silhouettes with rifles moving through the brush. He dropped one then the next in rapid succession.

"Dismounts flanking right and left!" he called out.

The cartel sicarios exited their pickups and spread out as infantry support. Pierce scanned the scene ahead, counting at least ten men maneuvering in the dark. The rocky, uneven ground provided just enough cover for them to leapfrog effectively toward the hacienda.

Pierce gritted his teeth and slammed a fresh magazine home.

Suddenly, the wall ten feet from him exploded inwards as he heard the unmistakable *thud-thud-thud* of a heavy machine gun.

"Turtle has a Fifty-Cal!" someone shouted.

Pierce knew the M2 would chew the hacienda's wall to dust in moments.

"Where is that drone?" he yelled.

An operator kneeling behind a boulder and sighting through a gap in the wall, barely broke his rhythmic firing as he radioed for an update.

"Four minutes!" he yelled.

"Four minutes to Hellfire!" Pierce yelled.

Just then, a grenade bounced across the tile and detonated five feet from an operator. He went down, groaning.

"Medic!" he yelled.

Their medic dove into action, slinging his rifle and pulling the wounded man by the drag handle on his vest behind a set of concrete steps.

"Where are you hit?" he asked as he searched the man for blood.

"Leg!" he groaned through clenched teeth. "Left fucking thigh!"

Blood gushed from a ragged shrapnel hole in his pants. The medic cut the fabric open with a pair of sheers.

Back at the wall, Pierce crouched lower and covered his sector with accurate fire.

Suddenly, from the left came the high speed thumping of rotor blades.

An MH-6 Little Bird helicopter flown by the 160th Special Operations Aviation Regiment (SOAR) known as the "Night Stalkers" swept down like a roaring dragon, its door gunner lighting up the night sky with 3,000 round-per-minute from a minigun. Cartel foot soldiers collapsed in showers of sand and blood while others dove for cover.

Rounds peppered a truck causing it to swerve and crash into a ditch.

Pierce cheered silently, but still, the turtle rolled forward. Its reinforced grill and bulletproof hide protected the operators inside. Muzzles flashed from firing ports while the turret-mounted Fifty-Cal blasted, the weapon's operator directing fire with cameras and a joystick while sitting safely inside.

"Pop smoke," Pierce yelled, hoping to deploy a visual barrier between his men and the gun operator's camera lens. Men hurled smoke grenades over the courtyard wall towards the advancing tank.

"Predator status?" Pierce yelled again.

"Two minutes," the comms operator yelled back.

Pierce gritted his teeth, reloaded, and directed his fire at the gun ports, hoping to get lucky.

But the turtle kept coming.

The Fifty-Cal, blinded by the smoke, fired randomly, sending rounds high and wide.

He glanced back at the medic and saw him working feverishly with trauma pads and a RAPID tourniquet to stop the wounded man's bleeding.

The Little Bird swept back in, hammering the flanking trucks and dismounts while Pierce's men held their ground, bloodied but fighting, as the enemy tank bore down.

Rounds impacted and whizzed all around Pierce. He slammed his last magazine into his rifle, smacked the bolt release, gritted his teeth, and took aim.

Just then, a man in jeans and a T-shirt leapt out into the open twenty-feet from Pierce and opened fire with an AK-47.

Caught off guard, Pierce ducked back as rock chips peppered him and bullets ricocheted nearby.

"Shit!"

His rifle empty, Pierce dropped to a knee, drew his pistol, and quickly peeked out.

He caught the man trying to close the distance and put a tight group of hollow points in his chest, sending the man crumpling to the dirt.

More rounds impacted near the window.

Pierce leaned back and looked around as he popped a fresh magazine into his Glock 19.

His last one.

"Enemy in the open!" came the yell.

Two more sicarios tried to dash across the yard but his men cut them down.

"Black on ammo!" someone yelled.

The tank bore down on them as their ammunition ran out.

Pierce opened his mouth to order his men to fall back when suddenly—

"Hellfire inbound!" the comms operator yelled.

A streak of light flashed from high above followed by an earth-shaking boom. The turtle erupted in a fireball, flipped, and landed in a twisted burning carcass as the missile, fired from a Predator drone miles away, blew it apart.

"Yeah!" someone cheered. "*¡Toma, cabrones!*"

The Little Bird made tight circles over the destroyed convoy, finishing off stragglers with short bursts from its door gun.

Pierce keyed his comms.

"Rattlesnake to Exfil. Site secure. One wounded, one detainee, intel package in hand."

"Roger that," came the reply. "We're mopping up real quick. One more pass and we're ready to roll."

Pierce gave the courtyard one last sweep, then called his troops to head out.

A minute later, the sound of more rotors filled the valley. He watched a second Little Bird descend to the earth just outside the compound, landing as nimbly as a dragonfly.

Pierce waved, and his team moved to board the chopper. They shoved the prisoner roughly before as they helped the wounded man limp to the aircraft.

They climbed in, and as soon as the men positioned themselves in the doorways with their feet on the skids, the pilot ascended into the sky.

As Pierce's Rattlesnakes flew away, beneath them, the turtles burned.

The two Little Birds flew west for almost an hour to the coast of Mexico.

"Coastline abeam. Feet wet. Forty miles to Mother," the pilot transmitted as they continued out to sea.

The waters of the Northern Pacific were as black below as the night sky above. After a few minutes, Pierce saw the lights of "mother" below—a US Navy Littoral Combat Ship (LCS) anchored thirty nautical miles due west of Aticama, just outside Mexico's Territorial Waters.

"Mother, Raptor One, ten miles, inbound, feet wet. Request deck status and wind," the pilot radioed.

"Raptor One, this is LCS Corvus, deck status ready. Wind 230 at 12, deck angle stable. H-pad two. You are cleared inbound, advise fuel status," the ship's Combat Information Center Air Boss called back.

"Fuel state: 30 minutes. Request straight-in, will call final," the pilot replied.

As they approached the ship, Pierce saw the LCS's flight deck, a flat, dark slab of non-skid paint, pocked and salt-streaked, with a white landing circle and an H stenciled squarely in the center. Flood lamps cast bright light across the pad while the ship's wake churned beneath. The deck pitched with each ocean swell, and the Little Bird's skids dipped and rose as the pilot skillfully timed the touchdown.

As the bird settled, the downwash kicked up a cloud of brine that smelled like JP-5 fuel. Crewmen moved to secure the chopper to the deck as Pierce's men dismounted. As soon as boots hit the deck, a group of Navy corpsmen rushed to the helicopter with a gurney to take the wounded man away. They loaded him half-conscious onto the stretcher and quickly rolled him toward the sick bay.

Minutes later, Pierce stepped into a wardroom and closed the steel door behind himself. Still wearing his dusty plate carrier, the sleeves of his blouse dark with grime, he smelled of sweat and cordite. A few feet away, a large touch-screen table displayed a top-down sat image of the raid site. Heat blooms still registered from the burning turtles.

At the head of the room stood a man in civilian attire with a coffee mug and a face like carved granite. He had short-cropped hair, crow's feet, and no visible rank.

"Pierce," the man said without looking up.

"Sir."

"Sit."

Pierce slid into the metal chair across from the screen.

The man looked at him. "Your man?"

"Shrapnel in his leg. No major arteries hit. He'll make it."

The man gave a small nod.

"Debrief me."

"We hit the hacienda at 0200 local. Three tangos outside, three inside. All killed except the one prisoner we took in the basement. We secured the site and captured intel from the office upstairs, including this—"

He pulled a small pouch from his chest rig, unzipped it, and withdrew the letter and photo.

The commander took them between his fingers. His forehead wrinkled as he studied the photo intently.

"Recognize that?" Pierce asked.

"Jesus," his commander muttered.

The image was grainy and monochrome. A cratered compound ringed by scorched concrete and twisted steel. Beneath it, a single word in Persian script.

Pierce leaned forward. "That's Fordow, the Iranian nuclear facility we recently bombed."

The commander's eyes didn't leave the photo. "That is what it says."

"Positive. We studied every angle of that site when Iran buried it a decade ago. That's the centrifuge hall after we dropped bunker-busters on it."

The CIA officer laid the photo flat on the table and tapped the corner with his knuckle.

"You telling me cartel oil thieves had this photo in their possession?"

"Not just this," Pierce said. "They had a satphone, maps with pipeline schematics, shipping manifests—some in Persian—and a Getac laptop like I carried in Afghanistan."

"What about the detainee?" his commander asked.

"Claims to be a logistics guy. Says he just moves oil and equipment for the cartel, but when we pushed him about foreigners, he admitted there were some around. Muslims, he called them."

"Iranians?"

Pierce shook his head.

"Didn't say. Whoever they are, they're working side-by-side with the Jalisco cartel."

The commander leaned back, the ship creaking faintly around them.

"This isn't about stolen diesel, is it, sir?" Pierce asked.

The commander leaned in, resting both hands on the edge of the table.

"Maybe."

Pierce looked up.

"Langley suspected this might happen, am I right?"

The commander gave a humorless smile.

"Some junior analyst at Langley fed ten years of cartel data into an AI system. Trafficking routes. Comms intercepts. Banking transactions. The model came back with a prediction: if we push the cartels too hard, they'll call for backup. And not from each other. From hostile nation states."

Pierce raised an eyebrow.

"Like Iran."

"Like Iran," the commander agreed. "At first, folks thought it was nonsense. Too far-fetched. But the simulation kicked out a scenario with probabilities the brass couldn't ignore. So, they greenlit a sweep. NSA started pulling down comms, wire traffic, burner data, satellite chatter."

"And they found something," Pierce surmised.

The commander nodded.

"Encrypted chatter from cartel members talking to what looks like Iranian FIS assets."

Pierce shook his head.

"And so, the next move was to send Ground Branch to hit oil thieves in the middle of nowhere?"

The commander's eyes narrowed.

"That's where the intel led. The Jalisco cartel has many branches. The chatter with Iran all pointed to the oil theft branch. That's why they sent you in. To find proof."

Pierce looked at the scorched photo and the handwritten note one more time.

"Consider it delivered."

His commander grunted in agreement.

"Sir, respectfully, if Iran's helping Jalisco sabotage pipelines, smuggle weapons, or move radiologicals across the southern border, we need more than Little Birds."

"We're not there yet," the commander replied. "Langley's going to want this photo within the hour. The laptop's already on a bird to Panama. Your op just moved us up the chain."

Pierce exhaled.

"Copy that."

The commander stood.

"Get some rest. Your team rolls again tomorrow night."

Pierce nodded once, then rose.

As he stepped out into the corridor, the red lights of the LCS cast his shadow long across the bulkhead, like the silhouette of a cactus in a burning desert.

3

Chapter 3 – Family Man

Mason's home, Golden, Colorado, USA

The weight bar clanked in the quiet garage.

Travis D. Mason stood shirtless, forty-five-pound plates stacked on either side of a barbell, sweat slicking the carved muscle across his back and shoulders. The air smelled of rubber mats and cut grass. Morning sun streamed through the open garage door, catching on the power rack he'd bolted to the concrete floor.

He racked the bar after his final set of overhead press, veins standing out across his forearms, and peeled the plates off one by one. His brown hair stuck to his forehead, and his jaw darkened with gray-flecked stubble.

After draining a bottle of water, he rubbed Icy Hot into the old scar on his right bicep, the one the Canadian outlaw biker Rage had opened with a tomahawk years ago.

Some days the ache was dull. Some days it burned. Today wasn't the worst.

He tugged on a T-shirt, slung a tool belt around his waist, and stepped into the bright Colorado morning.

Inside their home, Lisa set their infant son Ryan gently into his playpen.

The baby shifted once, then settled, his attention caught by the soft shapes

24

hanging above him.

"You're okay," she said, brushing her hand lightly across his forehead.

She moved into the kitchen and turned on the faucet. Warm water filled the sink as she began stacking dishes.

She turned on music and sang along as she worked.

Through the window above the steaming sink, she could see the front yard and the street beyond.

Movement drew her attention.

Across the street, a dark pickup idled at the curb, while another vehicle, a black SUV, parked behind it. Men moved between them and the house, lifting heavy duffel bags from the vehicles and carrying them inside.

Lisa slowed, her hands still in the water.

The bags sagged under their weight as they were passed from one set of hands to another. The men spoke little, their movements well-coordinated.

Just then, one of them stepped back from the truck and looked up.

His gaze seemed to settle on her.

Lisa froze holding a plate beneath the water.

The man' watched her for a moment, then turned and carried another bag toward the house.

Lisa flinched as hot water scorched her finger, snapping her back.

"Ow!"

She waved her hand in pain.

Ryan made a small cry from the living room.

She walked over and rested her hand against his chest, feeling the soft, steady rise and fall of his breathing.

"It's OK," she soothed him. "Momma's OK."

Outside, a truck door shut with a muted thud.

"New neighbors," she told him. "That's what I get for being nosey."

Thirty minutes later, Mason was on a ladder in the backyard pounding nails into a new patio cover when a baby laughed behind him.

He looked over his shoulder.

Lisa stood at the sliding door in a white robe, burp cloth on one shoulder,

Ryan balanced on her hip. The baby waved his fists and kicked.

"You've got a fan," Lisa called.

Mason grinned.

"Just the one?"

"Don't get cocky."

She stepped out barefoot, smiling.

The backyard was clean and quiet. Fresh flower beds and new trees lined the neat space. Ponderosa and scrub oak lined the wooden privacy fence, and beyond that, the Rockies shimmered in the distance.

"The patio looks good," she said.

"I'll finish framing today," he said. "Put the roof on next weekend. Trying to get it done before it gets cold."

Lisa adjusted Ryan in her arms.

"Looks like someone's moving into the house across the street. The one that's been up for rent?"

Mason nodded.

"I saw some men moving in earlier," she noted.

"I just hope they're good people," he replied.

Lisa nodded while Ryan squealed and Bud lay panting in the sun.

The next morning, Mason, Lisa, and Ryan went to church.

Lisa wore a soft blue dress and a silver cross. Ryan wore a onesie while Mason, in a white shirt and black slacks, tied his hair back and slipped on his gold wedding band.

The church was new, all brick and glass, and nestled near the edge of town. Inside, families wrangled toddlers, retirees smiled behind coffee cups, and ushers in blazers handed out bulletins.

When service started, Lisa sang while Ryan clutched her necklace and yawned.

Mason stood rigidly, hands by his side. He didn't sing. He swept the exits, then the men in the pews, reading their posture, their hands, the tension in their shoulders.

It was habit.

When the music faded, the preacher stepped to the pulpit.

He looked the part, with silver hair, a dark sport coat, and cowboy boots under his slacks.

"Joel, Chapter Two," he said. "There's a line in there that stuck with me this week. It says: *'I will restore to you the years the locusts have eaten.'* That's God talking."

He paused, his hands on the podium.

"Most of us have lived through a few locust years. Things got taken from us. Sometimes because of what we did. Sometimes because of what we didn't. And sometimes just because the world's not fair."

He looked over the crowd.

"But there's a promise in that verse. Not just that God will forgive us. But that He'll *restore* us. Give back the time we thought was wasted. Redeem the years we lost."

He spoke a while, then stepped away. A soft *amen* rolled through the room.

Lisa leaned in.

"Baby's sock," she whispered.

Mason looked down, picked it up, and slid it back onto Ryan's foot.

The boy grinned.

Lisa touched his hand. Her eyes were soft.

Mason felt a warmth inside his chest he'd never known before.

After service, he buckled Ryan into the car seat and drove them home.

Lisa didn't speak until they were halfway there.

"Do you ever think about stepping back? At work?" she asked.

Mason glanced over.

She kept her eyes on the road ahead. "Not quitting. But not being, you know, the one out front all the time."

He didn't answer.

"You're a part-owner of Green Zone now," she said. "You've got a company. A team. Trainers, contractors, specialists. You don't *have* to be the one taking the jobs anymore."

He shifted in his seat. His arm ached.

Lisa looked at him. "I want you to be home more. For Ryan. For me. I want to grow old with you, not light candles for you."

Mason stared ahead.

The truck rumbled uphill.

"I hear you," he finally said.

He reached over and took her hand, squeezed it, and held it the rest of the way as they rode in silence.

Meanwhile, in Jalisco, at the scene of the motor pool raid, a sharply-dressed young man in his thirties stepped through the broken gate of the hacienda and stopped. He wore a lightweight gray suit over a crisp white shirt. His hair glistened with gel, his wrist glinted with a gold watch, and his Italian leather loafers gleamed in the afternoon sun. He looked fit and youthful, like a young stockbroker or executive, but the right side of his face was scarred, the skin twisted like a river of molten flesh under his Gucci sunglasses.

Like his face, the courtyard was burned and scarred.

Black scorch marks crawled up the stucco walls. The Christmas lights that had once hung across the yard now drooped in melted strands like dead vines. Pools of dark blood stained the tile. Flies buzzed over the bodies.

The turtles were finished.

One of the armored trucks lay upside-down in the dirt road outside the compound, its heavy steel plating peeled back like a tin can. The missile had blown the vehicle open like Jiffy Pop. Charred rubber still smoked from the tires.

More turtles sat slumped next to the courtyard, their engine blocks eaten through by thermite. Their hoods sagged inward where molten metal had burned straight into the cylinder heads.

Octavio stood quietly, hands clasped behind his back.

A group of Mexican Federal Police officers wandered the compound. Their dark uniforms were dusty and sweat-stained, rifles slung casually over their shoulders.

One of the investigators approached Octavio.

He was a narrow man with a trimmed mustache and mirrored sunglasses.

His badge hung openly from a chain around his neck.

"*Señor* Octavio," he said politely.

Octavio gave a slight nod.

"How many dead?" he asked.

"Twenty confirmed," the investigator replied. "Three inside the house. Two near the gate. The rest outside the walls."

Octavio looked toward the road.

The crater from the missile strike had turned the earth black. The twisted remains of the turtle still crackled as the metal cooled.

The man crouched and held something up between two fingers.

A brass cartridge case.

He handed it to Octavio.

Octavio turned it slowly in his fingers.

The casing was longer than a normal rifle round. Thick at the base. The brass still held faint heat from the sun.

Stamped on the bottom:

SIG SAUER — 6.8

Octavio exhaled slowly.

".277 Fury," he said.

The investigator looked surprised.

"You know it?"

Octavio nodded once.

"New American military rifle."

He rolled the casing in his palm.

"They are not sold in Mexico."

The investigator glanced toward the hacienda.

"The men inside were killed very cleanly," he said. "Most with two or three rounds. Chest or head."

Octavio studied the damage again.

Thermite burns in the engines.

Entry breach on the gate.

He looked toward the road again.

"The turtle was hit by a missile or bomb," the investigator said. "The neighbors heard helicopters and machine guns."

Octavio nodded and handed the cartridge casing back.

The investigator slid it into an evidence bag.

Octavio walked slowly across the courtyard.

The front door of the hacienda hung crooked on its hinges.

Inside, the house smelled of gunpowder.

Furniture was shredded. Feathers from ruined cushions floated in the sunlight pouring through the broken windows.

He stepped over a dead bodyguard and climbed the stairs.

The upstairs office door was open.

The room had been searched.

Drawers were pulled out. Papers were missing. The wall where the pipeline map had hung was bare.

Octavio studied the empty spot for a long moment.

Then he walked to the desk.

The laptop was gone. The satellite phone was gone.

He opened the desk drawer. Empty.

Octavio's expression hardened slightly.

"They took intel," he murmured.

Behind him, the investigator shifted his weight.

"What does it mean?"

Octavio turned toward the window.

Outside, smoke still drifted from the destroyed turtles.

"It means," Octavio said quietly, "that this was not the Mexican army. Not the police."

The investigator waited.

"This was special forces."

The investigator swallowed.

"Mexican?"

Octavio's brow furrowed.

"No."

He stepped past the man and walked toward the stairs.

Outside, a warm wind swept across the valley, carrying the smell of burning rubber.

His jet touched down in Zacatecas just after sunset that night.

From the window, Octavio watched the city lights spread across the hills like scattered embers. Church towers rose from the old colonial center, their stone facades glowing amber beneath the streetlamps.

Beautiful. Ancient. Untouched by the war that fed it.

An SUV waited on the runway when the plane stopped. Two bodyguards climbed out and opened the rear door without speaking.

Octavio stepped down from the jet.

The warm mountain air filled his nose as he walked toward a waiting Range Rover.

He slid into the back seat.

The SUV rolled away from the private airstrip and wound down the narrow mountain roads toward his neighborhood.

By the time they reached the house, the sky had gone fully dark.

The gate opened before they stopped.

Inside, courtyard lights glowed softly across the stone walls. Bougainvillea vines spilled down from the balcony in purple cascades.

Octavio stepped out of the SUV and dismissed the bodyguards with a wave.

Inside the house, the sound of children's laughter drifted from the kitchen.

He paused in the hallway.

For a moment, he listened.

Then he walked in.

His wife, Valeria, stood at the stove stirring a pot, her long dark hair tied loosely behind her neck. The kitchen smelled of garlic and simmering tomatoes.

Their two children sat at the table doing homework.

When Valeria saw him, her face softened.

"You're home."

Octavio stepped to her, leaned down, and kissed the top of her head.

The children jumped up from their chairs.

"*Papá!*"

He smiled as they hugged him, their small arms wrapping around his waist.

"How was school?" he asked.

They spoke at once, excited, telling him about teachers and friends and some argument over a soccer match.

Octavio listened, nodding.

For a few minutes, he let the noise wash over him.

Dinner was simple. Pasta. Bread. A bottle of red wine opened on the table.

The children talked and laughed. Valeria asked about the trip.

Octavio answered with small, vague replies.

Work. Meetings. Problems with shipments. Nothing unusual.

Eventually the children finished eating and wandered off to their rooms.

Valeria poured two glasses of wine and carried them to the balcony. He followed.

The night air was cool in the mountains. From the terrace they could see the cathedral towers lit against the dark sky.

For a while, neither of them spoke.

Valeria studied him.

"You're thinking about something."

Octavio stared out over the city.

"I saw something today," he said.

"What?"

He shook his head slightly.

"Something... concerning."

Valeria leaned against the railing.

"Dangerous? For us?"

He nodded.

"Yes."

The word hung in the air.

Valeria looked down at the wine in her glass.

"I don't like this life anymore," she said quietly.

Octavio turned toward her.

"The children are getting older," she continued. "They ask questions now."

Octavio watched her. She looked back at him.

"We could leave," she said. "We've talked about it before."

He sighed and looked past her toward the dark mountains.

Valeria touched his hand.

"Octavio? Talk to me."

He forced a small smile, but his eyes drifted back to the horizon.

4

Chapter 4 – Orders

Zacatecas, Zacatecas State, Mexico

The estate didn't exist on any map. It sat in the dry hills outside of town, hidden behind a ridge of basalt rock, flanked by withered agave. No cell signal reached there, and no eyes but God's.

Octavio stepped through the towering wooden front doors. Inside, the *hacienda* felt more like a monastery than a cartel base. It had tall, arched ceilings and stone floors. Spanish guitar music echoed softly through the halls. Religious icons lined the walls. Jesus crowned in thorns, the Virgin of Guadalupe, Saint Jude with his flaming heart.

He was led down a corridor to a study with high ceilings and no windows. An expansive wooden desk sat in the center. Books in shelves lined the walls. In one corner, an old Bible sat on a carved lectern.

At the desk sat el Obispo—the Bishop—head of the Jalisco cartel's oil theft branch.

He wore all white linen with pearl buttons, a neat black beard, and hair combed straight back. A single gold ring on his left hand bore a diamond cross.

The guards left without a word, closing the door behind them.

The Bishop stared at his visitor with eyes as black as ink.

"Octavio, join me. You've come from Jalisco. I already heard. They hit the compound. Fancy weapons. Thermite. Neighbors heard helicopters and bombs. Then they vanished with no trace."

"*Sí, patrón,*" Octavio confirmed.

"And?"

"We lost a lot of men and four armored trucks. They may have taken a prisoner, too. They took a satellite phone and a laptop. A map and some other files. We're trying to find out what else. The shell casings were not five-five-six or seven-six-two. They are a new caliber used by U.S. special operations. The boot prints were mixed but mostly from expensive brands."

The Bishop nodded.

"So, *los gringos* have come to Mexico."

"*Sí. Most likely, patrón.*"

The Bishop leaned back. He laced his fingers and stared at the candle burning beside his desk.

"Then they must know what's coming next. What we've been working on."

The young lieutenant exhaled.

"We must assume so."

The Bishop rose and walked to the lectern. He flipped forward through the massive, old Bible, first many pages, then fewer as he dialed into the passage he was searching for. Then he placed a pair of frameless reading glasses low on his nose.

"Have you read the book of Joel?" he asked.

"*Sí, patrón.*"

"Good. Chapter two, verse three."

He said it slowly, measuring each word.

"*Before them, the land is like the garden of Eden. Behind them, a desert waste. Nothing escapes them.*"

He let the verse hang for a moment. Then he removed the glasses and turned back to face Octavio.

"The Americans will try to destroy us and all we have built. There is no time to wait. The plan we've made with our Muslim friends must begin now.

But before they release the funds, they want to see proof we can do our part. You are responsible for the operation, as we discussed."

Octavio stared back, his jaw clenching and unclenching.

"*Sí, patrón.*"

"Our friends have prepared a target list," the Bishop continued. "Follow the plan. I will instruct El Mano to assist you."

Octavio frowned but nodded.

"Understood," he said.

The Bishop crossed back to his desk and sat down.

"You look troubled, *mijo*. What concerns you?"

"It is only that you mention El Mano. I wish he was not involved."

"Oh? El Mano is our best *sicario*. Why wouldn't you want his help?"

"*Ese cabrón está enfermo*," Octavio objected. "He's a crazy bastard."

The Bishop grinned.

"*Sí*, but he's *my* crazy bastard, and that's all that matters. *¿Verdad?*"

The candle flame danced between them.

"*Sí, patrón*," Octavio answered.

The Bishop stared, as if to see into Octavio's soul.

"Then go in peace, my son," he said finally.

Octavio nodded and left the room.

5

Chapter 5 – No Peace

Zacatecas, Zacatecas State, Mexico

Octavio didn't sleep that night. Instead, he sat on his hotel room's balcony overlooking the plaza below, watching the cars drive by and the people walking here and there, his mind racing until the sun rose.

He showered, dressed, and had his bodyguards drive him to church.

It was a small, whitewashed stone chapel. Inside, candles flickered in the alcoves, and an old priest with white hair stood at the altar.

The pews were only partially full of mostly women, with a few old men and a crying baby near the back.

He sat on a worn wooden pew, hands folded, eyes lowered.

The priest spoke with a fiery tone.

"My brothers and sisters," he said, "I must speak today about a sin that has brought sorrow to our people."

Octavio looked up.

"We have seen the fires. We have buried the dead. Fathers, mothers, children, lives ended in an instant." The priest paused. "These are not accidents. They are the fruit of greed and lawlessness."

His gaze moved slowly across the pews.

"Men tell themselves they are only taking what can be replaced. They tell themselves, the violence belongs to someone else. But theft and blood always walk together."

His voice hardened.

"That criminal path promises power and respect, but it leaves only fear behind. And there will be a reckoning for those who walk it while those who use their talents for righteousness shall be rewarded with eternal peace."

He bowed his head.

"Let us pray."

Octavio swallowed hard, then prayed.

After mass, he stood, genuflected, and walked out.

As he stepped from the church into the sunlight, he saw the priest shaking hands and wishing everyone a blessed day. He got in line. When it was his turn, the young cartel boss offered his hand to the priest who took it gently.

"My son, what has brought you here today?"

Octavio's mouth moved, but no words came out.

The priest continued to hold his hand only releasing it when the bodyguards stepped in.

"Your car is ready," one said.

The priest looked to the guard, then to Octavio. His eyes locked on the burn scars on his face. The old priest blinked in shock as recognition hit him.

Unconsciously, Octavio brushed his cheek with his hand.

Then he nodded to the priest and walked briskly to the Toyota Land Cruiser idling at the curb where another guard held the door open.

The priest stared wide-eyed as they pulled away, his open-mouthed gaze reflected in Octavio's sunglasses.

He rode in silence until his phone buzzed. He answered it.

"*¿Cómo estás, Valeria?*" he said. "How are you, *mi amor*? And the kids?"

A pause on the line.

"We're fine," she said. Her voice was tight. "We're always fine."

Octavio shifted slightly in his seat, eyes flicking to the driver, Roberto, then to Ramón in the passenger seat.

"Diego asked about you this morning," she continued. "He wanted to know if you were coming to his game this weekend."

Octavio looked out the window at the dry hills rolling past.

"Tell him I'll make the next one."

"You said that last time."

He exhaled through his nose. "Valeria—"

"And Luisa," she cut in, "she doesn't even ask anymore. That should tell you something."

He said nothing.

"She is growing up, Octavio. She talks about school, about friends. About boys. You should hear it. You should be here."

Octavio sighed.

"I'm doing this for them," he said, keeping his voice low. "For you. For all of us."

"No," she said. "You tell yourself that. But you're never here to see any of it."

Ramón shifted slightly in his seat. Octavio turned his head just enough to see him, then looked forward again.

"I will be home in a few days," Octavio said. "We'll spend time together then."

"For how long?" she asked. "A day? Two? Before you disappear again?"

He didn't answer.

"When does it stop?" she pressed. "When is it enough?"

His jaw tightened.

"It's business," he said.

Silence stretched between them, filled only by the hum of the engine and the tires on pavement.

"I don't want our children growing up thinking this is normal," she said more quietly. "A father who is never there. A man who calls and says he loves them but is always somewhere else."

Octavio swallowed.

"*Tranquila*," he said, softer now. "I'll be home soon."

"You always say that."

He looked out the window again. A church steeple passed in the distance, white against the morning sky.

"Tell the *niños* I love them," he said.

Another pause.

"I will," she said. "They still believe you."

The line went quiet for a moment.

"I love you," he added.

She didn't answer right away.

"I know," she said finally.

The call ended.

Octavio lowered the phone slowly. No one in the vehicle spoke. The road stretched ahead, empty and bright.

He stared forward, his brow drawn tight, the words still hanging in the air.

Over a thousand miles away in Denver, the chill morning air over the Green Zone Defense training yard carried the first hint of winter.

A line of men stood on the concrete pad, sweat darkening their shirts despite the cold.

Training blades hung at their sides.

Mason walked past them, one sleeve rolled high enough to expose the thick scar along his bicep. He flexed his hand once, feeling the pull in his shoulder.

"Never underestimate a blade," he said.

He stopped, turning to face them.

"I've been in firefights, rocket attacks, IEDs. Nothing came closer to killing me than a hatchet to the arm. I lost nearly half my blood before they got me closed up."

No one moved.

"At this distance," he said, "a knife beats a gun. No noise. No jam. No warning."

He drew his blade.

"You will get cut," he said. "The only question is how bad."

He shifted his stance, blade hand low, off-hand high.

"Blades out."

Steel rasped as the trainees drew their dulled practice blades.

He stepped toward one man with his knife raised too high.

"Lower it."

The man adjusted.

"Lower."

Mason nodded once, then stepped back.

"You don't fight like the movies," he said. "It's fast. It's close. It's ugly."

He turned.

"Cole."

Darius Cole stepped forward, blade in hand.

They squared off.

"Watch the hands," Mason said. "Not the blade."

Cole moved first. A quick jab toward Mason's midsection.

Mason slipped off-line and snapped his blade across Cole's wrist.

"Target hands first."

They reset.

Cole came again—higher, faster.

Mason dipped inside. His blade cut low, stopping just short of Cole's thigh.

"Femoral artery. Dead."

They moved again.

Cole pressed harder this time. High slash. Low follow.

Mason met it, turned the angle, and stepped in tight. His elbow checked Cole's chest. The blade drove in under the ribs.

"Heart. Dead again."

Mason didn't step away.

"You don't win it out there," he said quietly. "You win it in here."

He closed the distance until they were chest to chest.

"Inside. No space. No time."

He broke contact and turned back to the line.

"Pair up."

The yard came alive. Boots grinding. Steel tapping. Breath steady and controlled.

Mason moved between them, making small corrections.

"Too wide."

"Step. Don't reach."

He caught one man drifting off-line and pulled him back just as a blade cut through the space his ribs had been.

"That's how you live," Mason said. "Inches."

"This isn't about winning," he said. "It's about ending it."

Steel moved faster.

After the training session, Mason showered in the locker room, dressed in clean khaki tactical pants and a dark green GZD polo.

He went to the break room, retrieved his lunch container from the fridge, and placed it in the microwave.

As it heated, he looked up to see a news channel playing muted on a flat screen TV.

The president of Mexico had given a speech objecting to any proposed American military action in Mexico against the cartels.

The number of estimated casualties in the cartel drug wars flashed by.

Over 350,000 homicides. More than 110,000 missing.

Mason gawked at the scale of the carnage, not across the globe, but right across the border.

What if that war ever crossed the Rio Grande? he wondered.

He pictured Houston, Dallas, Los Angeles, Chicago—burning, explosions, tears, screams.

Suddenly, the microwave beeped.

His lunch was ready.

6

Chapter 6 – Los Tejanos 1

U.S. Penitentiary, Beaumont, Texas, USA

The recreation yard smelled of fresh-cut grass and hot concrete.

Bruno sat at a steel table in the far corner, sun cooking the crown of his shaved head. Sweat ran down the back of his neck and soaked into the collar of his state-issued shirt. He picked at the label on an orange Gatorade bottle, stripping it into thin curls, letting them fall and stick to the damp tabletop.

The yard moved in its usual rhythm, but something underneath it was off.

It wasn't loud enough to name. Not yet.

The Paisas crowded near the pull-up bars, tighter than normal. No laughter. No shit talk. Just quiet conversations and furtive looks.

Across the yard, Los Tejanos held the handball courts. A couple of them casually swatted the blue handball against the wall, the hollow pop echoing across the concrete, but nobody was really playing. The ranking members stood together near the fence line, backs half-turned, heads low, speaking intently.

Everything was too still.

The tension pressed down on the yard like the Texas sun.

Even the DC Blacks on the other side ran their dice game low, voices muted, hands quick and efficient.

The Woods by the weight pile cast long, measuring looks toward both Mexican cars, then back to their own group, everyone pacing and watching.

Bruno shifted in his seat. His tongue dragged across dry lips. His hands trembled enough he had to press them flat against his thighs to steady them.

But Bruno wasn't looking for trouble.

He scanned again.

Looking for *it*.

Needing it.

A spark. A sign. Anything to break the pressure building in his chest.

A man walked past him too fast, then slowed, like he caught himself. Another adjusted the waistband of his shorts, checking the weight of something tucked inside. Everywhere Bruno looked, men were carrying themselves just a little tighter, a little closer to the edge.

The yard was a powder keg, but Bruno needed to get high.

The whistle blew. Rec was over.

The sound cut cleanly through the tension.

The yard broke apart into movement. Lines formed. Men funneled toward the sally port in tight groups, each car clustering naturally, instinctively, like schools of fish.

Bruno stood with the rest, slipping into the middle of the flow. Not too close to anyone.

He kept his eyes up, hands loose at his sides. He felt the shape of the shank tucked into his waistband, wrapped in cloth, the hard edge pressing into his hip.

Everyone carried. You didn't walk a USP naked.

As they shuffled forward, a Paisa brushed shoulders with a Tejano. Neither looked at the other, but the contact lingered a fraction too long.

Bruno felt it.

That little shift.

The gate clanged shut behind them.

Inside, the unit swallowed them whole.

The noise hit first.

Radios screamed *Norteño* music from open cells. Dominoes cracked against steel tables. Men shouted up and down the tiers, voices layered over each other forming a constant roar.

But underneath it—smoke.

That blessed, bitter, chemical bite.

K2. Spice. Deuce.

Bruno inhaled before he could stop himself.

His body reacted instantly. Skin tightening. Jaw clenching. Eyes sharpening, scanning harder now, faster, searching.

He spotted them.

Two inmates in the dayroom, folded over, nodding into themselves, one drooling, the other staring at nothing, eyes wide and glassy, trapped somewhere deep inside his own head.

Above them, a CO leaned on the second-tier rail, arms folded, watching without watching, his face blank, like none of this concerned him.

Bruno turned down the tier.

Music blasted from a cell halfway down. *Corridos*, loud enough to rattle the steel door. The bass thumped through his chest, syncing with his pulse.

He knocked.

Payaso lay stretched on his bunk in boxers and tennis shoes, his body covered in tattoos, triangles inked above and below his eyes. He puffed a thin joint, smoke curling slowly in the stale air.

"*Qué pasó*, Bruno?" Payaso said, smiling. "Damn, you look rough, homie."

Bruno stepped in, lowering his voice, glancing once over his shoulder before turning back.

"I need something," he said. "Can you front me till store."

Payaso chuckled.

"You know I got you, dog. Here, hit this."

He passed the joint.

Bruno hit it hard.

The smoke burned going down, harsh and chemical, but then it spread through him, loosening something tight in his chest.

His shoulders dropped.

His jaw unclenched.

Payaso watched him, grin widening, eyes sharp despite the lazy posture.

"You worry too much, *ese*," he said. "Relax. The world keeps spinning."

He reached for a Bible on the bunk and flipped it open. Then he tore a page out, slow and deliberate.

The paper whispered.

Then he worked the razor with practiced ease, slicing a long, thin strip.

"You're in luck. Fresh *Biblia* just landed," he said.

He handed the strip to Bruno.

Bruno took it greedily.

"Good lookin' out."

"*Siempre,* homie. Enjoy that," Payaso said with a big grin.

Bruno hesitated for just a second, looking at him.

Something about the smile.

Too wide.

Too easy.

Then the need hit him again, sharp and insistent, and the thought slipped away.

Bruno headed straight to his cell, his body tingling with anticipation of the high.

Day shifted into evening. The cell block dimmed, but it never went quiet.

Bruno sat on his bunk, hands shaking as he worked the strip.

The sounds around him stretched, warped, like they were coming from far away and too close at the same time. Laughter echoed wrong. Metal rang too sharp.

He used a pencil lead to create a spark from his outlet, catching a piece of toilet paper on fire. The flame flickered weak and yellow.

He brought it to the strip.

Smoke.

He pulled it in deep.

Too deep.

The hit slammed him sideways.

His chest tightened. His heart raced hard enough to hurt, pounding against his ribs like it wanted out. The walls leaned in, then away, breathing with him.

He lay back.

The ceiling warped.

Voices stretched, slowed, twisted into something unrecognizable.

Not right.

Too much.

He sat up.

Too fast.

The room spun, tilting hard to one side. His stomach rolled.

He needed air.

Needed space.

He pushed off the bunk and stumbled to the door and out onto the tier.

The rail caught him before he hit the floor.

Everything waved. The lights were too bright, drilling into his eyes. The sounds cut sharp, each one separate now, too loud, too clear.

The tier stretched long and warped in front of him, like it had no end.

Men moved like shadows. Too fast. Then too slow. Faces blurred, then snapped into sharp focus, then blurred again.

Everything was wrong.

Then it started.

It kicked off with a shout.

Sharp. Angry.

A Paisa swung first, catching a Tejano across the face with a razor shank. The blade opened him up from cheek to ear. Blood splattered onto the floor.

For a split second, everything froze.

Then the cellblock exploded.

Shouting. Sneakers squeaking on waxed floors. Bodies thudding on floors and tables.

Knives flashed. All sizes, from short icepicks to full-size "bone-crushers".

The deuces hit. A high, piercing alarm screamed through the unit. Lights strobed.

"DOWN! DOWN!" the COs shouted from above.

No one listened.

Fighting spread like a grease fire.

Bruno turned in place, his heart racing.

Too much. Too fast.

A man slammed into him, blood pouring from his neck. Bruno staggered back.

Another body hit the rail. A blade punched in.

Again. Again. Again.

Grunts. Screams. The wet sound of steel working through flesh.

"Get him—!"

"Stab him—!"

The words broke apart in Bruno's head.

Fragments. Noise.

He reached for his waistband.

Missed. Tried again.

His fingers felt thick. Slow. Useless.

Tear gas popped. A sharp crack.

Thick smoke billowed.

White clouds rolled through the dayroom, burning eyes and lungs.

Men coughed, choked, but kept fighting, even blindly.

Bruno stumbled into the haze. He couldn't breathe. Snot poured from his nose.

He couldn't find his cell.

Then—

"Bruno!"

A hand grabbed him hard.

Payaso.

"Come on, Bruno," he said. "We gotta move."

Two more Tejanos flanked him. Big men with blades watching in all directions.

Payaso pulled him through the smoke, past bodies, past fighting.

He dragged him down the range. His feet barely worked. The world narrowed.

A tunnel.

Noise blending.

The deuces still screaming.

They reached his cell and pushed him inside.

The door clanged shut.

Bruno sagged onto the bunk, his chest heaving and eyes streaming.

He tried to speak, but he couldn't form words.

Payaso stepped in front of him, smiling.

"I told you—I got you, homie," the Tejano gang member said.

Bruno had a moment of clarity.

Something had shifted.

Too late.

The first blade went in low, hard, under his ribs.

Heat bloomed in his side, white-hot, sudden. His breath caught, and his eyes widened, his pupils dilated.

He looked down. The sharpened piece of steel was buried to the cloth-wrapped hilt.

"What the—" he tried to say.

Another blade punched into his chest. Then another. The air filled with grunts, quick and low, like men digging a pit.

Bruno gasped, twisted. He drove a knee into one man's gut, cracked an elbow into another's jaw. Teeth snapped, blood sprayed. With raw instinct, he fought through the haze. For a moment he thought he could break free.

Then the weight crushed him. Their bodies pinned him as their blades worked. The jagged steel of their shanks tore his side, sliced his arm, ripped his shoulder. Warmth poured over his shirt and down his legs.

He slid off the bunk to the concrete floor, deflating like a popped water balloon. His fists opened and closed, slick with blood. His chest heaved and bubbled, his lungs collapsing.

Payaso leaned in close, his grin stretched wide. His breath stank of weed and coffee.

"El Mano sends his *saludos, tu pinche rata.*"

7

Chapter 7 – Los Tejanos 2

Rural South Texas, USA

The trucks rolled in just after sunrise.

Dust trailed behind them in long, pale ribbons, hanging in the still air before settling over the scrub. The ranch stretched wide and empty in every direction. Mesquite, thorn brush, and hard-packed earth baked under a flat South Texas sky.

They parked in a loose semicircle.

Engines idled for a moment, then shut off one by one.

Oso stepped out of the lead truck. He was broad and heavy with a shaved head and tattoos covering his body.

He didn't rush. His boots hit the dirt, and he stood there a second, taking in the horizon.

Behind him, the others moved.

Flaco came out of the passenger side with a rifle already in his hands, not raised, just held low and natural. His eyes worked constantly, scanning the tree line, the low ground, the edges where someone might hide.

Tigre popped the tailgate on the second truck and started unloading gear—hard cases, a cooler, a shovel.

Chino walked around to the rear of the Suburban.

He opened the hatch and pulled out a black case. He set it gently on the tailgate, flipping the latches with practiced hands. Inside, a drone sat, carbon frame, camera angled forward like a staring eye.

He smiled faintly.

On the far side of the vehicles, Joker opened the trunk.

The man inside started screaming before the lid was fully up.

"Mmmph! MMM—!"

They dragged him out hard, dumping him face-first into the dirt. He rolled, coughing, gagging, his wrists zip-tied behind his back, ankles bound. A strip of duct tape covered his mouth, already soaked through with spit.

He twisted, panicked, trying to get his bearings.

Oso walked over slowly.

The man saw him and froze.

Even through the tape, the pleading started again.

"Mmmph—please—please—!"

Oso looked down at him.

Joker reached down and ripped the tape off the man's mouth.

The man sucked in air like he'd been drowning.

"Oso, please," he said, voice cracking. "Please, I didn't do nothing. I swear to God, I didn't—"

Oso let him talk.

"I didn't take nothing," the man rushed on. "I didn't skim, I didn't— someone's lying, *carnal*, you gotta believe me—"

Oso tilted his head slightly, studying him.

Chino didn't look. He was already powering up the drone, fingers moving across the controller, checking systems, adjusting feed.

A soft electric whine filled the air.

The man heard it.

His eyes flicked toward the sound, then back to Oso.

Fear sharpened.

"Please," he said again, quieter now. "I got kids. I got a family—"

Oso crouched in front of him.

Close enough now that the man had to lean back slightly, his breath hitching.

"You were given a job," Oso said.

His voice was calm.

The man nodded fast.

"I did it—I swear I did—"

"Yeah, but you also took some of the money," Oso said.

The man shook his head violently.

"No, no, I didn't—"

"And you've been getting high after I told you to chill on that."

"That's not true—!"

Oso watched him for a long second.

The wind moved through the brush behind them, dry and hollow.

"You think I don't know?" Oso asked.

The man broke.

"I was gonna fix it," he said, voice collapsing. "I was gonna put the money back—just give me time—please—"

Oso stood.

He stepped back and nodded once.

Joker stepped in and cut the zip ties at the man's wrists.

The man blinked, confused.

Then the ties at his ankles.

He pulled his hands forward slowly, rubbing his wrists, not understanding.

"What... what are you—"

Oso pointed out toward the open land.

"Run," he said.

The man stared at him.

He didn't move.

Flaco raised his rifle slightly.

"Run, *pendejo,*" Oso yelled.

The man's breathing quickened.

He looked from Oso to the rifle to the open scrub.

He shook his head.

"Oso... please... don't do this..."

Flaco pulled the rifle's trigger with a *boom*, the round passing close to the man's face.

He stumbled to his feet, hesitated, then ran.

At first, it was clumsy. His legs unsteady from being bound, feet slipping in the loose dirt. He nearly fell, caught himself, kept going.

Faster now.

Pushing through the brush.

Branches tore at his clothes. Thorns raked his arms.

Behind him, no one moved.

No shots. No shouting. Just the wind.

The man ran harder.

He crested a low rise and disappeared into thicker scrub.

Still nothing.

Back at the trucks, Oso waved casually and Chino lifted the drone.

The motors spun up with a rising whine.

He glanced at Oso.

Oso gave a small nod.

"Go ahead," he said.

Chino grinned.

The FPV drone lifted clean off the tailgate and hovered for a second, steady as a held breath. It carried a small explosive charge on its back.

Then it shot forward, low and fast, skimming just above the brush.

The camera feed filled his screen.

Green and brown blur.

Then—movement.

There.

The man crashed through the scrub, stumbling, gasping, glancing over his shoulder now.

Chino eased the stick.

The drone slowed. Hovered. Watched.

The man didn't see it at first.

He kept running, lungs burning, legs starting to fail.

Then he heard it.

That high, electric whine.

He turned. Saw it.

Floating there in the air behind him.

He froze.

Then he yelled and ran again.

Chino followed.

He kept the drone just behind and above him, matching his pace, letting him hear it, feel it.

The man zigged left, crashing through a stand of mesquite.

Chino adjusted smoothly, banking around the branches.

The camera dipped, corrected, locked back on.

The man stumbled, fell to his knees, scrambled up again, sobbing now.

"PLEASE—!"

Chino laughed under his breath.

"Run, homie," he murmured.

The man veered right, hitting thicker brush now, trying to lose it, trying to disappear.

Chino pushed forward.

The drone surged ahead, cutting distance.

The man glanced back again—

Too close now.

He tripped and fell hard.

He rolled onto his back, hands up, pleading.

The drone hovered above him.

For a moment, everything held.

The man stared up into the camera.

Into that black, unblinking eye.

"Please," he whispered.

Back at the trucks, Oso watched the horizon.

Flaco stood beside him, still as stone.

Chino's thumb pressed forward.

The drone dropped.

Fast.

A streak of motion—

Then impact.

The explosion punched down into the earth with a sharp, contained blast. Dirt and brush kicked up in a tight column. The sound rolled across the open land a second later, low and final.

Silence followed.

Dust drifted.

Chino lowered the controller slightly, still watching the feed as it cut to static.

He smiled.

"Got him," he said.

Oso nodded once.

"That's enough," he said.

Tigre was already moving, grabbing the shovel.

Joker lit a cigarette.

Flaco turned his gaze back to the horizon.

Oso looked out over the land, then back at his men.

"Los Tejanos never forget. Remember that."

8

Chapter 8 – El Mano

Huehuetenango, departamento de Huehuetenango, Guatemala

The city was dressed for a king.

Huehuetenango's narrow streets shimmered in the noon sun, a patchwork of cobblestones and shadows beneath sagging electrical lines. Vendors sold roasted corn and plastic cups of *horchata*, the air thick with cinnamon and fried pork fat. Marimba music rolled from speakers wired to a crumbling balcony, loud and distorted.

Desfile hípicos, or "horse parades," were traditional in this mountainous pocket of Guatemala. The government banned them after a cartel shootout the prior year, but the local narcos, called *Los Huistas*, don't ask for permission. Here in the mountains, they are the law.

Peasants lined the main avenue, pressed tightly to the curb. Some waved. Most didn't. Their eyes stayed low, respectful.

Then came the famous dancing horses.

They pranced two by two through the dust, hooves kicking rhythmically in time with the marimba. Their manes were braided in cartel colors. Green and silver on some, red and gold on others. Saddles were stitched with luxury monograms like Louis Vuitton and Gucci. The finest gold spurs were masterfully engraved. The men, all representing the cartel elite, rode tall with cowboy hats tipped forward, black sunglasses, teeth gold, gold-plated automatic pistols with extended magazines in leather holsters around their ample waists.

Their women rode their own prancing ponies, their bodies sculpted and inflated by the best plastic surgeons in Colombia, wearing bodysuits so tight they looked spray-painted on, sunglasses the size of satellite dishes, their outlined lips over-plumped with filler.

Security was everywhere. Each boss had his own ring of sicarios, village boys in tight shirts with SCAR rifles or AK-47s with duct-taped magazines. They walked with loose hands and tight jaws, scanning windows, balconies, and crowds as the procession crawled along.

Watching from the shade of a bakery doorway stood a foreigner. He wore a baseball cap low over his eyes and a gray windbreaker, a bottle of Mexican Coke in one hand, the other hand tucked in a coat pocket. His posture was lazy as he watched the parade closely.

His eyes followed one man in particular—a man on a dappled gray horse.

Don Chepe was one of the five Huista kings. He was heavyset, about 60 years old, with a drooping silver moustache and deep lines on his tanned cheeks. He wore a diamond horseshoe ring on his trigger finger and a gold-plated Glock on his hip. His saddle was hand-stitched red crocodile. The crowd watched in wide-eyed awe as he passed.

The foreigner raised the Coke bottle and took a sip. The hiss of carbonation bled into the tiny radio transmitter he held in the same hand next to the bottle's neck.

"Eyes on. Third from front," he whispered in English. "Gray horse. White hat. Red saddle."

Far up the block, on the roof of the Hotel San Rafael, a figure reclined in a folding chair beneath an awning. He looked like a drunken European backpacker, shirtless in floral shorts, flip-flops, and headphones. At his feet sat a custom ground station, twin antennas tilted upward like an insect. An electronic controller with joysticks and buttons rested on his lap.

As soon as the target was confirmed, he leaned down and lifted a towel, revealing a custom-made quadcopter drone and a pair of modded goggles.

He placed the goggles over his shaved head, the device covering the top half of his face. Then he lifted the controller, pressed a button, and with the buzz of a thousand bees, the FPV drone spun to life.

The flying machine had four rotary blades driven by the most powerful motors on the market. It carried a small explosive charge. The camera was clear in his heads-up display as the drone whipped over the edge of the roof in a blur and sped off like a hawk.

"ETA fifteen seconds," said Sergi, former Ukrainian Armed Forces FPV drone pilot, now mercenary-for-hire.

The spotter downed the Coke and set the bottle on the counter.

From the roof, Sergi angled the headset forward. The drone sliced over powerlines and rooftops, humming low. It slipped through a gap between an awning and a tree, its nose angled straight at Don Chepe.

"Visual confirmation of target," Sergi said in thickly accented English. "Nice hat."

On the street, Don Chepe leaned over and slapped the rear of a dancing mare ridden by a beautiful young woman. The horse reared. He laughed and waved at the crowd.

Suddenly, the drone screamed into view, head height, banking hard.

Chepe saw it at the last second. His eyes went wide, and he yanked hard on the reins.

The gray horse reared, and the drone missed by inches.

Chepe kicked hard. The horse bolted sideways, shoving through the crowd.

Vendors screamed. Tables toppled. He veered down a side street.

Sergi corrected quickly and gave chase.

"Target is running," the spotter transmitted.

"I see him," Sergi replied.

The drone surged around the corner, brushing past laundry lines and buzzing light bulbs. It rocketed over tin rooftops and ducked under a dangling tarp.

Chepe kicked the horse again, racing onto a downhill slope, horseshoes sparking against the cobblestones.

The drone followed. Sergi feathered the throttle around the corners.

Chepe looked back and saw the buzzing killer tracking him.

He pulled his pistol and fired over his shoulder.

A wild shot ricocheted off a wall, zinging into the sky.

Sergi sent the drone zigzagging over a fruit cart.

"He's trying to lose me in the alleys," he said.

"Don't lose him," the spotter replied.

Chepe shot down another narrow path. The drone followed. It passed under a wooden beam, then over a parked motorbike.

Don Chepe turned into a plaza full of people. He charged through them, trampling people in a panicked race from flying death.

Maneuvering now in the open, the drone surged forward, over the top of the scrambling crowd.

Chepe raised his pistol again as his face filled Sergi's screen.

When the distance closed to mere inches, the drone exploded.

The blast hit Chepe squarely in the chest. His torso vanished in fire. The horse crashed into a wall, skidding sideways in a spray of blood and dust. Windows blew out.

The screen flashed white. A moment later, the sound of a distant boom carried up the street to Sergi.

"Got him," he whooped through the comms.

First there was shocked silence, then women screaming, but soon after, armed men sprang into action.

Gunfire broke out as sicarios raised their rifles toward the roofs, firing blindly.

Crowds scattered in all directions, knocking over food stands and elderly villagers alike. Bottles shattered. A man staggered from a shop, bleeding from a stray round.

The Coca-Cola-drinking spotter turned and walked away quickly.

He kept his head down, moving with the surge of the crowd away from the parade route toward an alley. No one noticed him. Just another foreigner caught in the madness. He was nearly clear when a voice barked behind him in Spanish.

"*¡Oye!*"

The spotter didn't turn, but he looked down. His sleeve had ridden up during the push, and the silver edge of his metal wrist glinted in the sunlight.

The voice came again.

"*¡Oye! El Mano!*"

He pushed into the alley while behind him, boots pounded pavement.

Two Huista bodyguards in red T-shirts and blue jeans with radios clipped to their belts were closing fast. One carried an AKMS rifle with the buttstock folded over, the other a huge chrome Desert Eagle pistol drawn from a shoulder holster.

The spotter cut through a courtyard and into the back kitchen of a bakery, startling a cook.

He shoved through a curtain of beads and burst onto another street.

The Desert Eagle fired with a thundering boom. A bullet snapped past his ear and shattered a window.

The spotter spun in the alley, planted his feet, and raised his left hand.

The lead sicario turned the corner, gun up—and caught a gout of fire to the chest.

The spotter's prosthetic steel arm hissed as the integrated flamethrower roared to life. A plume of burning gel shot across the alley, catching the man full in the torso. He screamed and went down, body twisting, skin bubbling, slinging flaming globs of accelerant and melted flesh. The air filled with the stench of burning napalm and sizzling meat.

The second guard rounded the corner just in time to see his compadre crumple in a burning pile, screaming in agony. He skidded to a stop, shocked.

The spotter closed the distance in a flash. Jumping in the air, he delivered a steel-fisted superman punch to the center of the sicario's face. A wet crack. The body folded, twitched, and went still.

Up above, Sergi spoke again.

"You're hot. Get out."

"No shit," the spotter growled.

He pulled a locator fob from his coat and pressed the activation button.

"I've got your signal," Sergi said, and reached down for a different controller and headset.

From his rooftop perch, a much larger six-rotor drone rose into the air. The DJI Agras T100 heavy-lift drone raced forward like a monstrous prehistoric insect, a tether rope dangling beneath its thorax. It whirred over the buildings and the chaos in the streets below in a direct path to the spotter's location.

Rage heard it arrive and looked up and saw the drone position over the alley. He reached up and grabbed the tether rope. Opening his jacket revealed the straps of a harness. He yanked a lanyard tipped with a carabiner from his pants leg and deftly linked it to a ring on the end of the massive drone's tether.

"I'm hooked," Rage radioed.

With that, the drone lifted, motors whining under the strain, rising into the hot blue sky over Huehuetenango with the spotter dangling beneath. As he cleared the rooftops, rising fifty feet, then one hundred feet into the sky, he took a moment to appreciate the carnage below.

Crowds ran. Babies screamed. Fire licked the walls near the explosion site. Sirens clawed the air. Huista bodyguards looked up in amazement to see the assassin flying away. One raised his AR-15 rifle and fired.

Bullets whistled past his head. He chuckled.

With his right hand, he raised a Ukrainian FORT 230 submachinegun from a sling under his jacket, extended it toward the street below, and let off a burst of automatic fire. The stream of 9mm bullets rained down like deadly hail.

One of the cartel gunmen clinched his neck as a bullet pierced his throat.

Near him, an elderly woman collapsed, blood pumping from a hole in her skull.

Hollow points impacted the street around them, kicking up dust and rock chips.

The rest of the bodyguards scattered.

Dangling from the umbilical high above them, the spotter laughed.

Years ago, he had crossed a river in the north from Canada into the US with the Dead Wolves Motorcycle Club and his blood brother, Raison, to commit the robbery of the century. But it hadn't gone well. After escaping the street battle in Denver, he had crossed another river—this time the Rio Grande as he headed south into Mexico.

In his new life as a sicario for the most powerful cartel in Central America, few knew him by his real name—Rage.

Instead, they whispered his new nickname in terror.

El Mano.

The Hand.

With the rotors whipping his long hair about his scarred, weathered face, Rage laughed, reloaded, and with a *BRAAAAP!* emptied another magazine onto the panicked crowd below. At this distance, he could just barely hear people screaming in fear and pain from the searing rounds as the drone whisked him away to safety, his mission complete.

Hundreds of meters away, seated on the rooftop watching through the drone's camera as people trampled each other to flee Rage's fury, Sergi chuckled.

"And now... he is gone."

9

Chapter 9 – Home 1

Zacatecas, Zacatecas State, Mexico

Hours later, a private jet landed at Zacatecas International Airport in central Mexico. When the fuselage door opened, Rage stepped out onto the airstairs wearing a black Adidas tracksuit and a scowl, his long hair pulled back into a ponytail, his flamethrower prosthesis now swapped for a composite myoelectric hand.

He looked around briefly, then descended the steps to a convoy of black Suburbans waiting for him.

Sergi followed wearing a black T-shirt and track pants and carrying a backpack.

Without a word, Rage walked to the SUV where a cartel bodyguard wearing a cowboy hat and a pistol in his belt opened a door for him.

After men loaded their gear into the back, the Suburban pulled out of the airport parking lot and merged into the night, its headlights cutting through dust and heat.

Inside, Rage sat back in silence, a cigarette ember glowing between his fingers. The city slid past in fragments. Stucco walls, iron gates, and stray dogs drifting through shafts of light.

"Has Arturo reported from Colorado?"

"*Sí*," the driver replied. "He said they made it and are set up at the house, waiting for your orders."

"Good," Rage replied.

They rode in silence while he thought and smoked.

After a minute, he asked, "Is she home?"

The driver glanced at him in the rearview, then back to the road.

"*Sí*. She's back from her trip."

Rage took a slow drag, then released it.

Smoke filled the cabin.

"What's she like?"

The driver hesitated. His hands adjusted nervously on the wheel.

"*Señora* is like usual."

Rage watched the reflection of passing lights crawl across the glass.

Sergi looked up from his phone.

"What's next for us, boss?" he asked.

"I've got a meeting with the Bishop. Some big job he put together with that asshole, Octavio," Rage replied.

"Ah," Sergi said. "Your favorite guy. Why do you hate Octavio so much?"

Rage thought for a moment.

"He reminds me of somebody I trusted once. Somebody close to me. My own blood. But he couldn't be trusted because he was always scheming."

Sergi nodded.

"Always keep an eye on the ones who want to call shots," Rage advised. "They'll sell out anyone—even their own blood—to get what they want. Don't forget that."

"Sure thing," Sergi agreed. "But you know, I just do what I'm hired to do. I trust you to handle the politics."

After a drive through the rocky hills, they arrived at a secluded, walled property. The automatic gates opened before they reached them. Wrought iron, black and heavy, they rolled back into the stone walls as the convoy swept through.

Inside the wall, a mansion rose ahead. Spanish-style, with white stucco glowing under exterior flood lights and a red tile roof, its arches cast long shadows across the courtyard.

The Suburbans stopped. One of the bodyguards stepped out, scanning, while another opened Rage's door.

He stepped onto the gravel. Music drifted faintly from the back.

He crushed the cigarette under his boot and walked toward the house.

Inside, the air was cooler and thick with the scent of perfume. The entryway was pristine, with tile floors and antique artwork.

A half-empty champagne bottle sat on a side table beneath it. Rage passed it without looking.

From the back of the house, he heard the whining electric guitar of a Guns N' Roses track.

He passed through the house. Living room, kitchen, then French doors thrown open to the night. The music grew louder as he approached.

Suddenly, a gunshot boomed from the backyard.

Rage quickly drew a pistol from his waistband and froze in place, listening.

Voices echoed faintly. Splashing. Laughter.

Cautiously, he stalked toward the patio doors.

He stepped into the backyard.

The pool glowed turquoise in the dark, and the ripples cast flickers of light around the gardens.

Clothes were scattered across the patio. Heels, a dress, a man's shirt. An overturned wine glass bled onto the concrete.

In the water was a woman.

Bare shoulders above the surface, auburn-hair-gone-gray wet and slicked back, laughing loudly at something.

In the water with her arms wrapped tightly around her waist, was a young man. He was maybe twenty. Lean. Tanned. Handsome as a model with a head of thick black hair.

The woman was holding a pistol—a stainless revolver—and pointing it away from the house at a concrete statue of a topless maiden. The concrete figure's arm was laying broken on the ground where it had been blown off at the elbow.

A pink pool float carried a mirror with a straw and a half dozen white lines laid out. An empty champagne bottle floated upside down near the steps.

Rage stepped to the edge of the pool and stared at them.

After a moment, the woman noticed.

Her smile widened instantly, bright and unbothered.

"Rage!"

She lifted one arm from the water, waving loosely, splashing.

"There he is."

The young man turned, squinting toward the patio.

Rage glared from the edge of the pool.

She held out her arms, her enhanced breasts decorated with aging blue and red tattoos. Mascara dripped down her cheeks, and red lipstick was smeared around her mouth.

"Come here," she said holding out her arms as she made her way to the side of the pool where he stood. "Don't just stand there glaring like a cop."

Rage's eyes moved once across the scene, then back to her.

The young man looked uneasy.

She grinned, unfazed, then reached for a champagne glass and took a long drink, water running down her arm.

"You're late," she giggled. "We started without you."

Axel Rose's voice screeched through the outdoor speakers as Rage stood silently at the edge of the pool, glaring at her.

She tilted her head back and sang along at the top of her lungs, using the empty glass as a microphone.

"Welcome to the jungle, it gets worse here every day. You learn to live like an animal in the jungle where we play. "

Then, suddenly, she stopped.

Her eyes got big.

"Oh, no," she said under her breath.

She looked at the wounded statue with the severed arm, then looked back at Rage.

"I—I—I was aiming for her head," she started to explain. "I can't believe I—I—shot her arm off."

She looked at Rage, cutting her eyes down to his prosthetic hand.

Her male friend was frozen in fear.

"I swear, sweetheart, I didn't mean it," she continued.

Rage's face tightened like a fist.

Then she tilted her head back and laughed uproariously.

"Holy, shit! You should see the look on your face right now," she howled, the veins sticking out in her thin neck. "You have to admit, that's pretty fucking funny."

She cackled harder, struggling to catch her breath.

"I shot the arm off of a bitch that belongs to a man with one arm. Can you believe that shit?"

Rage glared.

"Hello, mother," he said.

10

Chapter 10 – Home 2

Green Zone Defense Training Center, Denver, Colorado, USA

Just outside Denver, Mason sat quietly on the stone bench, the crisp morning air dry in his throat, sipping coffee from a paper cup with a plastic lid. His ball cap and sunglasses sat on the bench beside him. Everything was quiet except for Bud sniffing around. Facing west toward the mountains, the rising sun behind him glinted on the polished marble and bronze of the GZD Memorial Park.

South of the main buildings, tucked in a grove of aspens, the garden featured trimmed grass and sculpted shrubs ringed by red and gold flowers in mulched beds. In the center stood a bronze statue of GZD's founder, The Colonel, framed by the Rocky Mountains towering above like gray-blue shoulders under a scarf of snow. In front of the statue stood a marble podium topped with a bronze plaque.

In raised letters, the plaque read:
IN HONOR OF THOSE WHO STOOD
BETWEEN ORDER AND CHAOS
AND PAID IN FULL
THEIR NAMES LIVE HERE
AND IN OUR HEARTS

FOREVER

Beneath the inscription were the names of every GZD officer who had died in the line of duty.

Mack Radford. The Colonel. The definition of an officer and gentleman.

Ali Carver. Combat veteran. World class athlete. Courage personified.

Michael Reynolds. Big Mike. Husband. Grandfather. As loyal a man as ever lived.

All three gave their lives that fateful day over a decade ago when the Dead Wolves Motorcycle Club decided to cross the Saint Lawrence River and bring hell to Colorado.

Since fending off their attempted heist, GZD had become legendary in the security industry.

He couldn't help but think that, knowing The Colonel, he would sacrifice himself all over again for the good of others.

But that brought his heart no relief.

Mason stood. Bud's ears perked. He said a silent goodbye to his friends, then walked back to the training center to start the workday.

The Green Zone Defense Training Center sat at the edge of the Rockies, fenced, hardened, and humming.

Mason walked the main hall with Bud at his heel.

Steel doors. Cameras in every corner. The place smelled like coffee and gun oil.

He passed the kill house—shots cracking inside—then the range below, the steady rhythm of a rifle echoing up through the floor. Offices buzzed with calls. The place ran like a machine.

He pushed outside.

At the far end of the property, a Quonset hut stood open. Inside, a netted tunnel stretched across the concrete.

Caleb stood in the center, a backpack bristling with antennas.

"Mason! You're gonna like this."

Mason stepped up to the net.

"Show me."

A quadcopter lifted into a hover.

"Zulu-9 jammer," Caleb said. "Takes control of anything on common frequencies."

He tapped his controller.

The drone twitched, drifted, then slammed into the net and dropped.

"We call that move 'signal denial'," Caleb said.

Mason nodded once.

"Again."

The drone lifted.

Caleb worked the jammer's controller.

The drone turned, then followed a false path and crashed again.

"That one is known as 'GPS spoofing'. The jammer gives it a false destination and the drone falls for it."

Mason watched, arms folded.

"Can you take control?"

Caleb grinned.

"Watch."

The tablet chirped.

The drone rose again, steadied, then moved cleanly, landing exactly where Caleb guided it.

"Now it's mine."

Mason gave a slight nod. "What about bigger ones?"

A larger hex drone spun up, heavier, louder.

It lifted. Held.

Caleb worked faster this time.

The drone resisted then finally bent to his control and came down hard.

"The bigger they are, the harder they fight," Caleb said. "But anything with a signal, we can grab it."

Mason studied the machine.

"And if you can't?"

Caleb reached over his shoulder, pulled a short-barreled shotgun from a scabbard attached to the jammer, and shouldered it in one motion.

The smaller drone lifted again.

One shot.

It dropped out of the air in pieces.

"Tungsten bird shot works every time," Caleb said.

Mason gave a faint smile.

"That's more my speed."

Caleb lowered the weapon.

"Either way," he said, "this is the future."

Mason looked at the wreckage on the concrete. Then at the backpack.

"Yeah," he said. "I bet you're right."

That evening, hickory smoke hung low over the yard. Mason stood at the grill, turning ribeyes as fat hissed over glowing coals. The smell drifted across the fence. Behind him, voices blended with country music and the sharp bursts of kids running through the grass.

Bud lay nearby, head on his paws, tail thumping.

Caleb held court by the picnic table, a beer in one hand, talking loud enough for three conversations at once.

Lisa moved between the kitchen and yard, setting out food, smiling as she went.

Mason stepped back from the grill with a plate and found an empty lawn chair to sit in while he ate. Bud pressed against his leg. The noise carried around him.

Lisa sat beside him.

"I talked to your dad today."

Mason glanced at her.

"Yeah?"

"He's not doing well. He's having a hard time getting around."

Mason nodded once.

"Surprised he admitted it."

"He trusts me," she said. "We could think about moving back to Houston. Be closer to him."

Mason looked out over the yard.

"Hell, we just built this house. This is our home."

"Yes," she said. "But maybe not forever."

He shrugged.

"Maybe."

By ten, the yard had gone quiet. Chairs were folded. Lights turned off. The house settled.

Lisa moved upstairs with the baby.

Mason stood at the kitchen sink drying a platter with a dish towel when Bud let out a low growl.

He turned.

Bud stood at the sliding glass door, rigid, ears forward.

Mason stepped beside him.

Across the street, a figure stood on the dark porch of the rent house. No light. Just a shape.

For a moment, the figure lifted something to its face.

Then it turned and disappeared inside.

Mason stayed there a second longer.

Was that binoculars?

Then he slid the lock closed and watched his reflection in the glass, the street beyond gone still again.

11

Chapter 11 – Meeting

Texas/Mexico Border

The river was down to a trickle.

Summer heat had shrunk the Rio Grande until it was little more than a ditch cutting through the scrub rather than a boundary of nations.

Its surface barely moved, the sluggish water reflecting the stars. Trash clung to the reeds here and there, plastic bottles bobbed against the banks, and the smell of algae and mud rose in the still night air.

On the Mexican side, three pickups idled with their lights off, engines thumping low. Men stood in the beds, scanning the darkness with thermal scopes mounted on rifles.

Octavio stood on the bank, hands tucked in his jacket pockets. He wore plain clothes and looked like a local rancher.

On the American side, six men slipped into the water and began wading across, holding their phones and valuables above their heads. Octavio's men tracked their progress the whole way through their sights.

Once they exited the water on the Mexican side, one man walked directly toward Octavio. He was short but powerfully built, nearly as wide as tall. His head was shaved smooth, and his face, head, arms, and neck were covered in blue-black prison tattoos.

Oso.

The rest of the Tejanos gang members looked similar. Hair cropped or shaved bald, beards and goatees, eyebrows scarred. They wore denim jackets, khaki pants, and sneakers.

Octavio shook hands with their stocky leader.

"*Mucho gusto, Oso*," Octavio said.

"*Mucho gusto, Octavio*," Oso replied. "Well. We're here."

Octavio gestured to the trucks, and the men loaded into the backs, still dripping from the river.

The meeting place was a half-burned down shack set a few hundred yards back from the water. Only the frame and a few charred boards remained. Inside, someone had thrown together a table from plywood and set down a six-pack of Tecate.

Oso opened a beer and chugged it quickly. He belched, then opened another. He called to one of his men and offered him the remaining cans to share with the crew.

"So, what's up, Octavio? What can Los Tejanos do for our friends in Mexico?" Oso asked.

Octavio opened a folder and spread photographs across the table. Satellite images, photos of industrial equipment, and company logos.

Oso picked up a photo of a drilling rig and smiled.

"Hell yeah, that's an all-electric H&P rig. That's what they drill horizontals with. You know, I was a tool pusher in the Permian after I got out the first time. Fuck that, though. That's some hard ass work," he said.

"That's why you're here and not one of your other *carnales*. You were chosen because you have shown loyalty and courage—and because you know about oil," Octavio said.

Oso studied the other photos one by one.

"The Bishop has a plan," he continued, "and he expects full cooperation from Los Tejanos."

The prison gang shot-caller studied the company logo.

"TexOil. I know the name. But it's not like Mexico over there in the U.S.

We can't just tap into pipelines like y'all do. They'll shut that shit down instantly."

"We're not going to tap their pipelines, Oso," Octavio began. "Tell me this: in prison, when a weak inmate comes onto a cellblock, what do your *carnales* do to him?"

"Shit, we make that *puto* catch a ride. He pays us protection or we fuck him up every day until he gets with the program, you know what I'm sayin'? It's no mercy on the weak in there."

"Exactly," Octavio said. "Now, we're going to do the same thing, but on a larger scale. We tell the oil companies that they pay up, or we burn their operations down."

Oso chuckled and slid the photos around the table, thinking to himself.

"Man, that shit is crazy. If we roll like that, the feds will be all over us," he said.

"Listen. We're targeting companies that are already under pressure to sell their assets. They can't afford to call the feds because any word of problems will scare off buyers. TexOil invested heavily in oil instead of natural gas, and now the price-per-barrel is down by almost half. They're out of money to operate, and they've maxed out their credit lines. They have to divest wells to even stay afloat. They're trying to sell their Eagle Ford shale wells in South Texas right now," Octavio explained.

Oso frowned.

"OK, bossman. What do you want us to do?"

Octavio looked around the burned-out shack. The roof was open to the night sky. This far from civilization, every star was visible, and Octavio thought that of all nights, God could probably see him the clearest tonight.

"The same thing you did to those weak men in prison," he replied. "We're going to break TexOil. We're going to make them pay."

Oso chuckled.

"If you say so, bossman. Los Tejanos are always down for whatever. So, what's the plan?"

Octavio handed Oso a piece of paper.

"This is a numbered target list. Memorize it, then burn it. I will let you know when to hit each one.”

Oso read the list, his eyes widening.

“Holy shit...”

12

Chapter 12 – Talent

Colotlán, Jalsico State, Mexico

A few miles outside Colotlán in southwestern Mexico, a ranch house crouched low against the earth, half-lost in dust and scrub. A thin ring of mesquite trees clawed at the wind, offering what little shelter they could. Beyond them, the land fell away into dry, rolling hills that disappeared into the dark.

Inside an equipment shed, a single fluorescent tube buzzed overhead.

Sergi stood at a folding table, sleeves rolled up, hands steady.

A drone lay open in front of him, its carbon fiber arms spread like a crucifix, wiring exposed. A small camera faced forward, its glass eye black and unblinking.

He adjusted a connection with a jeweler's screwdriver, then paused, listening.

Behind him, something hissed.

He finished tightening the contact, then clipped the panel back into place with a soft click. Only then did he glance over his shoulder.

Rage stood near the open bay door, half in shadow. The steel prosthetic extending from his right arm caught the light in dull flashes. The service panel inside the device was open, exposing its inner workings.

The housing was compact but dense, layered with heat shielding and machined plates. The fingers were fixed in a relaxed, half-curled position. A small nozzle protruded from the middle knuckle. Braided fuel lines ran inside the wrist into a reinforced forearm chamber. The forearm itself was a sealed pressure vessel, built to carry a limited charge of custom gel—a thick, flammable adhesive engineered to burn intensely, even underwater.

Sergi cut his eyes from his own work to watch Rage refill the flamethrower with a hose from a pressurized container.

When it was full, Rage dropped the hose and tilted his wrist.

A soft ignition tick sounded and a tongue of flame spilled out, bright and controlled, like a large cigarette lighter.

He held it there. Watched it.

Then he smacked the service panel closed, aimed his outstretched arm across the room, and unleashed a jet of fire.

Instantly, the temperature in the room increased.

The flame licked across a rusted oil drum twenty feet away. The paint blistered, then blackened. Heat shimmered in the air.

Rage cut the flame.

Silence settled again, broken only by the faint buzz of the light.

Sergi turned back to his table.

"You should not run it too long in bursts like that," he said in accented English. "You overheat the nozzle, you lose pressure consistency."

Rage said nothing.

Sergi reached for a handheld controller and thumbed a switch.

The drone on the table chirped alive. LEDs blinked. The small camera flickered, then steadied.

On a rugged tablet propped against a crate, a live feed appeared. The inside of the shed. Rage stood in the background, distorted by the wide-angle lens.

Sergi studied the image.

"Signal is clean," he said. "No interference out here."

Rage stepped closer to the oil drum.

He lifted his arm again.

Another burst, longer this time.

The flame roared louder, thicker, turning from orange to a deeper, almost white core. The drum glowed where the heat concentrated. A line of fire crawled across the concrete floor where fuel residue had pooled.

Rage angled the nozzle, guiding it.

When he released the internal trigger, the flame snapped off.

The fire on the floor continued to burn.

Rage watched it spread for a moment, then ground it out with the heel of his boot.

Sergi glanced over.

"You like fire," he said.

Rage's voice came low, flat.

"Fire can be useful."

Sergi picked up the drone and carried it toward the open bay door. Outside, the night stretched wide and empty. A pickup sat parked near the fence line. Rage's bodyguards smoked beside it, their silhouettes barely visible.

Sergi set the drone down on a flat section of packed dirt and stepped back.

The rotors spun up with a rising whine. Dust lifted in a tight spiral.

The drone rose clean off the ground, hovering at eye level for a moment before Sergi nudged the controls. It drifted forward, then accelerated out into the darkness.

On the tablet, the feed shifted. Now it showed the ranch from above. The shed. The truck. The bodyguards looking up.

Sergi guided it higher.

"Range is about ten kilometers with this setup," he said. "More if we push it, but signal becomes unreliable."

Rage stepped beside him, eyes on the screen.

The ranch shrank beneath them.

"What about payload?" Rage asked.

"Depends what you want to carry," Sergi replied. "Grenade is easy. Thermite, also possible. Shaped charges with the proper mount."

He adjusted the drone's pitch, sending it forward over the ridge.

The terrain beyond opened into a long stretch of desert.

"Fast," Sergi added. "Hard to see. Hard to stop."

Rage nodded.

"In Ukraine, we used them every day," he said. "Sometimes dozens. Sometimes hundreds."

Rage didn't look at him.

"And now?" Rage asked.

He brought the drone into a slow orbit, the horizon tilting on the screen.

"Back home," he continued, "they say we fight for freedom. For country. For future."

He smirked.

"But while we are fighting, the politicians are buying apartments in Paris. Ferraris. Sending money out of the country. Money for missiles and body armor is spent on yachts."

He shook his head.

The drone dipped slightly, then corrected.

"So, you left," Rage said.

"Yes."

"Why Mexico?"

Sergi smiled without humor.

"I got an offer."

He tapped the side of the controller.

"Good money. Very good. A gentleman here, he understood what I could do. He knew money talks."

The drone swept back toward the ranch.

"So, I decided to leave the war in Ukraine," Sergi said, "and go into business. Like everyone else."

The drone descended, dropping low over the mesquite trees, then sliding back into the open space near the shed. Dust kicked up again as it settled to the ground. The rotors slowed, then stopped. Silence returned.

Sergi powered it down and lifted it back onto the table inside.

"And you?" he asked. "Why are you here?"

Rage walked back to the oil drum, now blackened and warped.

"Same as you. Because they pay me," he said.

Rage studied the scorched steel.

"And because I'm good at it."

The fluorescent light buzzed overhead.

Outside, the wind picked up, whispering through the mesquite.

"I've learned a lesson over the years about fire," Rage continued. "Fire's only useful when it's controlled, aimed. Left loose, it just destroys. That's the difference between a combustion engine and a forest fire. Same with your drones. You use that skill with purpose, it gets you somewhere. You don't, it's just wasted energy. I'm the same way. This—" he held up the metal hand "—is what I'm built for. Killing is my talent."

Sergi set the drone down carefully, aligning it with the edge of the table.

Rage turned toward the open night.

"Get those drones ready," he said. "We'll be back to work soon."

Sergi nodded once.

"They will be."

Rage stepped out into the darkness, the faint smell of fuel and burned paint lingering in the air.

13

Chapter 13 – The Clown

USP Beaumont, Texas, USA

The interview room at USP Beaumont smelled like bleach and old sweat.

Fluorescent lights hummed overhead. The cinderblock walls were painted a dull gray that swallowed everything—colors, shadows, time.

A scratched steel table sat bolted to the floor between two chairs.

Payaso sat on one side.

His wrists were cuffed in front and looped through a ring welded to the tabletop. A fresh scrape ran along his cheekbone, still red beneath the brown of his skin. This time, there was no signature grin. Instead, he kept his eyes cast down.

The door opened.

A man in a white shirt and tie stepped in, followed by a correctional officer. The officer stayed by the door, arms folded. The man in the tie set a thin folder on the table and sat down across from Payaso.

"You know why you're here?" the investigator asked.

Payaso leaned back as far as the chain would allow.

"For being a handsome motherfucker?" he said.

The investigator didn't react.

"You're here because three men got stabbed to death on the yard," he said.

"One of them bled out in a cell. Multiple witnesses put you in the area."

Payaso shrugged.

"Lotta people on the yard," he said. "Hard to see who's doing what."

The investigator opened the folder.

Photos slid across the table.

Blood on concrete. A body facedown near the rec tables. Another inside a cell, shirt soaked dark, arms twisted at bad angles.

Payaso didn't look at them.

The investigator watched him anyway.

"Bruno," he said, tapping one of the photos. "That was you."

Payaso's eyes flicked down for a fraction of a second.

Then back up.

"Don't know him," he said.

The investigator closed the folder halfway.

"Here's how this goes," he said. "You're looking at a homicide charge inside a federal penitentiary. Add gang enhancement, you're buried. You cooperate, maybe I can talk to the U.S. Attorney."

He let that hang.

Payaso shifted in the chair. The chain scraped softly against the steel ring.

"You got the wrong guy," he said.

The investigator leaned back.

"No," he said. "I've got the right one."

Silence settled between them.

The fluorescent light buzzed.

The investigator slid the folder the rest of the way open and turned it around.

"This wasn't random," he said. "Bruno had nothing to do with the riot that day. It was a hit."

Payaso said nothing.

The investigator tapped the table lightly with one finger.

"I know you're not calling shots here. I know you have no choice but to do what you're told. That's the way it is in here, right? Convict rules. So, tell me—who called the shot to hit Bruno?"

Payaso's jaw tightened slightly.

"Lotta people call shots," he said.

"Yeah," the investigator replied. "But this one came from somewhere else."

Payaso looked at him.

The investigator held his gaze.

"You're not killing people on the yard for nothing," he said. "So, who wanted Bruno dead?"

Payaso's eyes dropped to the table.

He rubbed his thumb along the edge of the cuff.

The room stayed quiet.

Then—

"Wasn't about him," Payaso muttered.

The investigator didn't move.

"What was it about?" he asked.

Payaso shook his head slightly, like he was already regretting saying anything.

"Some business," he said.

"What business?"

Payaso exhaled through his nose.

"Something big," he said. "Outside. In the free world."

The investigator leaned forward just a little.

"Outside where?" he asked.

Payaso hesitated.

His eyes flicked to the mirror on the wall. Then back.

"You gonna protect me?" he asked.

The investigator didn't answer that.

"I can put it in the report," he said. "After that, it's bigger than me."

Payaso let out a quiet, humorless breath.

"Yeah," he said. "That's what I figured."

Another pause.

Then he leaned forward, lowering his voice without meaning to.

"They wanted it done for somebody," he said. "Not us."

"Who?"

Payaso hesitated again.

Then—

"They call him El Mano."

The investigator's expression didn't change, but something in his eyes sharpened.

"El Mano," he repeated.

Payaso nodded once.

"Top sicario in Mexico," he said. "Works for Jalisco sometimes. Not one of them, though."

"Then what is he?"

Payaso gave a slight shrug.

"White boy," he said. "Biker. From Canada."

The investigator stayed still.

"Go on."

Payaso lifted his cuffed hands slightly, then let them drop.

"He's missing a hand," he said. "Got something else there. Metal. Heard he puts different shit on it."

"Shit like what?"

"Like—like—weapons and shit, you know?"

The investigator didn't interrupt.

Payaso's voice dropped another notch.

"They say he uses drones, too. And that he burns people alive. They say he never misses."

The fluorescent light buzzed louder in the quiet.

The investigator closed the folder slowly.

"You ever seen him?" he asked.

Payaso shook his head.

"No," he said. "Just heard."

"From who?"

Payaso leaned back again, chain pulling tight.

"Doesn't matter," he said. "You ain't gonna find him like that."

The investigator watched him for another second.

Then he stood, gathering the folder.

"You've been very helpful," he said.

Payaso let out a short laugh.

"Yeah," he said. "We'll see."

The investigator nodded to the officer by the door.

"Take him back."

The officer stepped forward, unlocking the chain from the table and guiding Payaso to his feet.

As they led him out, Payaso glanced once more at the mirror.

Then he was gone.

The door shut.

The room fell quiet again.

The investigator stood there for a moment, the folder in his hand.

Then he opened it again, flipped to a blank page, and wrote:

"El Mano"

– White male – biker

– Canadian

– Prosthetic hand

He stared at the words for a second, then closed the folder and walked out.

14

Chapter 14 – Cotulla

Cotulla, La Salle County, South Texas

The pumps worked through the night like iron metronomes.

On the flat scrubland outside Cotulla in South Texas, three wells rose out of the dirt. Pumpjacks, like skeletal horses, dipped their heads and rose again, steel groaning as they pulled crude from deep below the earth. At the edge of the site, six cylindrical tanks, each the size of a small house, sat in a row, their curved sides catching faint starlight.

The night was hot enough to make the asphalt tacky. The bitter-sweet smell of bitumen hung low over the ground. Coyotes barked somewhere out in the dark.

A set of headlights appeared miles away, then vanished as they dipped behind a rise.

The lease went back to its rhythm.

The headlights reappeared, close now, then vanished in the night.

A white F-250 rolled down the caliche road with its lights off, tires grinding softly over crushed rock.

The driver eased it to a stop short of the first well, cutting the engine before the truck fully settled.

Silence returned.

Both doors opened at once.

Two men stepped out.

One carried a duffel heavy enough to pull his shoulder down. He dropped it beside the first wellhead with a muted clank and unzipped it. The other man took a knee at the tree of valves, gloved hands running along the steel, feeling for seams, fittings, pressure points.

The first device came out wrapped in black tape, about the size of a shoebox. There were magnets fixed along its base. The man pressed the device into place at the entry point where the polished rod fed into the wellhead assembly.

It snapped into position with a dull click.

They attached the second device to the second wellhead, and then same for the third.

The kneeling man gave a nod.

They moved.

They crossed the pad to the tank battery.

One man climbed the ladder two rungs at a time before swinging onto the catwalk.

He moved along the tops of the tanks, placing charges at the seams where the steel plates met.

Each device locked in place with the same magnetic certainty.

Then they jogged back to the truck, boots crunching over gravel, urgency replacing patience.

Doors shut.

The engine turned over once, then settled into a low idle.

The truck rolled out, lights still off, disappearing back down the caliche road.

As it passed the lease sign, the lettering flashed briefly in the moonlight.

TexOil, Inc. – Leonard Lease – Wells No. 1, 2 & 3

The first explosion blasted the wellhead apart, a column of fire and shattered steel erupting into the night. The polished rod shot free like a spear, spinning end over end before vanishing into the dark.

The second charge detonated a fraction of a second later.

Then the third.

The wells didn't just explode—they ruptured.

Pressure that had been contained for years found release all at once.

Fire blossomed into the sky.

The tank battery ignited next.

The tanks burst open, spilling crude oil, each one adding fuel to a growing inferno spreading outward in waves.

Fire rolled across the ground, catching brush, licking up mesquite trees that snapped and cracked in the heat.

Two miles north, at an active TexOil drill site, an elderly gate guard stood outside his camper, pouring coffee into a chipped mug.

The drilling rig loomed above him, lit by floodlights that turned the pad into artificial daylight. Diesel engines rumbled. Draw works screamed as pipe turned deep in the hole.

He leaned against the doorframe and took a sip.

Too hot.

Too bitter.

He spat into the dirt and muttered under his breath.

When he looked up, he saw it.

At first, just a glow on the horizon.

Then it grew.

Orange. Red. Rising fast.

A fireball pushed upward, swelling into the night.

He froze, mug still in his hand, the reflection of the flames flickering across his glasses.

Then he set the mug down, fumbled for his phone, and started dialing.

On Highway 83, a Border Patrol unit rolled northbound.

The explosion hit seconds later.

A low concussion rolled across the land, followed by a second, sharper blast that carried farther.

The driver braked hard, tires skidding as the truck fishtailed onto the shoulder.

Both agents stepped out and stared.

Columns of fire tore into the sky, twisting as pressure vented from the ruptured wells.

The younger agent raised his phone without thinking, recording.

"What the hell is that?"

The older agent's eyes tracked the base of the flames, the spread, the pattern.

"I don't know," he said finally. "There was no drilling rig there earlier. Those are old wells over there. I don't know what could've happened."

He keyed his radio.

At the Cotulla volunteer firehouse, alarms erupted.

Men moved fast.

Boots on, jackets pulled tight, helmets grabbed as they ran for the trucks.

Engines roared to life, sirens cutting through the night as the bay doors rolled open.

The first engine cleared the lot in under thirty seconds.

They saw it before they reached it.

The sky glowed.

The closer they got, the worse it became.

The tanks had ruptured, crude spilling across the ground and igniting in sheets of flame that rolled through the mesquite. The wells screamed as pressure bled off through fire, jets of burning gas twisting in the updraft.

The lead engine slowed, then stopped.

Too hot.

The driver cursed under his breath.

"Hold here!"

The heat hit them even at distance like a wall. Tires softened against the asphalt. Paint on the hood shimmered.

"What are we supposed to do?" the firefighter in the passenger seat asked.

"Our hoses can't reach from here."

"Hell if I know," the driver said.

Above the inferno, a small quadcopter hovered.

Its camera tilted, capturing everything—the engines, the flashing lights, the men standing back from the heat.

Miles away, inside a black Suburban, the feed filled a pair of FPV goggles. Chino smiled.

Prison ink crept up his neck and across his jawline, disappearing beneath the headset. His hands worked the controller with practiced ease, small inputs keeping the drone steady in the rising thermals.

"Hell yeah, *carnal*," he said. "It's burning now. Whole place is lit up."

He adjusted altitude, circling wide to capture the spreading flames.

"All the cops and fire are rolling in. They can't get close though."

In the front seat, Oso watched the road ahead, face unreadable.

"Let it run another pass," he said. "Then bring it back."

Chino nodded.

The drone dipped lower, heat distortion warping the image as it passed over the tanks. Flames licked up toward it, the air churning.

"Good shit," Chino said quietly.

Oso glanced once in the rearview mirror, watching the glow on the horizon grow brighter.

"Call it back," he said. "Let's get out of here."

The drone climbed, turning away from the fire.

Behind it, the wells burned unchecked.

The email came in at 12:08 a.m. the night before where it sat unread for over seven hours.

At 7:17 a.m., a help desk associate clicked it open.

She worked reviewing general inquiries desk—low-level stuff, mostly. Lease questions, vendor forms, the occasional complaint about truck traffic or noise. Nothing that mattered. Nothing that ever reached past her desk.

She almost deleted the message without opening it.

No subject line.

No company signature.

Just an address she didn't recognize.

Something about it made her pause.

She clicked.

The message was short.

No greeting.

No formatting.

Plain text.

We know about your Leonard Lease in La Salle County.

We know all your wells.

You will pay us $1 billion or we will burn everything you have.

This is not a warning. This is business.

We will contact you again. Be ready.

She frowned.

"What the hell..."

She leaned closer to the screen, reading it again.

The wording was off. Not quite broken English, but not corporate either. No attempt to sound legitimate. No phishing links. No attachments.

Just a threat.

She glanced at the timestamp.

12:08 a.m.

Seven hours ago.

She hovered her mouse over the sender address.

Encrypted domain. Random string. Nothing she recognized.

Probably spam.

Or a joke.

She almost closed it.

Then her phone buzzed on the desk.

A news alert.

She glanced down, half-distracted.

BREAKING: Explosion reported at oil site near Cotulla, TX. Multiple fires burning.

Her eyes flicked back to the screen.

Then back to the phone.

Then back again.

For a moment, she didn't move.

Didn't breathe.

A cold, slow realization worked its way up her spine.

She stood abruptly, chair rolling back behind her.

"Okay... no..."

She grabbed the phone, opening the alert.

No details yet. Just footage. Someone filming from the highway. Flames tearing into the sky.

She looked back at the email.

You have already seen what we can do.

15

Chapter 15 – Green Light

TexOil, Inc. Headquarters, Downtown, Houston, Texas

The conference room was on the twenty-third floor of TexOil Tower, a high-rise in downtown Houston. Outside the walls of glass, sunlight glimmered across the city below, red taillights crawled along Lamar Street, and concrete stretched as far as the eye could see.

A long table cut the room in half, its black glass top polished to a mirror sheen. At one end sat the oil executives, ties tight, jackets buttoned, their expressions carved in stone.

At the other end sat federal agents, men and women in FBI jackets with serious expressions.

Special Agent Kim Wright wore a navy blue suit and black heels, her jet hair pulled back into a tight bun, her skin nearly as smooth and dark as the tabletop.

Next to them sat two agents of the CIA. Pierce, Mason's old leader from Ground Branch, the CIA's tactical arm, was one of them, skin tanned and eyes sharp.

Caleb and Mason took two seats across from the federal contingent. Mason tugged uncomfortably at the lapel of his blazer while Caleb shifted excitedly.

Files and laptops lay open, and half-drained coffee cups steamed faintly.

No one spoke until the projector screen on the wall flickered to life.

The first image was satellite stills of South Texas taken the night of the inferno. Plumes of fire and black smoke reached skyward. The ground below was charred.

A middle-aged woman executive with TexOil spoke first.

"Three wells, six storage tanks, and one pipeline valve house were destroyed by sabotage. No casualties, but production is down. Costs will run into nine figures. And it's an environmental disaster."

"How do you know it was sabotage?" Caleb asked.

Kim Wright answered.

"We know it was sabotage because the bombers emailed TexOil right before the bombing telling them they were going to blow up that exact wellsite. They sent it before the explosion."

A young land manager with TexOil spoke up.

"TexOil owns and operates about 30,000 wells globally. It could have been any one of our sites from Texas to Nigeria."

"Who was it? Environmentalists? Terrorists?" Caleb asked.

"Extortionists," the woman from TexOil spat. Her auburn hair showed streaks of gray, and the lines around her mouth emphasized her scowl. "Common criminals. They have demanded a sum of money, or they threaten to blow up more wells."

"It appears they timed this attack just as we're moving to divest our Eagle Ford assets," the young man added.

"After years of work, we have a buyer interested in acquiring our South Texas assets," the woman explained. "We are days away from signing a Purchase and Sale Agreement."

"Our counsel is reviewing, but we assume we'll have to represent to our buyers this threat exists," the younger TexOil manager continued. "Which may cause our buyer to pause."

"We cannot have the buyer pause," the woman executive stated plainly.

Caleb nodded understandingly.

"Do you have any leads?" he asked.

"Yes, we do," a man from the CIA piped up. He was overweight, balding, and red-faced. Next to Pierce's chiseled and tanned physique, he looked unhealthy. "The Jalisco Cartel. In particular, a man named Rafael Mendoza-Hernandez, known in Mexico as 'the Bishop.' He runs the oil theft wing of the Jalisco cartel."

Caleb's gave a confused smirk.

"The cartel is trying to extort a US oil company?" he said in disbelief. "That has to be a first, right?"

"Threats against infrastructure occur all the time," Kim Wright said. "But bombings do not. Also, the CIA has gathered additional intel pointing to this being a very real and continuing threat."

Pierce spoke up, his voice like rolling thunder.

"We suspect the involvement of a hostile foreign regime," he said plainly while staring directly at Mason, who still hadn't said a word. "This isn't just a cartel shakedown. There's more at play. Somebody wants to cripple American energy from the inside out."

The oil execs muttered curses under their breath.

Pierce let the silence stretch before continuing. "POTUS has been briefed, the Joint Chiefs, everyone. Direct action is authorized. We have the green light on the cartel."

Mason held Pierce's gaze, wondering what more he knew.

The oil execs exchanged relieved looks.

Pierce continued directing his words to Mason. "Direct action is my field. Defense ops will be yours. We need GZD to secure the oil sites and prevent more bombings."

Mason blinked.

"You said TexOil has over 30,000 wells around the world. I'm not sure Green Zone Defense can provide that scale of protection."

"Not globally," Kim Wright responded. "We believe the cartel is targeting South Texas oil fields because they're both close to the border and up for sale. Easy for them to launch cross-border attacks."

Mason chuckled and shook his head.

"So, we have the Mexicans and an unnamed foreign power launching attacks across the southern border into Texas? I did not have that on my

Bingo card for the year."

"The only Bingo we're worried about is which well they'll blow up next, and how to stop them," Kim Wright said matter-of-factly.

Caleb exhaled deeply and sat back in his chair, his mind racing.

"Ok, so we focus on South Texas. It's still a tall order. I doubt any firm could secure all your wells. But we can provide back up and reinforcements."

"Understood," Kim Wright said. "That's why the rest of us are putting everything we have toward stopping the threat where it lives."

Mason locked eyes with Pierce.

"'Stopping the threat where it lives.' I thought I smelled tacos and margaritas," Mason cracked. "They say the surfing in Puerto Vallarta is top tier."

Pierce chuckled.

"I'll let you know when it's time to wax your board," he said. "But for now, better leave the Hawaiian shirt activities to me."

"Gentleman, we need your expertise," the woman oil executive said. "Our employees and shareholders are counting on a smooth deal. Can we count on you?"

Mason leaned back in his chair, eyes still locked on Pierce.

"If we step into this," Caleb said, "we're not guarding gates and checking badges. We're stepping into an active conflict with a cartel that's already proven they'll use explosives on U.S. soil."

The room held still.

"That means casualties are on the table," he said. "Yours. Ours. Anyone standing in the wrong place when they make their next move."

One of the executives—a gray-haired man at the end of the table—leaned forward, hands clasped.

"With respect," he said, "the cartel already made this a war. We didn't bring this to them. They brought it to us."

The woman executive followed without hesitation.

"They attacked our assets. Our employees," she said. "We have a responsibility to keep operations running and people safe. Shutting down isn't an option."

Silence settled again.

Mason looked from one face to the next, then back to Pierce.

Caleb exhaled quietly.

"If we do this," he said, "we do it our way."

The woman executive didn't hesitate.

"Whatever you need," she said.

Caleb held her gaze, then leaned forward, forearms on the table.

"Alright," he said. "We're in."

"Just understand something," Mason said. "This is going to get deadly before it gets better."

No one at the table argued.

16

Chapter 16 – War

TexOil, Inc. Headquarters, Downtown, Houston, Texas

The meeting broke without ceremony.

Chairs slid back. Laptops snapped shut. The oil executives clustered together in low, urgent voices, already talking numbers, disclosures, and contingencies.

The FBI agents peeled off in pairs, murmuring into phones. The CIA man with the red face wiped his brow and disappeared through a side door.

Mason stood slowly, one hand resting on the table a moment longer than necessary. His shoulder ached—a dull, familiar pull where Rage had nearly taken his arm from him. He ignored it.

Pierce was already moving.

No goodbye. No handshake.

Just a glance over his shoulder.

Mason followed.

They stepped out into the hallway, the door sealing behind them with a soft hydraulic hiss. The noise of the room died instantly, replaced by the sterile quiet of corporate carpet and recessed lighting.

Pierce didn't slow.

"Walk with me."

They moved down the corridor side by side, past glass offices and framed photos of drilling rigs and offshore platforms. A receptionist looked up, then quickly back down at her screen.

Mason kept his hands loose at his sides.

"What aren't you saying?" he asked.

Pierce didn't answer right away. He pushed through a stairwell door instead of waiting for the elevator.

Concrete. Echo. The heavy door slammed behind them.

Now that they were alone, Pierce stopped halfway down the first flight and turned.

"This isn't just pressure," he said. "It's shaping."

Mason leaned against the railing, watching him.

"Meaning?"

"Meaning they're not trying to get paid and walk away. They're trying to move markets. Disrupt supply. Drive fear into the sector right when assets are changing hands. Force the deal to collapse."

Mason's eyes tightened.

"Cartel doesn't think like that," he said.

Pierce gave a faint smile.

"No," he agreed. "They don't. But Iran does."

The word hung in the stairwell like a bad smell.

Mason looked at him harder now.

"You're sure?"

Pierce shrugged slightly.

"Sure enough."

"That's a hell of an escalation."

"It is."

They stood in silence for a moment. The hum of the building filtered faintly through the concrete.

Mason pushed off the railing.

"So, what's the real play?" he asked. "Because you didn't drag me in here just to babysit pumpjacks."

Pierce studied him, measuring.

"Forward defense," he said. "You lock down the fields. Harden targets. Force them to miss. Every failed attack buys us time."

"For what?"

Pierce's eyes didn't move.

"For me to kill the snake at the head."

Mason let out a quiet breath.

"Bishop."

"And anyone standing next to him," Pierce said.

They started down the stairs again.

Mason spoke without looking at him.

"You've got a location?"

"Working on it."

"That means no."

"That means not yet."

Mason gave a faint, humorless smirk.

"Same thing."

They hit the next landing. Pierce stopped again, turning just enough to face him.

"I can't be everywhere at once. Neither can you. I need you and your guys to hold down the fort while my Rattlesnakes and I hunt. Can you handle that? Or have you gone soft in civilian life?"

Mason took a deep breath.

"That's what Lisa wishes."

"She's a smart girl," Pierce said. "But she better have known what she was getting into when she married you. Come on now. It's time to get to work."

Pierce continued down the stairs to the garage while Mason walked back up to the conference room floor. As he stepped through the door, Kim Wright saw him.

"There you are. I've got something else to tell you. In private."

"This just keeps getting better and better," Mason sighed.

They stepped into a corner of the hallway where nobody passed.

Kim cast her voice low.

"Your nemesis has popped back up. He may be involved in this mess."

Mason scrunched his brow.

"Who?"

"Rage," she replied.

17

Chapter 17 – La Quemazón

Zacatecas, Zacatecas State, Mexico

The Bishop's stone and adobe hacienda had been a sugar estate once, long before cocaine and stolen petrol replaced cane and molasses in the local economy. Its plaster walls were yellowed and cracked, but the gates were steel, the cameras modern, and the guards armed with black rifles. A fountain trickled in the moonlit courtyard, its water bubbling gold from the bulbs glowing overhead.

Rage waited outside the doors, his lean silhouette framed by the carved archway. He wore black jeans, a gray flannel shirt, and a black cowboy hat. The polished steel of his prosthetic hand gleamed below his shirt cuff.

The doors opened and out stepped a beefy bodyguard with a bald head in a black suit. Stone-faced, he motioned for Rage to turn around. Once Rage had assumed the position, the guard patted him down thoroughly, double-checking everything in his pockets, even flipping up the collar of his shirt and searching inside his ponytail.

When he was done, he spun Rage back around by the shoulder. Facing each other, he motioned for him to open his mouth, which he searched with a penlight. Finally, with a grunt, he instructed Rage to present his prosthetic hand. The fingers were wired to flex whenever he thought about it. The guard inspected it closely, turning the metallic hand over, searching for buttons, blades, nozzles, or other threats.

"Don't worry, Manuel, *amigo*," Rage said with a grin. "This one's gentle."

The bodyguard glared at him. His search completed, he jerked his head for Rage to enter.

Inside, the Bishop sat in a high-backed chair behind a wide, map-covered desk. A soot-blackened crucifix stood on a console behind him.

He looked up when Rage entered, a thin smile across his face.

"*El Mano*. Have a seat. *Bienvenido*. Welcome back from Guatemala."

"Gracias, *patrón*," Rage replied.

Rage lowered himself into a chair before the desk, his metal fingers clicking against the wooden armrest.

The door opened and in stepped Octavio wearing brown slacks and a white linen shirt, his black hair combed into place, his eyes tense.

"Octavio, just in time," the Bishop said. "You know *El Mano*."

Octavio and Rage exchanged nods.

"We are waiting for one more visitor. One of our new friends from Iran. While we wait, did you know, Octavio, that Iran used to be called Persia, and was once a great empire?" the Bishop asked.

Octavio nodded.

"In the Book of Isaiah," Octavio recited, "King Cyrus of Persia is named as God's chosen to cause the reconstruction of Jerusalem—a prophecy made long before Cyrus was born. Then later, in the Book of Ezra, Cyrus issued a decree allowing the Jews to return to Jerusalem and rebuild the Temple, just as prophesied."

The Bishop smiled and clapped, his large hands echoing in the stone chamber.

"*¡Excelente!*" he said. "You know your Old Testament well, *mijo*."

The Bishop stood and walked to the lectern where his Bible sat, his white suit flawless.

"When a new opportunity presents itself, I always turn to God for guidance," he said.

Standing over the open book, he said a brief prayer in Spanish, made the sign of the cross, then ran his fingers slowly down the page.

"When the Iranians first reached out to me, I asked, 'Father God, what do these men from this foreign land, with their strange gods and their strange customs, offer my people? Trade or treachery? Friend or foe?' Then I turned to the Bible, and I was reminded that God used the Persians to help His people long ago."

He turned a few pages, his dark eyes drifting over the text meditatively.

"The Americans came to Mexico—to Jalisco—and destroyed our property. Our Persian friends have suffered the same atrocities at the hands of *gringo* imperialists. Just recently, the *gringos* bombed their nuclear facility at Fordow. But now, just as in the days of Cyrus, they offer us a supporting hand."

Octavio shifted and opened his mouth to speak, when the door opened once again.

In walked a darkhaired man. Middle-aged and swarthy, he wore a blue pinstriped suit, white shirt, and blue tie. His trimmed black beard and thick hair held flecks of gray.

"Gentlemen, meet Reza Farhadi," the Bishop said as he walked across the room, hand extended. "*Bienvenido, señor.* Please, join us."

The Iranian operative shook the Bishop's hand, then crossed to the last waiting chair.

The boss gestured to the other seated men. "This is Octavio, my best commander. He has many years' experience organizing operations and negotiating payments with the oil companies. And this is our friend, *El Mano*. He eliminates any trouble wherever it is found."

"*Mucho gusto*," Reza said. His eyes were as clear and dark as the night sky, and he wore a silver ring with a large turquoise stone.

Still standing, the Bishop poured two fingers of mezcal each into four *jícaras*—small traditional drinking bowls made from dried gourds.

"Drink up, *compadres*," he said with a grin, and each man took their bowl.

Raising his *jícara*, he said, "*Que Dios nos juzgue después. Hoy bebemos.* Let God judge us later. Tonight, we drink!"

The men drank mezcal, savoring the flavors of smoke, earth, and fire.

When they were done, the Bishop sat and held his hands steepled in front of his chest.

"I have brought together the very best Jalisco has to offer. And also, as you instructed, we've proven our capability to strike with the action in Cotulla. We have done our part. So, *compadre*, what have you brought me?"

Reza reached into his pocket and removed a folded paper. He slid it across the desk to the Bishop, who picked it up, unfolded it, and studied it closely.

"I bring you proof of funds. You are holding a statement for a bank account in Panama. The operation known as *La Quemazón*—The Burning—is fully funded, as we agreed," Reza stated.

The Bishop's eyebrows raised as he studied the paper. A huge grin spread across his face.

"So, I see, *compadre. Bien!* With these funds, we can wage guerrilla warfare against our shared enemy—*los Estados Unidos.*"

Reza nodded. Then his eyebrows lowered.

"My commanders wish to make clear they expect nothing less than maximum effort," Reza said sternly.

"Don't worry, *amigo*," the Bishop assured him. "Octavio has already laid the plans. If he runs into any problems, that's what *El Mano* is for."

Reza turned to Octavio.

"What was the result of the operation in Cotulla?" he asked.

Octavio glanced at the Bishop before answering.

"The mission was a success on the ground. We destroyed three of their wells, some oil tanks, and other machinery. But, as we expected, TexOil has not responded to our demand for payment yet."

"As we expected," Reza agreed. "So, what is your next move?"

Octavio looked Reza directly in the eye.

"TexOil needs us to go away quietly," Octavio said. "So, we escalate. Cotulla was merely the spark. Now, we set the fire. Eventually, they will pay our demands."

Reza nodded.

"Continue with the target list. My commanders in Quds Force want maximum effect for their investment."

"And that is exactly what they shall get," the Bishop said with a wide grin. "Am I right, Octavio?"

"*Sí, patrón,*" Octavio replied. "That is exactly what we planned. With Los Tejanos providing soldiers, and myself providing administrative and logistical support, we will attack TexOil again and again until they break."

Reza raised his drinking bowl to Octavio.

"May God's will be done," Reza said, and the Bishop smiled.

After the meeting, outside the gate, Rage stepped up to the curb where his convoy waited.

Octavio followed a few paces behind.

They stood in the night air without speaking. The engine of the Suburban idled low.

Rage lit a cigarette. The flame flared, then died. He took his time with the first drag and let the smoke drift sideways—into Octavio's face.

"Two things I don't get," he said. "Since when does Jalisco conduct terrorist attacks, and why are the Iranians using the cartel and not some Muslim group?"

Octavio didn't look at him. His jaw tightened once, then settled.

"You think El Obispo cares about Middle Eastern politics?" Octavio replied. "Jalisco wants money—from Iran or TexOil, it doesn't matter—while the Iranians want to hurt the Americans by any means. They couldn't care less about the money. They get terror. We get paid. That's it."

Rage smiled and adjusted his cowboy hat.

"And when the Americans send everything they've got against us, what then? You think the cartel can stand up to that? You think the Iranians will stick around for the big show?"

Octavio's glared at him.

"I am here to serve El Obispo," he said. "Not to question. Just like you."

Rage's grin came back, thinner this time.

"Are you now?"

He took another drag, then flicked ash onto the pavement between them.

"Look, I don't give a shit what the reason is. Just don't get into shit so deep I can't drag your ass out of it. OK, *amigo*?"

Octavio chuckled and looked down the street.

Rage studied him another second, then turned, opened the back door of the SUV, and climbed in.

Before the door shut, he paused and looked back out.

"If you fuck this up," he said, "the Bishop will order me to peel you and your family's skin off and leave you in the desert. You know that, right?"

A thin stream of smoke curled out past his face.

Octavio kept staring down the road.

"You know what else?" Rage asked.

Octavio turned to glare at him.

"I'll enjoy it," Rage finished.

Octavio stepped forward.

His voice stayed even.

"You touch my family," he said, "and I won't need the Bishop's permission. I'll kill you myself."

Silence settled between them.

Rage held his gaze.

Then a slow grin spread across his face.

He pulled the door closed.

The window rolled down as the Suburban eased forward.

Smoke poured out into the night.

"Don't fuck up," he said.

18

Chapter 18 – Blood

Zacatecas, Zacatecas State, Mexico

Later that night, at Rage's mansion, he stood on the balcony outside his bedroom smoking and staring into the hills. Below him, the courtyard fountain trickled softly.

"Are you going to brood all night?"

The voice came from the bedroom behind him.

His mother stepped out onto the balcony in a silk robe tied loosely, a glass of red wine in her hand. Her hair was brushed and her face bare. Deep creases lined her gaunt cheeks, and her teeth were yellowed.

She leaned against the railing beside him.

"I heard about the oil well bombing in Texas," she said. "It's all over the news."

Rage exhaled smoke.

"It wasn't me."

She reached up and brushed imaginary lint from his shoulder.

"I know. You're smarter than that. That kind of shit only brings heat."

He glanced at her.

"You don't bring more heat than necessary," she said. "Everybody knows that."

She sipped her wine.

"You watch too much TV."

She laughed.

"It's important to stay informed."

They looked out into the dark hills.

"You remember Montreal?" she asked casually.

"Why?"

"No reason. Just... sometimes I think about it. That tiny apartment I raised you and your brother in. How cold it got when the radiator went out. You boys having to sleep on the floor."

She took another sip.

"You used to tell me you'd get us out of there. Even when you were little."

He flicked ash over the balcony.

"That was a long time ago."

"Yes," she agreed, "and look at you now. Even with your hand chewed off, you didn't let that stop you."

She stepped closer, her hand around his upper arm. He could smell the wine on her breath.

"You did it. Just like you said. You provide for your mama better than any man ever could. You protect your family. You're a good man."

She tilted her head.

"But you've been gone a lot lately."

"I have to work."

"Of course. Important man. You work too much."

"You drink too much," he replied.

She squinted at him for a moment, then the smile returned.

"Is that what this is about?"

She set her wine glass down on the railing.

"After a lifetime of scraping by, I try to have a little fun, and you hold that against me?"

"You bring strangers into my house."

"They aren't strangers. They're my friends."

"They're boys."

She shrugged.

"They're harmless."

Silence.

She reached for his cigarette, took it from his fingers without asking, and inhaled.

"You used to hate when I smoked."

"That was Raison," he said quietly.

She went still for a breath.

"Yeah," she said. "That's right. It was your brother."

She handed the cigarette back.

"He always worried too much. Always had a plan to fix things."

Rage's gaze hardened slightly.

"Not anymore, he doesn't."

She looked out over the balcony.

"I don't like when you talk about him like that. Raison was mean to me. I guess he blamed me for a lot. But he loved you very much. He always looked out for you."

She placed her hand on his shoulder.

"But you're not him. You're stronger," she continued. "You always were. Even when your father left. Even when the club turned its back on us, when you lost your hand, when Raison died—you were always the strongest. Stronger than me even."

She squeezed his arm.

"No matter what, we don't betray or abandon blood."

Rage stiffened.

She reached up and kissed his cheek.

"I'm proud of you."

Then she drifted back toward the bedroom.

At the door, she paused.

"You know," she said lightly, "if your brother had listened to you more, maybe he'd still be here."

Octavio parked two blocks away and walked the rest of the way home, cutting through a narrow alley that smelled of damp concrete and old oil. He paused once at the corner, letting a pickup pass, his eyes tracking the reflection in its dark window.

Inside his home he heard the television murmuring from the living room and the clinking of dishes in the sink. His children's voices drifted down the hallway, cheerful and unaware. He stood there for a moment, listening.

Then he stepped into his office and closed the door without a sound.

He took a phone from a locked desk drawer and scrolled to a number saved under a single initial.

The line clicked once.

"*Sí*," came Oso's voice from the other side.

"*Buenas noches, sobrino*," Octavio said, his tone easy, conversational. "I was looking over the plans for the celebration."

A pause on the other end. Oso breathed heavily.

"I think the first location is too small," Oso continued. "The fee is too high."

"*Sí.*"

"You should move it," he said. "Use the third place on the list. It's more... appropriate for the celebration you have in mind."

The line was quiet.

"*Entendido*," Oso finally said.

"*Bueno*," Octavio said. "Make sure the guests have a good time."

"I will," Oso confirmed.

The call ended.

Octavio set the phone down. For a moment, he sat there, his reflection staring back at him from the glass. He looked older than he remembered, his eyes harder than they used to be.

Then he stood and left the room.

He found Valeria in the bedroom, folding laundry at the foot of the bed. She looked up as he entered, reading something in his face immediately.

"Octavio?"

He crossed the room and took her hand.

"Come with me."

He guided her toward the closet, closing the door behind them. The space was tight, the air warm with the scent of fabric and cedar. He reached up and pulled the chain on the overhead bulb. The light flickered once, then steadied.

Valeria watched him now, her hands still.

"What is it?"

Octavio knelt and moved a stack of shoes aside, revealing a small seam in the hardwood floor. He pressed two fingers into the groove and lifted. The panel came free with a soft creak, exposing a recessed safe beneath.

He spun the dial. The lock clicked. He opened it and reached inside.

He stood with a pistol in his hand, a subcompact nine-millimeter.

Valeria's expression tightened immediately.

"What's going on?"

He held it out to her.

"Take it."

"No, Octavio."

"Valeria—"

"I said no." She shook her head, taking a step back until her shoulders touched the hanging clothes behind her. "We have Roberto and Ramón. They're outside all the time. We're not alone."

Octavio's jaw flexed. He lowered the gun.

"They are not here for you," he whispered.

She stared at him.

"What are you talking about?"

"They are here for me." He pointed to his chest. "To watch me. To report. If something happens. If someone decides I've become a problem, they won't protect you."

"That's not true."

"It is." He stepped closer, forcing her to hold his gaze. "You think they would die for us? For our children? They work for the Bishop."

Valeria flinched as the realization hit her.

Octavio extended the pistol again.

"You cannot trust anyone except me. Not them. Not anyone."

Valeria's eyes filled, her voice breaking.

"I don't want this life anymore, Octavio. I don't want guns in my hands. I don't want these men outside my door, watching my children—"

"I know," Octavio consoled her. "I know."

He reached for her, placing the pistol gently into her trembling hands. She didn't take it at first, her fingers curled in against her palms.

"You think I want this?" he said. "You think I don't see what it's doing to us?"

A tear slipped down her cheek.

"Then let's leave," she whispered. "Please. We can go. Take the kids and go somewhere else. Anywhere."

Octavio closed his eyes for a moment, just long enough to feel it. The weight of it. The impossibility.

When he opened them, the hardness was back.

"It's not that simple."

"It could be."

"No." He shook his head once. "It's not."

Silence filled the small space between them, thick and suffocating.

Finally, Valeria looked down at the gun in his hand, then back up at him. Her shoulders sagged.

"Everywhere?" she asked, her voice barely above a whisper.

"Everywhere."

She hesitated, then slowly reached out. Her fingers wrapped around the grip, unsteady at first, then firmer.

Octavio didn't let go. He held his hand over hers.

"Keep it close," he said. "And if anything feels wrong—anything—don't wait. Don't hesitate."

Tears spilled down her cheeks.

"I don't want it," she moaned.

Octavio's eyes flashed as his patience expired.

"You have to," he insisted. "For the kids."

He shoved the gun into her chest and held it there, pushing her back half a step.

Finally, she took the pistol, and he released her hand.

For a moment, they stood there in the narrow closet, surrounded by their ordinary things.

From down the hall, their children laughed.

Valeria closed her eyes.

Octavio turned off the light with a sharp, metallic click.

19

Chapter 19 – The Man Camp

Oil worker camp, Karnes County, South Texas

The camp had gone quiet after sunset. Dozens of white trailers lined the caliche lot, their aluminum skins dull under the halogen lamps. Pickup trucks were backed into parking spots in neat rows like horses at a hitching post, while boots and coveralls hung on clotheslines strung between campers. The smell of fried food lingered.

Inside, tired men lay on bunks watching TV or scrolling phones, their bellies heavy from barbecue and beer. Tomorrow would bring another dawn shift of driving to the rig, throwing chains, logging mud, checking gauges, and sweating under the South Texas sun.

Just under four-hundred yards out, up an incline and in a shallow cut of mesquite and limestone, Flaco lay prone behind a rifle, his eye pressed to the eyecup of a powerful night vision sight. The scope's reticle glowed faint green as he adjusted for wind. The rifle's suppressor jutted over a rock, the barrel wrapped in burlap strips.

Beside him, Chino monitored a tablet that tracked the slow drift of a drone circling high above. The drone's camera fed the sniper team a real time infrared overview of the camp—the grid of trailers, men laughing around porches, and a single dog pacing in the lamplight.

"Target?" Flaco asked.

The drone banked.

"Got a few," Chino replied as he studied his screen, counting the men. "Hold on just a second."

Below them, at the man camp, the dog stopped sniffing and stood at attention, ears perked, and stared into the brush.

Nearby, a group of oil workers were leaning on a pickup smoking and drinking beer.

One worker, a bearded man with a Cajun accent and jeans tucked into rubber boots, looked amused at the animal.

"What's she on?"

A thinner man with a handlebar moustache looked at the dog.

"Javelina, prob'ly," he said in a West Texas drawl.

The dog whined, turned to look at the men anxiously, then turned back to the brush.

The skinny man followed her stare, but all he saw was mesquite and prickly pears in the darkness beyond the security lights.

"What's got you, girl? Bobcat? Hog?" the Texas rig hand asked.

Then the shot came.

An off-shift worker walking past with a trash bag was struck in the sternum by a high-velocity .308 rifle round.

The sound came in three rapid staccato parts. First, there was a powerful *thump*, like the beat of a drum, as the round smashed open his chest cavity, followed by a metallic *smack-ping* as the round continued through his body and struck a truck's bumper, sending the round whizzing into the darkness. Finally, the rolling *boom* of the powerful rifle echoed to them through the night.

The shot worker crumpled mid-step and fell flat on the garbage sack, causing it to burst open, scattering paper plates across the ground.

The men standing by the truck froze.

The dog spun in the dust and ran.

Another shot cracked and a security light shattered, raining glass onto the men beneath.

They dropped their beers and dove for cover.

"What the fuck?" on yelled.

"Stop shooting!" the Texan shouted. "There's people down here."

The bearded Cajun squatted behind a truck, eyes wide, looking around frantically, when suddenly his left shin exploded, the jolt knocking him over.

The rifle's *boom* followed half-a-second later.

Laying in the dirt, he looked at his severed foot and ankle lying three feet away, then down at the bleeding stump.

He tilted his head back and screamed.

Flaco worked the bolt action with smooth precision. Through the scope he saw the ripple of panic, men ducking, scattering like chickens. He tracked the dog for a moment until it scurried behind a trailer.

The drone hovered at one end of the camp. Dozens of trailers laid out in a row beneath it.

"Go ahead, *carnal*. Run that shit," Flaco said.

Chino tapped his screen, and the drone eased forward.

Once it was above a row of trailers, it released its payload—one of two soda-can-sized bombs it carried.

The first improvised explosive struck a trailer roof, bounced, and landed with a metallic click against the gravel.

One second later, the device exploded between the second and third trailers.

Ball bearings rocketed in all directions, tearing through thin aluminum camper shells like paper.

Inside the second trailer, a man awakened by the commotion was standing groggily in his kitchen when the blast hit, knocking him across the room.

In the neighboring trailer, two men were hit with steel balls traveling at high velocity.

One died instantly. The other howled in confusion and pain.

The drone continued one-hundred more feet to the trailer where the Cajun and the Texan were hunkered, then dropped its second bomb.

The explosive bounced off a trailer roof and detonated beneath a pickup, lifting the truck's bed off the frame.

Shards punched through trailer siding and windows shattered.

"Shit!" the wiry Texan yelled from behind the back wheel of a blue Ford.

For a moment, the shooting stopped, and all the Texan could hear were the moans and cries of the wounded.

"Shit!" he spat again.

Suddenly, a trailer door flew open, and two men burst into the parking lot, rapidly taking up firing positions behind trucks. One man was wearing shorts, lace-up boots, and had a full plate carrier loaded with magazines, tactical lights, and other gear over his bare chest. He carried an AK-47 rifle with an ACOG sight and laser mounted to rails. The other man was similarly armed with an AR-15 and a tactical vest over tan cargo pants and a green t-shirt. A United States Marine Corps Eagle, Globe, and Anchor tattoo covered his left forearm.

The Marine immediately took charge.

"Cover front!" he yelled to the other armed worker who immediately aimed in the direction of the shooter.

As he slid his rifle over the bed of the truck, he caught sight of the Texan lying in the dirt and the Cajun moaning in a heap.

The shirtless oil worker with the AK-47 reached into a pocket on his vest and retrieved a tourniquet. He tossed it, and it landed in the Texan's face.

The Texan picked it up and looked around in confusion, as if he were waking from a dream.

"Hey, shit for brains!" the shirtless man yelled. "Tie off your leaking buddy and get ready to drag him back."

The Texan looked at the wounded Cajun, took a deep breath, and grabbed the tourniquet.

The Marine pulled a cellphone from his chest pocket.

"Benson, Kelly, Monroe! Move!" he yelled into the phone.

Trailer doors burst open, and three more armed workers spilled into the night. Each man, armed with a rifle or pistol, took position behind a truck.

A bullet cracked past the Marine's head.

Spotting a brief muzzle flash in the distance, the shirtless man laid his rifle over the truck bed and bellowed at the others.

"Sniper, front, four-hundred yards!" he yelled, then laid into his trigger.

The AK-47 burst flames into the night, the overpressure of the muzzle scattering dirt and beer cans in the truck's bed. Flashes from each shot lit up his face as he fired round-after-booming-round of 7.62x39mm toward the distant shooter.

With that, the other oil workers opened fire in unison, sending hundreds of rounds into the brush in a deadly fusillade.

Another incoming shot cracked, but the men kept shooting into the darkness.

A worker armed with a deer rifle took a round through the forehead. He collapsed instantly, blood and brain matter spattering the white RV behind him.

"Hold fire! Hold fire!" the Marine yelled.

Once the firing paused, he called out, "Everybody, stay low!"

He looked up at the security lights.

"Damn it," he muttered and turned his muzzle toward the nearest bulb atop a thirty-foot telephone pole.

He shot the light out with a single round. Glass rained down. He turned to the next light. One by one, in rapid succession, he shot out four more lights, the man camp becoming darker with each shot.

"Everybody!" he yelled. "Kill your lights! Kill your generators!"

Lights in trailers started to click off. One brave man crawled from his camper and scurried between generators, shutting them off one by one.

As the man camp fell into darkness, the oil workers adjusted their positions, crouching lower.

"What the fuck, Mark?" yelled the man with the shirtless man with the AK-47. "Who's shooting at us?"

The Marine stared through his AR-15's scope and cursed.

"Fuck if I know. You got night vision? I can't see shit."

"Yeah, I do," the shirtless man replied. "I see right where he's at. Fifteen degrees right of your 12 o'clock, four-hundred yards out, behind some big rocks."

The Marine looked through his scope.

"I can't see shit with this. We need to get these men back and call 911."

"Roger that! But the motherfucker is still up there watching. And what the fuck with the explosions. They got a fuckin' mortar up there?"

"Fuck if I know. Just shoot anything that moves by that rock."

The Marine pulled his cellphone out again and called 911.

ZING!

Another round whizzed by them.

"Mother fucker!" the shirtless man yelled, and returned fire, his rifle thundering.

The other men joined, then stopped to reload.

"We either have to pull back or maneuver on this mother fucker," he spat as he changed magazines. "We're wasting ammo here."

"Just keep your head down," the Marine shouted.

"911 emergency, do you need fire, police, or medical?" the dispatcher asked.

"Ma'am, we need it all," the Marine said.

"Sir, what exactly is your emergency?" the dispatcher asked.

With a crash, a sniper round shattered a windshield, barely missing a worker's head. He ducked and cursed just before the other workers opened fire again.

The deafening roar carried into the darkness.

Unable to hear his own voice, the Marine held up his phone so the dispatcher could hear, then he returned it to his ear.

"Ma'am," the Marine continued once the workers stopped to reload again. "I've got thirty plus workers at the TexOil well site at the intersection of Boling and Cemetery Roads. We are taking direct and indirect fire from unknown shooters. I've got at least three casualties, probably more. We need everybody you can send."

The phone went quiet.

"Ma'am, are you there?" he asked urgently.

The silence continued. He was looking at the screen to ensure the call hadn't dropped when the dispatcher's voice came through again, shaking.

"I've got police and medical enroute to your location," she said. "How many people did you say were shooting?"

"Everybody," he replied, his jaw clenched. "Everybody is shooting."

Hundreds of yards away, up the ridge, the sniper team watched from their fighting position behind the rocks.

"I think that's good, homeboy," Chino said. "We should get the fuck out of here."

Through his scope, Flaco watched the Marines' reflection in a truck's window. He could see the light of his phone screen but couldn't get a clear shot.

"That motherfucker is lucky," he growled.

Chino looked around nervously.

"We've got to collect brass and burn off, *carnal.*"

Flaco exhaled.

"Call the drone back," he said. "Let's go."

Rising to his knees, he grabbed the bandanna his empty shells had fallen on, wadded them up, and stuffed them into a pocket. Then he lifted the sniper rifle, collapsed the bipod, and crept toward a Ford Bronco waiting on a trail near their position. He tossed the rifle carelessly into the open back of the SUV, then retrieved a milk jug filled with a dark liquid.

Keeping low, he crept back to the fighting position just as the drone landed at Chino's feet. As soon as the blades stopped whirring, Chino picked it up and ran to the SUV.

Flaco opened the jug and sloshed its contents across the ground and rocks, the putrid coppery smell of blood filling the air as the liquid splashed.

When he was done, he dashed back to the vehicle, jumped into the driver's seat, and donned a pair of night vision goggles. He cranked the engine and drove without headlights, steering by the green and black image in the goggles.

"Did you throw the blood?" Chino asked.

"Yeah," Flaco replied. "There's blood from about a bunch of motherfuckers mixed in there. It'll take them a hundred years to process that shit."

At the bottom of the incline, the man camp lay in ruins.

Trailers were torn and blackened from explosions, trucks sat tilted on flat tires, and men huddled in silence, staring wide-eyed into the darkness.

"Is it over?" somebody yelled.

"What do you see?" the Marine called out.

The shirtless man stared intently through the night vision scope on his AK-47.

"Thought I saw movement, but now I don't see shit. Think they moved," he yelled back.

The Marine thought for a moment.

"We need to get these men back and clear out these trailers," he finally said. "We're all sitting ducks out here. How many casualties can you see?"

The shirtless man looked around, then over to where he had last seen the Texan and the Cajun. The Texan's body was laying on top of the Cajun's, the tourniquet still in his hand, both men's bodies motionless.

"Well, damn," he muttered. "Two! I've got two. They're both done."

"Roger," the Marine called back.

"Bro, is this a dream?" the shirtless man asked, sighting through his rifle toward the sniper's nest again. "Are we back in Afghanistan?"

The Marine glanced to his left and right at the shattered glass and bullet-riddled trailers.

"Nah," he said calmly. "We're not back in Afghanistan. But this ain't no fuckin' dream neither."

20

Chapter 20 – After Party

Zacatecas, Zacatecas State, Mexico

Meanwhile, in Zacatecas, the courtyard was alive with men.

Octavio stood near the fountain with two other Jalisco cartel commanders, deep in conversation, their voices low.

Bodyguards drifted along the perimeter, rifles slung, eyes sharp.

Rage stood at the head of a long outdoor table, studying satellite photos spread across the stone.

"You don't hit them twice in the same place," he said. "You trick them into protecting one place, then you hit another."

A man nodded and started to speak but was cut off.

Laughter, loud and slurred, carried from the balcony above.

Rage didn't look up, but everyone else did.

His mother leaned over the wrought-iron railing, silk robe barely tied, a cigarette glowing between her fingers.

"Is this a war council?" she called down cheerfully. "Or are you boys just measuring yours dicks again?"

Octavio stiffened.

Rage's face turned dark. He looked up, glaring from under his brows.

"Go back inside," he said calmly.

She waved him off.

"Oh relax. I'm just saying hello."

She disappeared briefly from the railing.

Rage's teeth clenched as the other men looked at each other.

A moment later, the French doors opened.

She walked into the courtyard barefoot, robe flowing behind her, perfume cutting through the night air. A shirtless young man trailed awkwardly behind her, his eyes glassy from drugs.

She walked straight to the table.

"You never invite me to the interesting meetings," she announced.

Octavio stepped back half a pace.

"*Señora*," he said respectfully.

She smiled at him.

"Oh, well. At least *one* of you has class."

She sauntered around the table toward Rage. As she passed him, her hand landed on his shoulder.

"You should've seen him when he was little," she said to Octavio. "He was the toughest boy in Saint-Henri."

The men stood in silence.

Octavio stared at her.

"Go inside," Rage ordered.

His mother leaned closer, lowering her voice.

"You think I don't know when someone's planning something?" she murmured. "I was a biker old lady before most of you were born. A real outlaw. I've seen war before. More than most of you."

Rage's jaw flexed.

"You're drunk."

She laughed, then sniffled and wiped her nose.

"I'm *alive*."

She laughed.

Then her gaze drifted to the maps.

"Texas?" she asked casually.

No one answered.

She tapped one of the satellite images with her fingernail.

Rage's hand closed over hers.

"Enough."

For a brief second, their eyes locked.

She smiled again.

"You see?" she said lightly to the men. "Always so serious."

She kissed Rage's cheek.

He scowled.

She turned and walked back toward the house, her boy toy scrambling to follow.

The courtyard remained silent after she disappeared.

Octavio cleared his throat.

Rage picked up the map as if nothing had happened.

"Pass the word. The next phase of the plan is on."

Octavio said nothing.

He simply studied Rage as if seeing him for the first time.

The Tejanos safehouse was a one-story cinderblock duplex off South Zarzamora Street in San Antonio.

Outside, the paint was peeling, and two junk cars crowded the driveway. Inside, a plastic box fan hummed in the kitchen window, pushing the weed and cigarette smoke around the stagnant living room.

On the scuffed coffee table sat a half-eaten order of tacos wrapped in wax paper, empty Tecate cans, scattered crumbs of cocaine, and a gold-plated Springfield Armory 1911 pistol engraved with horses and topless women. A flat screen TV played rap videos in the corner.

Chino sat at a laptop swiping through drone footage, his grinning face pressed to the screen.

"Look at this one, bro," he said, angling the computer. "I dropped that shit right on top of those fuckers. I know whoever was inside that trailer got fucked up, homeboy."

On the screen, the drone's downward-facing camera recorded an improvised bomb falling away, tumbling down onto the white roof of a trailer below. The device bounced off and exploded next to the structure in a plume of dust and debris.

Sitting next to him, Joker, a muscular forty-year-old in a white tank top, slammed a beer and belched. He flexed one arm and mimed a headshot with his fingers.

"Boom. Next time, we're torchin' the whole fuckin' thing."

In the kitchen nearby, Flaco sat at a round dining table, quietly cleaning his black Remington 700 sniper rifle, the bolt removed and laying on a red shop rag. His eyes were sunk into his head, and his cheekbones protruded. He slowly cleaned the weapon with cotton swabs, the stench of solvent mixing with the smoke.

Tigre, the crew's driver, leaned over a coffee table and snorted a line off his phone screen.

"In and out like nothing. You did that shit clean, *ese*."

From the kitchen, a deep voice boomed.

"You fools think you really did something, huh?"

The room fell quiet.

Their leader, Oso, stepped out of the shadows. Thick-shouldered, menacing, and quiet as a grave. His head was bald and tanned, his face pock-marked and tattooed.

Joker set his beer down.

"We dropped six of them, *carnal*. We sent a message, like you said."

Oso stepped into the living room.

"That's real serious to you. But in Jalisco, they go into a village, load all the people—men, children, old ladies—onto buses, take them into the desert, and kill every one of them. Then they put them in a hole, bury them with a bulldozer, and go eat *tamales*. They kill a hundred people a day like it's nothing. That little shit last night, that's child play in Jalisco."

Nobody spoke.

Chino bristled.

"Octavio said we'd get paid for doing the work no matter what."

Beto, who'd been pacing by a window in socks and basketball shorts with a pistol tucked in his waistband, spoke up. His pupils were black and dilated from cocaine, and his face glistened with sweat.

"One thing I wanna know—what about the taxes? We're doing all this work. We're taking the risk. But the *carnales* still want a percentage kicked to the big homies in the ADX. I feel like, we should get a break, know what I'm sayin'?"

Everyone froze.

Oso's eyes moved slowly to rest on him.

"What did you say?"

Beto hesitated.

"I'm just saying, man. ADX Florence is a long way from here. Those old fools don't do the jobs. Maybe it's time we—"

Flaco snapped the bolt shut on his rifle with a loud *CLACK!*

Oso walked over to Beto and stood face to face with him, their noses almost touching.

"Let me make this clear," he said. "You breathe because we've got respect. You move because you've got permission. *¿Entiendes?* You think I did all those years and put in all that work just to play out here? You think this shit is a game?"

He leaned in, his breath sour with beer and tobacco.

"Those 'old fools' see everything. You don't know what loyalty means till you've been in solitary your whole life eating bullshit trays through a slot. We pay our respects and our dues, Beto. That's how we fucking roll. *¿Entiendes?*"

Chino broke the tension with a chuckle.

"Hey, Oso. You should let me hit up your parole officer with the drone. BOOM! Right on top of the Bexar County parole offices. *¡A la chingada!*"

The others laughed.

Oso's face turned darker. He stood tall and his voice boomed like a drill sergeant.

"You fools are fucking joking, but I promise the cartel is not."

He looked around the room at his men, and his face turned to fury.

"You know what? Fuck this shit. Tejanos! Check in. What's your fucking status?"

Flaco lifted his rifle, racked the bolt, and sighted across the room through the scope.

"Flaco, ready. One shot, one kill."

"Chino?" Oso asked.

"Drone's ready. New payloads and everything. I upgraded the signal range, too."

Oso nodded.

"Good. You other fools need to tighten the fuck up."

He reached into his jacket, pulled a burner phone, and tapped out a text.

Then he looked around.

"The next orders are coming, and I want everyone sharp. No more sloppy shit. This is war. Fucking act like it."

21

Chapter 21 – Trust

Zacatecas, Zacatecas State, Mexico

The next evening, night laid across the hills of Zacatecas like a velvet sheet, but the Bishop's hacienda blazed with light and festivities.

Lanterns hung from the colonnades. Floodlights illuminated the courtyard fountains. Beyond the carved stone arches, dozens of guests drifted through the estate. Bankers, lawyers, money launderers, the courtiers of the underworld.

Music pulsed from hidden speakers, slow Latin jazz layered over a heavy bassline.

Money had gathered here tonight, and with it, sin.

The courtyard smelled of expensive cigars and roasted meat. Long tables overflowed with platters of roasted suckling pig, grilled lobster tails, pyramids of fruit, and crystal bowls filled with white powder. Ice buckets sweated around bottles of Dom Pérignon and aged tequila.

Women moved through the party like barely clothed exotic birds. Tall Colombians in silk dresses. Venezuelan models with shiny hair and glittering heels. Two Brazilian twins in matching gold bikinis floated through the pool with champagne flutes balanced in their hands.

Laughter rippled through the humid air as a Panamanian banker dumped

130

a handful of cocaine onto a mirrored tray and leaned down eagerly.

From the center of it all, the Bishop held court.

He stood beside the fountain in a cream linen suit, a glass of mezcal in one hand, the other resting lightly on the bare hip of a voluptuous young woman with dyed blonde hair. Around him clustered more offshore bankers.

One of them was drunkenly explaining something with elaborate hand gestures.

The Bishop listened politely, smiling his priestly grin.

Octavio entered the courtyard from a side entrance.

He walked through the wrought-iron gates and took in the scene. His black shirt was open at the collar.

The noise of the party washed over him.

The naked decadence. The drugs. The laughter. The bankers pawing at the women like tourists who had wandered into hell and discovered they liked it.

Octavio spotted the Bishop and crossed the courtyard.

A waitress stepped in front of him with a silver tray of champagne.

He waved her away.

The Bishop saw him approaching and excused himself from the bankers with a gentle raise of his hand.

"Octavio," he said warmly as the lieutenant reached the fountain. "You look like a man who has brought business to a celebration."

"I need a word with you," Octavio said quietly.

The Bishop studied his face.

"Of course."

He turned to the bankers.

"Please," he said with a gracious smile. "Enjoy yourselves. My home is yours tonight."

One of the bankers raised his glass.

"To Panama and Jalisco," he slurred.

The Bishop inclined his head.

Then he led Octavio through the arched doorway of the hacienda.

The music faded behind them.

Inside, the halls were cool and quiet. Oil paintings of saints and conquistadors watched them pass.

The Bishop stopped before a heavy wooden door and pushed it open.

A wine cellar lay below.

Stone steps spiraled downward into a vaulted chamber lit by amber lamps. Rows of dusty bottles filled the racks along the walls.

The door closed behind them.

The Bishop folded his hands behind his back.

"What troubles you?" he asked.

Octavio took a moment before answering.

He walked a few steps down the aisle of bottles, letting his fingers brush the wooden racks.

"I visited El Mano's house last week," he said.

The Bishop did not react.

Octavio turned.

"I saw something you should know."

The Bishop waited.

"His mother," Octavio continued. "She disrespected him."

The Bishop's face didn't budge.

"In front of the other commanders."

The Bishop's eyebrows raised slightly.

"How?"

"She mocked him. Spoke to him like he was a boy. Touched our mission files. She's an embarrassment. An aging whore. She brings young men into his home." He paused. "Men who are not careful about who they talk to."

The Bishop's eyes narrowed.

Octavio held his gaze.

"He cannot control her. She is his weakness."

The cellar felt colder now.

"You know how our enemies work," Octavio said. "The Americans. The intelligence services. The rival cartels." He gestured upward toward the party above them. "They don't attack the king. They attack the weak link nearest him."

Octavio lowered his voice.

"I know you trust El Mano, but a man who cannot control his own house can be compromised."

The only sound was the soft hum of the cellar lights.

The Bishop studied Octavio carefully.

Finally, he nodded.

"This is serious," he said.

Octavio inclined his head.

"I thought you should know."

"And I am glad you told me."

The Bishop stepped closer, his expression thoughtful now.

"El Mano has been... valuable."

"Yes," Octavio conceded.

"But weakness always surrounds power," the Bishop continued. "Family. Lovers. Friends. They become doors through which enemies may enter."

The Bishop placed a hand on Octavio's shoulder.

"You did the right thing bringing this to me."

22

Chapter 22 – Work

Mason's home, Golden, Colorado, USA

That same night in Colorado, Mason's truck rolled into his driveway just after dark.

The porch light was already on.

Inside, warm light spilled through the front windows.

He killed the engine and sat there for a second, hands resting on the wheel.

Everything was quiet except the ticking of cooling metal.

He stepped out.

Bud was at the door before he reached it. The dog's claws clicked against the hardwood on the other side, a low whine building in his chest.

Mason opened it.

The Dalmatian pushed through the gap and hit him hard, tail whipping, body solid. Mason dropped a hand to the dog's neck, gripping the loose skin under the fur.

"Easy," he said. "I'm here."

Inside, the house smelled like slow-cooked meat and fresh bread.

Lisa stood in the kitchen, one hand resting on the counter, the other holding a wooden spoon. She looked up as he came in.

"You're home so late," she said.

He closed the door behind him.

"Yeah."

She watched him for another second, then turned back to the stove and stirred.

"Wash up," she said. "Dinner's ready."

Mason set his keys down on the counter and moved to the sink. He washed his hands slowly, the water running hot over his fingers.

Bud stayed close, pacing once, then settling near his feet.

Mason dried his hands and turned.

Lisa was plating food. Two plates were already set.

"Did you eat?" he asked.

She shook her head slightly.

"I was waiting."

They sat at the table.

For a minute, neither of them spoke. Just the quiet sounds of forks on plates, the hum of the refrigerator, the soft clink of glass.

Mason chewed, swallowed, looked down at his plate.

Lisa watched him.

"Busy?" she asked.

"Yeah."

She nodded.

"How bad is this one?"

Mason took another bite, bought himself a second.

"Not bad," he said.

She held his eyes.

He didn't look away, but he didn't add anything.

A few seconds passed.

She picked up her wine glass and took a sip.

"Your dad called," she said.

Mason glanced up.

"Yeah?"

"He didn't say much. Just wanted to check in." She paused. "He sounded tired."

Mason nodded slowly.

"I'll call him."

"You should."

Another quiet stretch.

Outside, a car passed. Headlights swept across the front window and were gone.

Lisa set her fork down.

"You're going to have to go again, aren't you?" she asked.

Mason didn't answer right away.

He wiped his mouth with a napkin, folded it once, and set it down.

"Probably," he said.

"When?"

"Soon."

She nodded once, eyes drifting down to the table.

Bud's ears perked suddenly.

A low, quiet growl rolled out of his chest.

Mason's head turned.

The dog was staring toward the front of the house, body stiff now, muscles tight under his coat.

Mason listened.

Nothing.

"Hey," he said, reaching down, gripping Bud's collar lightly. "Easy."

Bud's eyes stayed fixed, his ears forward.

Mason watched the doorway a second longer, then let it go.

"Probably a cat," he said.

Lisa followed his glance, then looked back at him.

"Maybe," she said.

The dog settled somewhat, and Mason leaned back in his chair.

Lisa studied him again.

"You going to tell me what's going on?" she asked.

Mason held her gaze.

"Just work," he said.

Lisa's jaw shifted slightly.

"Just work," she repeated.

23

Chapter 23 – Move South

GZD Training Center, Denver, Colorado, USA

The conference room smelled of coffee and printer toner. Maps were spread across the table, taped edges curling upward, covered with notes in three different hands. Pins marked pumping stations, refineries, and drill sites from San Antonio down to the Mexican border. A laptop glowed with weather data, another with satellite feeds.

Mason leaned on the edge of the table with his arms crossed while Benito sat hunched over the map with a pen in his hand, making notes in the margin.

The door opened, and in walked Caleb.

"Just got off the phone with Kim Wright. The latest is six dead and twelve wounded at the TexOil man camp."

"Damn," Mason said gravely. "These guys are not playing. They may come even harder next time."

"Look," Caleb said, "we've got armed agents at every TexOil office in the country. We've assigned close protection agents to every executive. We have eighteen analysts chewing through data and cross-referencing against FBI intel. We've got nearly two hundred people assigned to this right now and we're trying to hire more. We've deployed all available assets. How the hell are we going to protect every TexOil well site, refinery, laydown yard, and everything else they've got? There are thousands of locations."

"We accepted the contract," Mason said. "There's no sense in wringing our hands now."

"What was I supposed to do? Turn down the biggest contract GZD has ever been offered?" Caleb replied, his hands clenching and unclenching.

Benito spoke up.

"All we can realistically provide is a quick reaction force. I heard a bunch of TexOil workers are calling in or walking off the job, so whether they like it or not, operations are getting paused anyway. For us, that should mean less targets to worry about."

"Benito's right," Mason added. "All we can do now is gather intel and provide QRF. Half the oil workers are veterans, and the other half are ex-cons. They've already proven they can and will fight back. Next time the cartel tries shooting up a man camp, I don't think it'll go as well for them. Did Kim say if they've gotten anything out of the crime scene?"

"Tire tracks, footprints, stuff like that," Caleb replied. "No shell casings. A lot of blood, so maybe the shooter took a round. Not sure yet. So, what's our next move?"

Benito tapped the pen against a red circle he'd drawn around Victoria.

"Next, GZD enters the ring. We are the heavyweight champ, after all."

"Benito's right," Mason concurred. "We need to set up tactical operations command in the area. The majority of TexOil's sites are spread across six counties in the South Texas Eagle Ford shale region. Victoria is the largest town near their holdings, so we should set up there."

"What do we need? Office space?" Caleb asked.

"No, something rural, private. A guest ranch or hunting cabin," Mason replied.

"Nobody thinks anything of a few out-of-town hunters carrying rifle cases in South Texas," Benito agreed.

"All right," Caleb said. "So, we move south."

"We need to get moving now," Mason said gravely. "We're already playing catch-up."

Mason knelt by the edge of the bed packing his personal items into a black duffle. He double-checked the side pockets. Clean shirts, med kit, extra socks.

Last of all, he made sure the Randall Model 1 fighting knife his father had given him was packed.

Outside the window, the first cold front of winter began to settle in.

Lisa sat on the corner of the bed, arms crossed over her sweater, watching him in silence.

"You sure I can't come with you?" she asked.

Mason paused, then pulled the zipper closed and stood.

"Not this time. I'll be too busy anyway."

She nodded, her lips pressed tightly together.

"This isn't just another consultation, is it?" she said. "There were attacks on oil workers in Texas. I saw it on the news. Now you're heading there."

Mason didn't answer.

Lisa stepped closer and rested a hand over his heart. Her eyes searched his.

"You're not the only one running this company," she said softly. "You've got a whole team now. Other people can do this part."

Still, he didn't respond.

"I want you home more. Not in pieces. Not in a coffin. Home. With me. With Ryan."

Mason rested his hands lightly on her hips. Her forehead touched his chest.

They stayed like that for a moment, hearts pressed together.

Then his phone vibrated on the nightstand.

Mason picked it up.

He answered.

"Talk to me."

"I found us a place," Caleb said. "Flights are booked. Take off in about 2 hours."

"I'm already packed. Leaving in ten."

Mason clicked off the call and looked at his wife.

Lisa's face changed the moment she saw his.

"It's bad, isn't it?" she asked.

He ran a hand through his hair.

"It's nothing I haven't faced before," he said.

She stood there, shoulders drawn in.

"Be safe," she said quietly.

Then she turned, crossed the room, and lifted Ryan from his crib.

Mason stepped into his boots, grabbed the duffel, and before he walked out into the frost, gave his family one last look.

"I love you," he said.

"I love you, too," she said as she bounced their son gently.

Bud stood near the door, watching him, tail low but moving, picking up the shift in the room.

Mason crouched and took Bud by the sides of the neck, pressing his forehead briefly to the dog's.

"Hold it down," he said.

Bud leaned into him, then licked once at his jaw.

Mason stood and looked back at Lisa and Ryan one more time.

Then he turned and stepped out into the cold.

The air bit hard outside. Frost clung to the grass and the edges of the driveway. The early morning was still and quiet.

Bud followed him out onto the porch.

Mason walked down the steps, crossed to his truck, and tossed the duffel into the passenger seat. The door shut with a solid thud.

Bud stayed close at his leg.

Suddenly, the dog stopped.

A low growl built in his chest.

Mason turned.

Across the street, the rent house sat still under the gray light. A figure stood near the mailbox bundled heavily against the cold, hood up, scarf pulled high across the face.

Mason watched the man flip slowly through a stack of mail.

Bud's growl deepened, weight shifting forward, ears locked.

"Hey," Mason said.

He rested a hand on the dog's neck.

"Easy."

Bud didn't break his stare.

The man across the street looked up.

For a moment, he just stood there—watching.

Mason gave a short wave.

The man hesitated, then returned the gesture before walking back toward the house.

The door shut behind him.

Bud's growl faded, but he didn't relax.

Mason watched the house a second longer.

It was quiet. Nothing appeared out of place.

He gave Bud one last firm pat along the neck.

"It's nothing," he said.

Then he climbed into the truck, shut the door, and fired the engine.

24

Chapter 24 – GZD South Texas

Centennial Airport, Denver, Colorado, USA

The Gulfstream lifted off from Centennial under a bruised evening sky. Denver's lights shrank into the dark as the jet banked south, smooth engines pulling it over plains and rolling hills. Mason sat by the window, hands folded, watching the land pass by below.

Caleb took a seat across the aisle, his leg bouncing restlessly. "Feels familiar, doesn't it?" he asked. "Flying south on a mission. Intel guys on one side, company men on the other. Us in the middle. Feels like Belize all over again."

"At least this time," Mason said, "we're not ghosts. We're on the books."

Caleb nodded.

"Does that make you feel better?"

Mason didn't answer.

They landed in San Antonio after sunset. The air was heavy with mesquite and exhaust. A pair of Suburbans waited on the tarmac. The drivers wore ballcaps and jackets to hide their holstered sidearms.

The first driver was Darius Cole, a tall, athletically-built man of dark complexion. Cole had been raised a devout Baptist in a rough neighborhood in Atlanta. A high school football and wrestling champ, he joined the Navy right after graduation, completed BUD/S on the first try, and became a sniper for SEAL Team 4, later rotating through multiple combat deployments across Central and South America. He'd worked for GZD for two years as a sniper, trainer, and security agent.

The other driver was Daniel Salgado. Born and raised in Laredo, Texas, Salgado knew the border better than anyone in the company. He enlisted in the Marine Corps at 18 and eventually earned a slot with Marine Special Operations Command (MARSOC) where he served with distinction in Afghanistan, Iraq, and across Central America during clandestine missions targeting narco-traffickers. After leaving the Corps, he joined the U.S. Border Patrol and quickly rose through the ranks to become a team leader with BORTAC, the elite special response team tasked with high-risk operations, cartel interdictions, and fugitive recovery. He had been with GZD for four years, held a senior security agent designation, and was a world-class Close Quarter Battle (CQB) instructor.

With their help, Mason, Caleb, and Benito carried their gear to the waiting SUVs. Backpacks, rifle bags, and hard Pelican cases carrying electronics filled both vehicles to their roofs.

The convoy rolled east out of the city, headlights cutting through dark ranchland. Highway 87 rolled under them in long stretches, lined with fences and occasional billboards half lit by failing bulbs.

A town of sixty-five thousand people built on oil money mixed with old cattle roots, Victoria was asleep when they rolled in. They passed through town, then headed Southwest on Highway 59 toward Goliad.

After a few miles, they turned down a county road to a rock driveway with a pipe cattle guard. The black outline of a hunting cabin appeared amongst the scrub oak and mesquite. A windmill stood crooked against the stars. To the right, a stock tank shimmered faintly in the moonlight.

The main building was one-story cabin with a tin roof and wraparound porch. The deck sagged in places, but the timbers were thick and solid. A string of yellowed bulbs ran the length of the eaves, illuminating a set of old deer racks mounted over the doorway. To one side sat a rusted pit smoker and a stack of chopped mesquite wood. The other side was stacked with plastic lawn chairs, duck decoys, and a pair of dusty generators.

Benito stepped out first, sweeping a flashlight across the clearing, then studying the horizon. "Good. No neighbors. No lights for half a mile."

Coyotes yipped far off in the brush.

Inside, the old cabin smelled like dry cedar and mouse shit.

"It'll work," Mason said. "Let's get the gear inside."

They hauled crates and bags into the main room which held a stone fireplace, a buckskin couch, and a beat-up pool table covered in dust. A deer mount stared from the wall, its glass eyes dull and accusing. Someone had left an orange hat on its antlers.

They unpacked, and, one by one, laptops and radios came online.

Caleb set up comms on the kitchen table, linking a satellite uplink to a GZD network relay node. One monitor showed satellite views of the surrounding counties. Another streamed FBI and DHS alerts. A third listed real-time TexOil site statuses: pump jacks, tank batteries, trailer camps, and rail hubs.

Benito stood at the mantle, rolling a fresh cigar between his fingers. "This place got Wi-Fi?"

"No," Caleb said. "But we've got cell and sat. We'll push encrypted signals through our own mesh. No one's hacking into this place."

"Good," Mason said, a cup of coffee in his hand.

Standing in the open back door, Benito exhaled smoke into the night. "You expecting contact soon?"

"I'm expecting a pattern," Mason said. "They hit Cotulla. Then a man camp. Next target will be bigger. They want headlines and chaos."

Caleb glanced over. "Yep. They want to jeopardize TexOil's deal."

"They want fear, yeah, but mostly they want money," Mason said. "The parasite never wants to kill the host, so their next move has to be big but measured. It does them no good to kill the deal now before they get paid."

The other GZD field agents began uncrating weapons and gear. Rifles were checked and body armor sorted. NVGs and radios were set on chargers, and maps were tacked to the living room wall.

By morning, the cabin had been cleaned, antennas mounted to the roof, and a folding table converted into a command terminal under the deer mount's blind gaze.

Mason stepped outside to watch the sun rise, staring out at the endless scrub beyond the fence line, wondering who this enemy was and what preparations he was making that same night.

25

Chapter 25 – Three Rivers

GZD South Texas cabin, Victoria, Texas, USA

Mason was up at 04:00 the next morning. He rolled out from under a blanket that smelled of mothballs, pulled on some sweatpants and a T-shirt, tied on running shoes, and brushed his teeth before tugging a cap over his shoulder-length brown hair.

He quietly stepped out onto the front porch, then stepped into the yard and took a moment to stretch. It was still about two hours until sunrise.

Mason took off jogging.

At the cattle guard at the end of the driveway, he turned left onto the dirt road, his rubber soles padding lightly on the hardpack. Normally, he would run five miles, but he'd learned to cut his training volume in half when on an operation.

He completed his run and was back at GZD South Texas—as they had begun to call the hunting cabin—before sunrise. He was scrambling eggs and frying sausage when Benito, Caleb, Cole, and Salgado awoke to join him. Over eggs and coffee, they made plans to finish preparing and testing their gear when Caleb's and Mason's phones both pinged.

The notifications were on their encrypted file transfer and messaging apps used to communicate with Kim Wright at the FBI.

There was a message and an audio file. Mason clicked the recording.

"Another attack on TexOil today. Three Rivers."

Then a click and silence.

A male voice, low and urgent, distorted through layers of digital noise.

He read the message from Kim.

The call had come through TexOil's stakeholder relations line at 08:03 that morning.

By 08:17, a recording of the call was routed to the FBI's San Antonio Field Office where Special Agent Kim Wright, on loan from the Denver Field Office, reviewed and uploaded the recording to a secure Department of Justice shared drive.

At 8:43, Caleb and Mason both received notifications on their encrypted apps.

Mason stood in the middle of the TOC's kitchen, the phone pressed to his ear, staring at a line of ants marching across the drywall as he listened to the recording again.

Caleb leaned against the counter, arms folded. "They must mean the refinery in Three Rivers, right?"

"Yeah."

"You believe it?"

Mason set the phone down. "We can't afford not to."

Both men walked from the kitchen to the living-room-turned-command-center where Benito was sitting at a laptop.

"How far is the refinery in Three Rivers?" Mason asked.

"Close," Benito responded. "About an hour."

At just past 10:00, two Suburbans rolled out of GZD's South Texas TOC. They took back roads to Highway 59, then headed Southwest.

The town of Three Rivers came into view just after 11:00 a.m., shimmering under the South Texas heat. A grid of low buildings and fast-food joints clustered around the highway, wrapped in dry grass and pump jacks. The entire southwest quarter of town was a TexOil refinery. It rose out of the scrubland like a steel mirage: tall flare stacks, pressure vessels, and silver-white tanks arranged like dominos. Chain-link fencing topped with razor wire ringed the entire facility. The main gate faced North and featured a small guard building.

Benito drove the lead Suburban up to the gate and rolled down the window. The gate guard, a young Hispanic man in a brown security uniform, approached.

"Green Zone Defense here to meet with Chief Hernandez," Benito said from behind his dark glasses.

The security guard looked nervous. He stepped back and raised a handheld radio to his face.

"I've got the contractors we talked about this morning at the gate for Chief Hernandez. Where should I send them?"

There was a pause, then the radio crackled.

"Send them to Lot B. We'll meet there," the call came back.

The guard pointed into the refinery.

"Go straight, then veer left at the yellow fire hydrant. There's a sign on the left that says Lot B. Just pull in there and somebody will meet you."

"Appreciate it," Benito said, and rolled up the window.

GZD's two black Suburbans pulled into the refinery's B parking lot and were immediately met by a stern older man in a crisp brown security uniform accompanied by three other guards and two uniformed Three Rivers police officers. They all carried sidearms, and one of the TexOil security men had an AR-15 slung across his chest.

The GZD South Texas team parked and unloaded. They all wore sunglasses and jeans or cargo pants over hiking boots with T-shirts or flannels, hoping to mix with the workers.

Mason approached the older TexOil security man with his hand extended.

"I'm Chief Hernandez," the man said. He had a thick head of iron gray hair and a rugged, tanned face.

"Travis Mason, Green Zone Defense," he replied with a firm handshake. "This is my team."

"This is Captain Williams and Sergeant Riley from Three Rivers PD," he said, and Mason shook their hands in turn. "We've barely been briefed about the threat. What do you know?"

"Unfortunately, not much. We received word from the FBI at about 08:45 this morning and got here as fast as we could."

The police captain spoke up. "This the same guys who shot up the man camp last week?"

"As far as we know, yes," Mason replied. "They've been known to use snipers and explosives. They have targeted both infrastructure and personnel. At the moment, the entire facility should be considered at risk."

"Can you clear the personnel out for safety?" Caleb asked.

"Not that easy," Chief Hernandez said. "You can't just pull people out. Safely shutting down a refinery takes days. If we pull people out, it could lead to a leak or explosion and jeopardize the whole town."

Mason exhaled.

"OK, then we need every security officer you've got on the perimeter. Do you have any contractors on site today? Anybody unusual?"

One of the other guards spoke up. "There are four outside contract crews working here today, but they've all been approved vendors for years."

"Ok, so nobody new inside the perimeter?" Mason asked.

"That's right," the guard responded.

"Then the attack will most-likely originate from outside the wire," Mason said. "Instead of waiting, we need to start searching for them now. It's probably a waste of time to set up police cruisers on the roads into town, but it could be worth it to ask around the local hotels, restaurants, or gas stations. Stage a few extra officers at the gate. Can Three Rivers PD beat the bushes and see what they scare up?"

"It would help a lot if we knew what we're looking for," Captain Williams said. He was a heavy-set man with a sun-reddened face and thin brown hair.

"A group of two to five males, Hispanic, between the ages of 18 and 50. Tattoos likely. Possibly in a stolen vehicle. They won't be from here, but they'll try to blend in," Benito replied.

Captain Williams looked sour. "You just described half the population of Live Oak County."

Mason thought for a moment.

"No, Captain Williams is right," he said. "We need his men on the perimeter, not out chasing shadows. Can you have men set up at all the cross streets leading to the refinery?"

"I can do that," he said matter-of-factly.

"Good," Mason said. "My team will take up overwatch from within the perimeter. The rule is, If you see something, say something."

"We need to share channels," Benito said.

"Seargent Riley can handle that," Captain William said. "Seargent, put all comms for this operation on Tac Channel 3."

"Yes, sir," the sergeant responded.

"We don't have a tactical team or armored car here," Captain Williams continued, "but I have calls into San Antonio PD and Bexar County for assistance. It may be hours before they can arrive. How soon are we expecting action?"

Mason glanced around at the distillation towers, flare stacks, and catwalks where hard-hat-wearing workers toiled in ignorance of the danger possibly headed their way.

"We're not even sure this is a credible threat," Mason said. "In past attacks, there was no warning."

"But there have been attacks," Chief Hernandez said.

"Yes."

"And deaths?"

Mason nodded, still casting his eyes around, studying the high ground.

"Yes."

The Chief exhaled.

"Where do you want to set up?" Chief Hernandez asked.

Mason pointed to a tower near the front gate with a winding steel staircase and a platform on top.

"Right there," he said.

26

Chapter 26 – Contact

TexOil, Inc. Refinery, Three Rivers, Texas, USA

After meeting with Chief Hernandez, GZD South Texas split up.

Mason and Benito parked their Suburban near the main gate on the north end of the refinery. Chief Hernandez had already called in all shifts of security personnel, and there were five armed guards covering the entrance. Mason and Benito set up fifty feet away with a clear view of the stream of pick-ups, delivery trucks, and tankers that passed through the red and white barrier arm.

Caleb was indoors, seated at a desk outside Chief Hernandez's office, running the UAS feed from a ruggedized tablet. Above them, their quadcopter drone orbited.

"Visual confirms seventy to eighty vehicles in Parking Lot D," he said into his headset. "People are trickling in for the noon shift. Benito, anything new from the FBI feed?"

"Nothing new on the federal chatter. Still no ID on the caller," Benito transmitted back.

At the south end of the facility, Salgado sat alone in the other Suburban. That end of the plant consisted of mostly storage tanks with few outbuildings or personnel. The easiest entry from the south was an opening for a single-track railway. Salgado scanned the perimeter fence with binoculars, an M4 carbine laying across his lap.

Fifty feet above them all, atop a refinery tower near the front gate, Cole lay prone behind a scoped Barrett Mk22 Mod 0 Advanced Sniper Rifle chambered in .338 Norma Magnum. The rifle was propped on a sandbag, and Cole was splayed out behind, feet wide apart to brace for the weapon's considerable recoil.

He panned across the buildings and streets surrounding the refinery through his scope.

Something caught his eye, and he stopped to study it.

"I've got eyes on three men loitering in a silver Tahoe on the east side of parking lot D," he said into his headset. "Front windows down, engine off. One of them keeps messing with something in the backseat."

At ground level below, Benito and Mason studied the silver Tahoe through binoculars.

"They're parked weird," Benito said. "Too far back from the other vehicles. I count three military-aged males in work clothes. They're moving about the vehicle. Nobody seems in a big hurry to head into work. No company markings."

Mason tapped his comms. "All elements, listen up. Possible target vehicle. Silver Tahoe parked in the northeast corner of the outside parking lot D. Caleb, let's get eye-in-the-sky on that Tahoe."

"Roger that," Caleb confirmed.

The GZD drone pivoted and dipped as it moved into position directly over the outside lot. Even at four-hundred feet above the earth, its main camera was so powerful Caleb could read the logo on a soda can on the ground.

Caleb leaned closer to the tablet, thumb and forefinger spreading the image as the drone settled into a slow hover above the suspect vehicle.

"Zooming," he said calmly.

The camera tightened. Through the windshield, the interior came into sharp relief. Torn upholstery, fast-food trash, and something sparkling in the sun on the dashboard.

"There's something reflective on the passenger-side dash," Caleb radioed.

"Could be pieces of broken glass. Looks like somebody busted in the passenger window. Vehicle might be stolen."

From his perch fifty feet up, Cole adjusted his cheek weld and let the reticle settle on the Tahoe. Three silhouettes. One in the driver's seat. One half-turned in the back. Another leaned forward, shoulders hunched, hands busy with something. He dialed in the zoom on his adjustable power scope until he could see the tattoos on the passenger's hands and neck.

"I spot prison ink on the passenger," Cole transmitted.

Mason didn't hesitate.

"Cole—stand by. Caleb, hold steady. Benito, with me."

Mason popped the Suburban door and stepped out while slinging a Daniel Defense DD4 MK18 RIII short-barreled rifle over his shoulder. He had slipped on a low-profile plate carrier with shooter cut ceramic plates and extra magazines, and he carried a Staccato HD P4 in a Kydex holster on his hip.

Benito was similarly armed with a Daniel Defense DDM4 V7 K with a short barrel and a Glock 19 in a drop-leg holster. He climbed out and racked a round into his rifle with a gloved hand.

"Flank wide left. I'm going up the right. Go!" Mason said.

Benito was already moving.

"Target vehicle has opened their doors," Caleb called out as he watched closely through the drone lens. "Three men exiting the vehicle...One is holding something down by his leg....Another is pulling something from the back seat...Rifle! I have confirmed visual on a gun. Over."

"I confirm visual on two long guns," Cole added as he watched through his scope. "Mason, they don't see you yet. They're heading straight toward the front gate."

27

Chapter 27 – Engage

TexOil, Inc. Refinery, Three Rivers, Texas, USA

As Benito passed the front gate at a trot, the guards looked at him in shock. There were two vehicles stopped at the barrier arm.

"Let them in! Clear the area! Get to cover!" Benito yelled.

The guards quickly lifted the gate barrier and waved the trucks through.

"Shooters have formed a skirmish line, over," Caleb said.

Mason mashed his push-to-talk button as he trotted across the street toward the Tahoe.

"Police are on the way," Caleb's voice came over Mason's earpiece as he sprinted across the street toward the threat.

He stopped and took a knee behind a white sedan.

"Cole," he transmitted, "talk to me."

"Shooters are coming to you. Nearest one is fifty-feet," Cole replied.

Mason leaned out and looked to his left. Benito was eighty feet away crouched behind a blue Dodge pick-up, waiting to strike.

"No time to wait for cops. Benito, on my 'Go!', we attempt to apprehend. If they flinch, flatten your guy on the left. Cole, drop the middle one," Mason said.

"Roger," came the responses from both men.

Mason peeked under the vehicle and spotted the approaching men's feet just twenty-five feet away.

He said a quick prayer then—

"Go!"

He stood up, shouldered his rifle, and centered his red dot over the chest of a young cartel gunman wearing a black sweatshirt and blue jeans. He wore a black ball cap pulled low and a bandana over the bottom of his face.

"Drop your weapons!" Mason yelled.

He heard Benito echo his command from the left.

"Drop your weapons! Drop your weapons!"

The shooter in black jerked to a stop, his eyes bulging with shock. He looked to the middle shooter.

Mason repeated his order.

"Drop the gun now or I shoot!"

The sicario started to back pedal, unsure where to go. Mason never took his red dot off the man's chest.

Suddenly, a familiar whistle zinged past Mason's head, and less than a second later, a distant boom carried down the street to him from a wooded park five-hundred yards away.

Mason ducked from the sniper round, and in that instant, the gunman in black raised his AR-15 and fired.

Bullets snapped past his head and smacked the truck behind him.

He returned fire, shattering car windows where the shooter had been, but the black-clad assassin ducked behind a red car.

"Sniper left!" Mason radioed.

At that, Cole went to work.

The .338 Norma boomed like a thunderclap. The supersonic 300-grain bullet passed through the center gunman's head at 2,700 feet-per-second, nearly ripping it off.

"Center shooter is down," he radioed calmly.

On the left flank, rather than getting popped by the sniper, Benito attacked. He stood, raised his rifle, and launched forward, hunting for the left-side shooter. As he trotted between cars, he watched intently for movement.

Before he could advance far, Caleb's voice snapped in his ear.

"Multiple drones inbound. West side. Low altitude."

Three drones flashed above them, mid-sized quadcopters flying in a single file. Caleb could see them clearly from his drone's position hundreds of feet above. He zoomed the camera in and set it to track one of the flying machines. He could clearly see the improvised bomb underneath its chassis.

"All three drones are carrying," he said with ice in his voice.

The enemy drones made a quick loop over the parking lot—

Then one dropped its payload.

The homemade bomb fell straight down, hit the side of a van five feet from Mason, deflected, and skittered across the pavement before detonating between two pick-up trucks.

The blast, mostly contained by the vehicles, nevertheless sent shards of rock and glass to pepper Mason's right side like a load of birdshot.

He went prone, gritting his teeth as the blast wave rolled over him.

Heat washed across his right side. It shoved the air out of his chest and left a sharp ringing in his ears.

He stayed down for a second.

Then forced himself to move.

"Contact front," he said, his voice raspy with pain.

28

Chapter 28 – Firestorm

TexOil, Inc. Refinery, Three Rivers, Texas, USA

Caleb watched through his drone's eye as the explosion kicked up a plume of dust.

"Mason, are you hit?" he called frantically over comms.

Mason took a moment to respond.

Though his ears rang and his side burned, he knew the difference between getting peppered with debris versus catching real shrapnel.

"I'm good," he called back.

Gathering himself, he pushed up to return to his feet when suddenly, the shooter in black stepped out from behind a Ford Explorer, rifle aimed.

Mason dove right just as a burst of bullets smacked the pavement, sending asphalt pebbles ricocheting off cars with metallic clicks.

He rolled, whipped the rifle up, aimed by instinct, and sent two rounds toward the shooter in quick succession, but they missed. Mason dashed right to flank from the outside. He raced down the length of a truck, then cut sharply north, scanning with his muzzle for a target.

He spotted the sicario a split second before the man spotted him. At full sprint, just as the killer spun to fire, Mason drilled him with three shots center mass.

Mason skidded to a halt, focused his aim, and shot the crumpled assassin in the head twice more for good measure.

"Right shooter is down," he said into his radio mouthpiece. "Cole, find that sniper."

"Roger," Cole said.

He repositioned himself on top of the tower's platform, pointing his scope toward the tree-lined park five hundred yards away, searching methodically for any sign of the shooter.

Above them, the enemy drones were circling the parking lot. Suddenly, as if they spotted something, they peeled off and headed toward the refinery, directly toward Cole.

"Cole, you've got in-bound," Caleb called over the radio.

"Shit," Cole muttered. He jumped to his feet on the platform high above the ground, shouldered his rifle, and scanned the sky quickly through his scope, but it was no use. He set the rifle down, drew his HK VP9 Tactical pistol, spread his feet in a shooter's stance, and prepared to battle the flying menaces.

Soon, he heard the buzzing of their rotors, but squinting into the bright noon sky, it was impossible to see.

He could tell by the sound they were circling him.

"Cole, get off that tower," Caleb called out. "They've got you zeroed."

Cole gritted his teeth.

"Bring it, motherfucker," he growled, gripping the pistol tighter, scanning for a target.

Caleb watched as one of the drones stopped, reoriented, and maneuvered into position directly over Cole's head.

"Get out of there!" Caleb yelled, but it was too late.

The drone released a bomb directly over Cole's position.

The bomb fell, its stubby winglets causing rotation.

Cole looked straight up, aimed, and fired into the sky.

Suddenly, three feet from where he stood, the bomb impacted the platform with a bang that vibrated up through his feet.

Inside the refinery's security office, Caleb leaped to his feet in terror. "Shit!"

Heart in his throat, Cole looked down.

The bomb had struck with enough energy to wedge itself into the platform—but it hadn't exploded.

Cole stared at it in shock.

Caleb was bent over the desk, eyes glued to the screen.

"Cole! What's your status?"

On top of the tower, the veteran sniper lowered his pistol, took several deep breaths, then mashed his transmit button.

"I'm good," he said. "It was a dud."

"Son of a bitch!" Caleb yelled, scattering an empty coffee cup from the desk. "There's still one more armed drone."

"Shit," Cole whispered, raising his pistol back up, searching the sky for the threat.

Then came Salgado's voice over the radio. "I'm on my way!"

At the far end of the refinery, Salgado had jumped in his Suburban and hit sixty miles-per-hour racing up the refinery road to the front gate, the SUV's big engine roaring, a cloud of dust behind him.

He barreled through the gate without touching the brakes and slid to a stop in the street.

Salgado stepped out, raised his rifle, and tracked the dark shape skimming just above the storage tanks.

The drone dipped, angling toward the catwalks—

Salgado fired.

The round caught the drone dead center. It cartwheeled into a tank berm where it sat twitching and sparking in the dirt.

"One drone down," Salgado said. "Two still airborne."

"Hell, yeah!" Caleb smacked the desk.

The remaining two cartel drones quickly gained altitude.

Cole resumed searching for the sniper while Benito and Mason hunted the last parking lot shooter.

On his tablet feed, Caleb could see the man hunkered behind a minivan looking frantically left and right, unsure what to do.

"Mason, Benito, last shooter is behind the blue van," Caleb sent.

Spotting the van, Benito stalked forward carefully.

The gunman spotted him and raised to shoot.

Benito saw him—then lowered his rifle and smiled.

The sicario hesitated.

In that moment, Mason popped out behind the shooter and jabbed his muzzle behind the man's ear.

"Drop. Your. Fucking. Weapon," he growled.

The man laid the rifle down and raised his hands.

Mason picked up the man's AR-15, removed the magazine and jacked the round out of the chamber, then tossed the weapon onto the ground.

"Secure this piece of shit," Mason told Benito as he approached.

Benito whacked the shooter hard in the head with his buttstock, knocking him to his face. Then he planted his boot in his back and ordered him to spread his hands and feet.

"Caleb, what's the sitrep?" Mason asked.

"Cole is searching for the sniper. No other movement spotted."

Cole calmly scanned the bushes, trees, benches, trash cans, and vehicles in the park, but didn't spot any movement.

"I've got nothing so far," he radioed back.

In that moment, police cars screeched into the streets surrounding the refinery, sirens blaring.

Cole lifted his head from the rifle.

Mason watched as police flooded the area. His body stung from the drone's bomb, and he could feel his muscles tightening from trauma. He looked down and was surprised to see his side completely soaked in blood.

"We'll, damn..." he said.

29

Chapter 29 – Carnales

Los Tejanos Safehouse, Southside San Antonio, Texas

The front door slammed hard enough to rattle the curtain rods.

Chino barreled in, pale with sweat, clutching a backpack that held his drone in a white-knuckled fist.

Flaco entered next, calmer, though his clothes were soaked with sweat and he was limping. He carried a dirty rifle bag over his shoulder.

Everyone in the room froze in place.

"Damn! You good, *carnal?*" Joker asked, standing from the couch.

Flaco nodded once.

Chino didn't speak. He bent over, hands on his knees, catching his breath, his eyes wide.

Tigre moved toward him. "You hurt?"

"No. I'm good."

Oso stepped forward.

"Where are the others? Where are Beto, Rafa, and Conejo?"

Flaco set the rifle bag down.

"Rafa and Conejo are dead. Beto got busted. They never even made it to the gate."

Oso's expression darkened.

"What the fuck?" Joker muttered and sat back down, shaking his head.

Chino dropped onto a stained recliner and lit a cigarette. He leaned forward, elbows on his knees, smoking intently.

"They were already in position when we got there," he said. "Had to be contractors, or the *pinche* Navy SEALs. Those fools had drones, radios, snipers... We didn't have eyes on the tower. Our *carnales* were wide open."

Oso stared at the floor. One hand rested on the butt of a pistol tucked in his waistband.

Flaco reached for a cigarette on the counter, lit it, and waited.

Oso finally spoke.

"You made contact with anyone on-site?"

"No." Flaco exhaled smoke. "I tried to cover them, and Chino dropped his bombs, but they were some real motherfuckers, not no local cops. Once the homeboys were all dead or busted, me and Chino took off. We ditched the van near Roosevelt. Nobody followed us."

Chino sat up suddenly.

"They knew. They were watching before we even parked. That's how they caught us."

Tigre frowned.

"You're saying they knew you were coming?"

"Fuck yeah, they did," Chino said, cigarette clutched tightly.

"Either that," Flaco spoke up, "or they have SWAT posted up at every TexOil spot. Seems unlikely. Think about it, *carnal*. They had a sniper on the tower. They were ready for us."

"Motherfucker," Tigre spat. "What's Octavio going to say?"

Oso didn't answer. The room fell silent.

After a minute of thinking, Oso walked to the kitchen table, picked up a burner phone, and stared at it.

"Where's the drone video?" he asked.

Chino unzipped his backpack and pulled out a flash drive.

"One of the drones got shot down, but here's the video from the ones that survived."

Oso looked at it, then slipped it into his pocket.

He took a deep breath.

Then he dialed.

The phone clicked. A series of encrypted relays chirped and whined. Then a male voice answered in Spanish.

"*Sí.*"

"The party today was a failure. Security wouldn't let us in," Oso said.

There was a pause.

Then Octavio's voice came slow and deliberate.

"You said you could handle it."

Oso's back stiffened.

"We've got this. They made their little move with their new players today, but we'll be ready for them next time."

Another pause.

"Move your men. Get ready for the next orders. Do you understand?"

Oso looked around the room at his brothers and shifted uncomfortably.

"Yes, I understand," he said.

The line went dead.

Oso tossed the phone on the table.

No one spoke. Chino stopped fidgeting.

Oso's eyes were as black as obsidian, and his fists were hammers as he glared at his remaining men.

"Pack your shit. We're moving."

30

Chapter 30 – Obsidian

Zacatecas, Zacatecas State, Mexico

Meanwhile, across the border in Mexico, the hacienda slept behind iron gates and thick adobe walls. A low wind whispered through the olive trees and over a trickling stone fountain.

Octavio stood barefoot on the balcony, white shirt unbuttoned, sleeves rolled to the elbows. His phone was warm in his hand.

He'd just taken the call from Oso about the failed attack on the refinery.

Now he stared past the courtyard, beyond the high wall, into the darkness.

Inside, Spanish guitar murmured from a record player.

From the bedroom, his wife, Valeria, appeared in a cotton nightgown, her black hair tied back, hands behind her back.

"I got you something," she said, a smile curving her lips.

Octavio smiled.

"*You* got *me* something?"

She brought her hands around revealing a square jewelry box.

He took it.

"Open it," she said.

Inside was a black cross pendant on a silver chain. About two inches tall, the cross was a simple design, but it had an interesting texture. It appeared as if it were carved from stone.

Octavio lifted the chain into the light spilling from the bedroom.

"I had it made. It's obsidian."

She looked into his eyes carefully.

"From the volcano in Tequila."

Octavio stared at it for a moment, taking it in. He raised his other hand to touch the cross when his wife grabbed his wrist.

"Be careful. The *artesano* said it is very sharp. Sharper than a razor," she warned him.

Octavio smiled, but she saw the tension in his eyes.

"You're thinking again," she said softly, stepping beside him.

Octavio let his hand drop as he was yanked from their moment back to reality.

"There is a new operation. One that has already brought American special forces and probably the CIA. I think this time the Bishop has gone too far. There will be no escaping this."

She waited.

"So, what are you saying? Is it—is it—"

She looked around, then lowered her voice.

"Our time yet?"

Still, he didn't answer.

She laid her hand gently on his chest.

"I can feel it. I see it in your face every day. Things are only going to get worse. What will we do when our time comes? When the CIA or Ramón and Roberto—our own bodyguards—come to butcher us?"

Her voice choked in her throat, and her body shook as she covered her face.

"Maybe we deserve what comes for us, but not the children."

After a moment, she composed herself. She wiped tears from her eyes and grabbed her husband by the arm.

"I packed the documents. The money. We could be on a plane within twenty-four hours."

Octavio stared into the night, brows so low his eyes were dark wells.

"You still believe we can walk away?" he finally asked.

She nodded. "If we move before *he* suspects."

"El Obispo always suspects," he replied.

"Ok, but he's distracted right now, right? Right? You've played the loyal soldier long enough, *mi amor*. But all his soldiers end up dead. We *have* to leave. Now!"

"Everyone I've ever known who tried to leave this life left in a coffin."

Valeria's eyes were steady, her jaw set.

"Not us, Octavio. We will survive. Our children will survive."

He sighed.

"Not yet, my love. I have one more thing to do."

She wilted at his words, as if the life had drained from her.

"And then?" she asked softly.

He reached for her hand.

"And then we run. I promise."

Two floors below, in the servant's corridor behind the kitchen, Ramón sat in a wooden chair, a pair of headphones over his ears.

The hallway smelled of cooking oil and bleach.

A plastic folding table was set up beside him. On it sat a small black receiver box with a blinking green light, a laptop, and an ashtray overflowing with cigarette butts.

Roberto leaned against the wall beside him, arms folded.

"You hear that?" Roberto asked.

Ramón didn't answer immediately.

In the headphones, Octavio's voice murmured through a faint wash of static.

"*...one more thing.*"

"*And then?*"

"*...and then we run.*"

Ramón slowly lifted the headphones off one ear and looked up at his partner.

"I hear it," he said.

Roberto exhaled through his nose.

"Chingado."

Ramón reached over and tapped a key on the laptop.

The recording file continued scrolling forward, capturing every word.

He removed the headphones and set them carefully on the table.

For a moment neither man spoke.

Then Roberto said quietly, "You think he's serious?"

Ramón shrugged.

"Doesn't matter."

He pulled out a burner phone.

Roberto watched as he dialed.

The line rang once.

A calm voice answered.

"Yeah."

Ramón straightened slightly in the chair.

"It's Ramón," he said.

A pause.

Ramón glanced toward the ceiling, toward the balcony two floors above where Octavio and his wife still stood in the night air.

"He's talking about running," he continued. "Soon."

Another silence.

"Send me the recording. Keep listening."

"Understood," Ramón said.

He ended the call.

Roberto looked at him.

"What did he say?"

Ramón slid the phone back into his pocket.

His expression was unreadable.

"He said keep listening."

Roberto rubbed his jaw.

"And? Did he say to stop him?"

Ramón looked down at the glowing recording screen.

The audio waveform continued moving across the monitor as Octavio and Valeria spoke softly above them.

"No."

Roberto frowned.

"Why?"

Ramón lit a cigarette and leaned back in the chair.

Smoke curled toward the ceiling.

"Because," he said quietly, "El Mano wants to see where Octavio runs."

Miles away, across another border, Rage sat alone in a dim room and listened to the first half of the conversation through a secure satellite feed.

The laptop screen illuminated the hard lines of his face.

On the desk beside him lay a long knife and a glass of whiskey.

He replayed one sentence again.

"We could be on a plane within twenty-four hours."

Rage leaned back slowly.

A smile crept across his scarred mouth.

"Run," he murmured.

31

Chapter 31 – El Topo

TexOil Tower, Houston, Texas

TexOil Tower, the company's global headquarters, gleamed above downtown like a polished blade—forty-three stories of glass and steel humming with air scrubbers and corporate secrets.

By day, it housed hundreds of oil and gas professionals: executives, geologists, engineers, and landmen. But after 7:00 p.m., all forty-three floors went quiet except for the elevator chime when the janitorial crew arrived.

María de la Luz pushed her cleaning cart off the service elevator and rolled it toward the glass double doors of the executive wing. She was fifty-three years old, wore gray scrubs, orthopedic shoes, and a laminated badge that said *Facilities – Third Shift.*

To security, she was invisible.

On the executive floor, a few lights glowed under motion sensors.

She started by vacuuming the hallways, then moved to the offices.

The CFO's office was first.

She pushed her supply cart inside and removed a vacuum.

As she set the vacuum cleaner down, her left hand slipped into her pocket and produced a matte black USB drive, which she deftly cupped in her palm.

She plugged the vacuum's cord into a wall socket, turned it on with a high-pitched roar, and began cleaning the room.

She started near the CFO's desk, making sure to do a good job for any camera that might be watching.

As she worked directly behind his desk, she spotted his PC tower on the floor. Quickly, she bent over as if to pick up a piece of trash and inserted the USB drive into the PC. She then returned to vacuuming as if nothing happened.

The USB drive contained specialized software written by Iranian intelligence. At its base, it was a worm disguised as routine maintenance software. It triggered no antivirus alerts, pinged no outbound traffic, and copied every file modified in the last seven days in less than thirty seconds directly onto the drive. Emails, attachments, browsers, spreadsheets, shared drives, and recycle bins were scraped and downloaded, even hidden folders.

While the program ran, María vacuumed. She never looked at the computer. When she was done with the floor, she came back around with a rag and cleaning spray to wipe the desk. She used that opportunity to remove the drive with barely a flick of her fingers, tucked it in her pocket, loaded up her cart, and moved to the next room.

She used the same USB to scrape every computer on the executive floor.

The COO's office. The Director of Security's office. The Deputy General Counsel's desk.

She also collected trash from every bin and placed it in a larger trash bag on her cart.

When that bag was full, she wheeled her cart to the service elevator and rode it down.

On the loading dock, she pulled the trash bag from the cart, tied it off, and carried it to the dumpster where she set it carefully just inside the opening.

María completed her shift like every other night, clocked out, said goodbye to her workmates, and strolled to the employee parking lot. There, she climbed into her old F-150.

She put the truck into gear, but instead of heading straight to the gate, she first drove around toward the loading dock and pulled in front of the dumpster. There, she made a show of getting out of her truck with an old fast-food bag and leaning over the dumpster to throw it away. She knew the location of the only camera that watched that direction—and she knew her truck blocked its view.

As she released the food bag into the dumpster, she grabbed the trash bag she had deposited earlier and pulled it back out. She tossed the bag filled with executive trash into the front seat, then climbed in after it, turned on the radio, and sang along all the way home.

Back at her apartment in Pasadena, she locked the door and dumped the trash bag on the tile floor. Then she slipped on latex gloves and began unfolding papers, flattened Post-Its, and wadded up drafts.

After laying each piece of unfolded trash on the floor, she photographed it with a digital camera.

By the time the sun rose, casting orange stripes through the miniblinds, María was sitting in front of a seven-thousand-dollar Getac X600 laptop, uploading everything she had scraped with the USB drive and photographed from the trash to an encrypted drive that only she and Octavio could access.

Back in Mexico, Octavio sat shirtless in front of his own laptop, mezcal sweating in a chipped glass beside him. A high-powered AI parser scrolled across the screen. It was trained to extract names, dates, keywords, and metadata from María's raw uploads in minutes.

After analyzing all the data, the system raised a pop-up signaling it had found something interesting. Octavio clicked to open the report.

The AI flagged dozens of mentions of a security firm found in sixty-three emails, two invoices, and one orange sticky note.

Green Zone Defense.

Octavio leaned forward.

Below that, it read:

Lead Contact – Travis Mason

A chill swept through him.

Everyone knew who Mason and Green Zone Defense were.

Especially Rage.

Octavio knew Rage's story, how he had been part of the heist attempt in Denver, how it had gone bad, how his brother had died.

Mason had been there.

He instructed the AI to search for more information on GZD. The system dug up an invoice for lodging in Victoria, Texas.

There was an address.

Octavio located the address using an online search. A guest ranch listed on a site for hunting leases. He pulled up aerial photos and zoomed in. It looked like a farm cabin.

He rose from his desk and walked barefoot into the courtyard where the night wind rustled the palms. The hacienda grounds smelled of roses.

Octavio opened his sat-phone and dialed a number from memory.

It answered on the second ring.

"TexOil has hired Green Zone Defense," he said.

There was a long pause.

"Are you sure?" the voice on the other side of the line asked.

"I've seen their contract, invoices, and emails myself. They're set up at a cabin near Victoria. I have their exact location."

The voice was dry, metallic, filtered through distance and encryption.

"Is he there?" the voice asked.

"Maybe," Octavio replied. "Travis Mason. His name is on the list."

There was a long moment of silence, then—

"You're going to need help."

"I already have help," Octavio replied.

A chuckle filtered through.

Then the unmistakable voice of Rage.

"Not enough."

32

Chapter 32 – Loyalty

Zacatecas, Zacatecas State, Mexico

The Bishop's private study overlooked the eastern courtyard of the hacienda.

Morning had come quietly. Uniformed servants moved like ghosts through the halls carrying dishes and linens.

Inside the study, the air smelled faintly of incense and polished wood.

A tall crucifix hung on the wall behind the desk.

The Bishop sat beneath it, reading.

Sunlight filtered through the shutters in narrow bands that crossed the room like prison bars. His cream-colored robe hung loosely on his frame, and a pair of reading glasses rested low on his nose as he studied a small leather-bound Bible.

The door opened.

Rage stepped inside.

He wore black jeans and a dark shirt. His prosthetic arm—sleek and metallic beneath the sleeve—hung relaxed at his side. In his other hand he carried a cellphone.

The Bishop didn't look up immediately.

He finished the line he was reading, closed the Bible gently, and removed the glasses.

"El Mano," he said.

Rage inclined his head slightly.

"Obispo."

The Bishop gestured toward the chair across the desk.

"Sit."

Rage remained standing.

"I won't be long."

The Bishop studied him.

Rage stepped closer and placed the phone on the desk.

"With respect," he said, "I thought you should hear something."

The Bishop folded his hands calmly.

"Go on."

Rage tapped the screen.

A recording began to play.

Static.

Then Valeria's voice.

"I packed the documents. The money. We could be on a plane within twenty-four hours."

The Bishop didn't move.

The recording continued.

Octavio's voice followed.

"You still believe we can walk away?"

The Bishop's eyes remained fixed on Rage.

Rage leaned against the edge of the desk, watching him.

The recording played the rest.

Valeria's voice again.

"If we move before he suspects."

"El Obispo always suspects."

The audio ended with Octavio's words hanging in the air.

The Bishop did not speak. He simply stared at Rage, his expression calm and unreadable.

Finally, the Bishop lifted his eyes.

"You recorded this?"

"My men did," Rage said.

The Bishop leaned back in his chair, his fingertips pressed together beneath his chin.

"That is… concerning."

The Bishop's gaze drifted toward the window.

Outside, a gardener pushed a wheelbarrow across the courtyard gravel.

"Octavio has served me well," he said slowly.

"So have I," Rage said.

"Yes," the Bishop agreed.

His eyes returned to Rage.

"Yes, you have."

He picked up the phone and replayed a small portion of the recording.

Valeria's voice echoed softly through the room again.

"We could be on a plane within twenty-four hours."

The Bishop stopped it there.

"You don't sound surprised," he said.

Rage gave a faint smile.

"I've had my reasons to doubt him."

The Bishop tapped the desk thoughtfully.

"And you allowed him to continue?"

Rage's expression did not change.

"I didn't have proof until now."

The Bishop slowly rose from his chair.

He walked to the window and looked out over the courtyard.

The olive trees rustled in the wind.

After several seconds the Bishop turned back.

"This is very serious," he said gravely. "I appreciate you bringing this to me."

Rage gave a small nod.

"I thought you would want to know."

"Yes."

The Bishop rested one hand on the desk.

"Yes, I do."

His expression turned sad.

"Loyalty," he said, "is a fragile thing in our world."

Rage didn't respond.

The Bishop folded his hands again.

"I will pray about this."

Rage straightened.

"Of course."

He turned and walked toward the door.

Just before he left, the Bishop spoke again.

"El Mano."

Rage stopped.

"Yes?"

The Bishop studied him carefully.

"Tell your men to keep listening."

Rage returned to his mansion.

The house was quiet. Only the faint clink of glass in the kitchen.

His mother sat at the island with reading glasses low on her nose, flipping through a travel magazine. A tumbler of bourbon sweated on the marble countertop beside her, the ice half-melted.

She looked up as he entered.

"Well. Look who finally came home."

"Only for a little while."

"You're going somewhere again?"

"Yes."

"For work?"

"Yes," he replied, "and more."

"Oh?" She raised an eyebrow. "Could it be for a girl?"

"No," he said coldly. "To kill the man who killed your other son."

The magazine slipped, clacking against the counter.

She went pale.

They sat for a while in silence. Then, little by little, her face twisted in hate and fury.

She gripped the magazine tightly, the tendons in her wrists flaring.

"You know what to do," she growled. "Avenge Raison. Avenge your brother."

After a moment, she relaxed. She downed her drink in a single swallow then leaned back to study him.

"You're still angry," she said.

"About Raison?"

"About me. About the other night. In front of your boys."

"I told you not to come down."

She exhaled softly.

"I just wanted to say hello. Plus, men love me. Especially Mexican men."

"You undermined me. Made me look weak."

A flicker of irritation crossed her expression, but she quickly masked it.

"They're men, not children. If they lose respect because your mother walks through a courtyard, they weren't worth having."

"That's not how this works."

"Oh, my baby boy. You've been running with wolves so long you forgot how to laugh."

"And you forget where you are."

"Don't talk to me like I'm one of your friends."

"I'm talking to you like you live in my house."

Their eyes locked.

She relaxed.

"You're right," she said. "I shouldn't have come down that night."

She slid off the stool and moved around the island to fix another drink.

"You get that look," she said quietly. "Same one you had when you were a boy back in Montreal—right before you did something stupid. You don't need to prove anything to these men."

"It's not about them," he growled. "Not this time."

She sighed.

"First, we were abandoned by your father. Then by your brother. Then by the club. I've been abandoned by everyone I ever called family. You don't need to die proving loyalty to these—these—*people*. I need you. Your mother.

The last of your family."

She smacked her glass on the table, the ice clinking.

"This is my choice."

She turned away.

"So, you don't choose *me*. That's what you mean."

The refrigerator hummed.

Rage stared into his mother's face as she poured another bourbon, spilling some.

Her pupils were wide. A tremor ran through her fingers before she steadied them against the counter.

"You've got the shakes," he said.

"I'm just hungry."

"Hungry for what? Food—or coke?"

She stiffened.

"A line here and there to take the edge off. Who cares? It's like sand in the desert here. It's everywhere."

Rage stared at her.

"I'm fine," she declared.

He exhaled and looked away.

"I'll be gone a few days," he said.

She nodded slowly.

"When?"

"I leave tomorrow."

She nodded.

He turned to walk away.

"Rage."

He stopped at the doorway.

"Come back," she said. "You're all I have left."

He held her gaze.

Then walked out.

She stood alone in the kitchen.

After a moment passed, she wiped her face with a trembling hand and reached for the rolled up one-thousand-peso bill beside the sink.

Neat white lines were laid out on a plate.

She took a breath, pinched one side of her nose, then leaned down.

33

Chapter 33 – Father, Warrior

GZD South Texas cabin, Victoria, Texas, USA

The next morning, dawn bled into the South Texas sky.

Mason sat at the kitchen table, opened his laptop, and eased into the chair as his muscles tightened.

A few clicks on the computer and he was in a virtual meeting with Kim Wright.

Her face was lined with worry.

"How hurt are you?" she asked. "Did you see a doctor?"

"I'm OK," he replied. "Caught some pebbles. I'll heal."

"Well, don't hesitate to seek medical attention on TexOil's dime," she said motherly, then switched to a professional tone. "I read your report, but I want to hear it from you. What the hell happened out there?"

Mason spent an hour walking Kim through the shootout at the refinery.

"So, the anonymous warning was legitimate," she said when he was through.

"Yes, it was. Any theory who it could be?" he asked.

"Not yet," she said.

"Where's the detainee? Do you have him?" Mason asked.

"We have him here in San Antonio. He's not talking, but his record says a lot. He's a repeat offender and known member of Los Tejanos, a major prison gang that originated in Texas but spread all over the Bureau of Prisons. The other two bodies were also Tejanos members. We know they work with the Jalisco cartel. The leaders of both organizations are in ADX Florence together."

"Hm," Mason grunted. "I guess felons have their networking events, too."

"I guess so," Kim said gravely. "Except this is no joke. The U.S. Attorney's office wants to treat this as terrorism. Only half the refinery's workers showed up to work since the attack. TexOil's employees are starting to raise questions."

"If you're a TexOil employee, it's a good time to take some PTO," Mason quipped.

"Well, don't you have all the jokes today," Kim admonished.

Mason shifted and winced.

"Yeah, the more I hurt the more jokes I tell. Eases the pain."

"All right, well hang in there," Kim said skeptically. "Call if you need some muscle relaxers or something. I'll have somebody bring them to you."

Mason thanked her, promised to rest, and assured her his men were ready to go again.

After that, he called his wife, Lisa.

She answered after one ring, and he put her on FaceTime.

Her face was pale, her eyes puffy and red.

"Hey, beautiful," he said with the biggest smile he could muster. "Tell me you didn't stay up crying all night."

Lisa laughed.

"You know I did," she said, wiping her nose. "How are you?"

"I'm fine. Just sore. How's Ryan?"

They talked for a while about their son, the house, and when he might come home.

"It's unclear right now, but I promise the entire weight of the USA is bearing down on this situation. They've got all the best people working on this, so it won't take long."

"Okay," Lisa accepted. "I just want you home."

Mason told her he loved her and then clicked off.

Then he limped to the kitchen, fixed a cup of coffee, and stepped out onto the back porch where he was surprised to see Cole sitting on a chair, his Barrett Mk22 sniper rifle laid across his lap. He had the bolt, magazine, and scope removed, and was busy pushing a cleaning rod through the barrel.

"How you holding up, big dog?" Cole asked.

"I'm fine," Mason said. "How about you? That was a close call."

Cole laughed.

"Shit, man. That's not even the first dud that's landed near me. Used to happen all the time in Afghanistan. Hell, in Helmand, I had an 82 mm round land not ten feet from me. Nothing. Dud. Just a bunch of debris from the impact."

"I bet you had some debris in your skivvies, too," Mason said.

Cole laughed.

Mason leaned against a wooden post supporting the patio roof and looked out into the scrubby, dry landscape.

"You've fought insurgents before. What do you think about this?" he asked.

"This job? These cartel shooters, or whatever—I think they're amateurs. They're sure as hell not Taliban," Cole replied.

"Why do you say that?" Mason pressed.

Cole finished cleaning the barrel, set down the cleaning rod, and picked up a rag and a small bottle of solvent. Dampening the rag, he continued cleaning the rifle's internal workings.

"That's easy," he said. "None of them came to die."

"What do you mean?"

"I mean, in Afghanistan, the Taliban were *ready* for it. They wanted to die in battle against us. But these cats aren't jihadis. I've seen it overseas. Common criminals with no honor join the war looking for a quick come up. They'll take shots at unarmed civilians or set off car bombs, but they're not going to strap on a suicide vest or drive a vehicle-based IED into a target. They're in it to score, not sacrifice. That's why they'll be easier to beat. At some point, the cost will get too high."

Mason chewed on his words while he watched the tall grass sway in the breeze.

"I grew up with dudes like that. They call themselves 'gangstas', but that's only when they get to be the bully. As soon as the tables turn—they fold," Cole continued.

They sat in silence for a moment. A red wasp buzzed around the porch, poking into all the nooks.

"How many kids do you have?" Mason asked.

Cole kept cleaning.

"Three. Two girls and a boy. Oldest is nine. Youngest just turned four. My wife keeps everything running while I'm out here playing army with you guys."

Mason laughed.

"She ever ask you to quit?" he asked.

"Sometimes, yeah," Cole replied. "Other times, she doesn't say it out loud, but I can feel it. Her eyes say it. Her hands when she hugs me goodbye, you know?"

Mason nodded.

"Yeah, Lisa wants me home, too. Wants me in church every Sunday, running the business from an office, not out here 'playing army'."

Cole laid the barrel into the crook of his arm, resting.

"Here's how I see it, Mason. I was made for this. Not saying I love war, but I've got a skill—a power really— most people don't: I can make sure the worst men don't hurt anyone else."

He looked out at the tree line.

"Being a dad means protecting your kids. It doesn't mean sitting in a safe office while evil roams free."

Mason met his eyes.

"My wife tells me a good father is present," he said.

Cole nodded.

"And she's right. But I think being present means more than geography. It means standing between your family and the wolves."

Mason took a sip of coffee, then asked, "You ever worry you won't make it back?"

Cole didn't hesitate.

"Every time. But I'd rather my kids remember a father who did something righteous than a father who was scared."

Mason sipped his coffee and looked out into the big Texas sky, squinting against the sun.

In Mexico, Octavio stood in the doorway for a moment before stepping into his son's room.

A lamp cast a soft yellow circle over the bed. Toy trucks were scattered across the floor. The ceiling fan hummed above, pushing warm air in slow, lazy circles.

His son, Diego, sat cross-legged under the blanket, waiting.

"Papá."

Octavio smiled and picked up the book from the nightstand. The cover was worn, the corners bent.

He sat on the edge of the bed, the mattress dipping under his weight.

"Alright," he said. "Story time."

The boy nodded, already settling in.

Octavio read.

His voice was steady, practiced. The story was simple. A farmer, some animals, something about patience and hard work.

Halfway through, the boy interrupted.

"Papá?"

Octavio stopped, thumb holding the page.

"What is it?"

The boy hesitated, then asked, "What did you want to be when you were little?"

Octavio thought for a moment.

"All I wanted was to make my parents proud," he said.

The boy studied him, eyes wide.

"My *mamá*," Octavio continued, "wanted me to be a priest."

A faint smile flickered, then faded.

"She used to say I had the face for it. That I was calm. That I listened."

"What happened?"

Octavio's jaw tightened.

"My father—your grandfather—died in an accident. After that... things changed."

He closed the book, resting it on his knee.

"I had to work," he went on. "To help the family. There was no time for school like a priest needs."

The boy pulled the blanket tighter around himself.

"Do you wish you were a priest?"

Octavio looked at him.

His mouth opened slightly. Then closed.

The silence stretched.

Finally, he leaned forward and kissed the boy on the forehead.

"Get some sleep," he said.

"But that wasn't the end."

"It is for tonight."

The boy frowned but didn't argue.

"Goodnight, *Papá*."

"Goodnight."

Octavio stood and turned off the lamp. The room fell into shadow, lit only by the faint spill of light from the hallway. He paused in the doorway, watching Diego for a moment longer.

Then he stepped out and closed the door.

He walked to the master bedroom and sat on the edge of his bed while his wife folded clothes into a worn duffel. The house was quiet but for the ceiling fan's slow tick and the distant bark of dogs on the street.

She moved with urgency, though she tried to hide it, slipping folded jeans between layers of shirts, pressing toiletries into the side pocket.

"You're sure about this man?" he asked.

She looked up, eyes tired but steady.

"His name is Jorge. He's moved many families across before— quietly—just like you said. He doesn't ask questions, and he doesn't work for the cartel. We pay him, we vanish."

He nodded.

"Tomorrow night," she whispered. "He can come to get us."

She slid the zipper closed and touched his hand.

"You must decide before then."

34

Chapter 34 – Ghosts

US/Mexico Border, South Texas, USA

Later that night, two DJI Agras T100 heavy-lift drones sat on the sandy earth one hundred yards south of the US-Mexico border, where the ground was covered in rock and thorns. The Rio Grande river ran a short distance away in a deep, narrow cut, the water flowing dark and fast, gnawing at the steep banks. This wasn't a place migrants crossed. It was too deep, too violent. Border Patrol didn't waste time watching stretches like this.

Sergi crouched next to one of the big drones, hands moving with quiet efficiency. Three feet tall and eight feet wide, the flying machines lay on the ground like prehistoric insects. He checked them once more, then nodded.

"They're ready," he said in his thick Ukrainian accent.

Rage stepped into a harness, the straps biting into his hips.

Both men were dressed top-to-bottom in black.

"You know I hate this part. If you drop me," Rage said, "I swear I'll come back and haunt you, you Borscht-eating bastard."

Sergi didn't look up.

"If I drop you, I'll join you as a ghost because the Bishop will kill me next."

Rage snorted.

Sergi slipped on the second harness, then he reached for a controller lashed to his forearm—then hesitated.

"Almost forgot," he said reaching into a pocket and retrieving a pair of goggles. "You're going to want these."

Rage frowned, then snatched them from his hand and slipped them over his eyes.

"I mean it," Rage said. "Don't fuckin' drop me."

"How many times have we done this?" Sergi grinned.

"Too fuckin' many."

"And I never dropped you once. Now, hold on and enjoy the ride. Remember to keep your hands below your head so you don't lose fingers."

Rage growled.

With a tap on his controller, Sergi brought the drones to life.

The machines shrieked as they spun up, a hair-raising, industrial scream, scattering sand and dried grass like a tornado.

The machines slowly rose, then strained, the straps snapping taut.

The harness bit tighter as Rage was lifted from the ground. He felt the vibration immediately, buzzing through the harness.

His stomach lurched as the riverbank fell out from under him. Brush and rock vanished below, replaced by open space and rushing water as he dangled from the umbilical. The downdraft flattened reeds and tore at the surface of the river, churning it into pale scars of foam.

The drone bucked once, twice, fighting the load.

They climbed straight up, awkward and shaking. Then the drone tilted forward.

The motion was sudden and violent, like being shoved in the chest. The river slid sideways beneath him, the far bank rushing closer, dark and jagged. The sound of the motors spiked.

"Now we go," Sergi said.

The drones lurched forward. Rage skimmed past the lip of the far bank, close enough to smell the mud and algae. The machine shuddered violently, the scream of the motors breaking into a ragged, dying whine.

Just as he saw his dangling feet pass the far riverbank, the drone died.

Rage dropped.

Branches tore at him as he slammed into brush, rolling hard, shoulder cracking against rock. The breath punched out of his lungs and for a second the world went white. He tasted dirt and blood and leaves.

Tangled in the brush behind him, the drone screamed one last time, a weak, dying howl, then fell silent.

Rage lay still, chest heaving, listening to his heart hammer and the river move on as if nothing had happened. The night closed back in, quiet and indifferent.

"See?" Sergi's voice carried through the darkness. "I told you. Nobody watches this place."

A quarter-mile or so from the riverbank, on the U.S. side, a white crew cab Ford Super Duty idled behind a ranch gate.

Oso leaned on the hood, arms folded, his eyes tracking the horizon.

Next to him, Flaco stood watching through a pair of binoculars.

In the truck's driver seat, Chino sat silently. A handheld radio hissed now and then from the center console.

"They're supposed to be here already," Chino murmured, checking the time on his phone.

The night was pitch dark.

"I see two men walking this way," Flaco said finally, the binoculars pressed to his face.

After a few minutes, Rage emerged from the darkness covered in scratches and dirt, his face a scowl. Sergi followed a short distance behind him.

Oso stepped forward.

"No weapons?" he asked.

Rage looked at him, annoyed.

"No. They're already here."

Oso gave a single nod and pointed to the truck.

"Checkpoint's soft tonight. We've got disguises, but you two have to ride in the box."

Rage walked toward the truck without another word. Sergi followed.

Flaco popped the tailgate. In the truck's bed, beneath a pile of hardhats, steel valves, and wrenches, was a welded steel box with just enough room for two men.

Rage scowled.

"I'm so sick of this shit," he spat.

He climbed into the bed and slid into the box.

Before following him, Sergi looked to Flaco.

"You sure this has air flow?" he asked.

Flaco stared at him.

"Right," Sergi said, then slid into the box next to Rage.

Flaco slammed the lid shut. Bolts clicked into place. There was a deafening cacophony as he spread tools over the box as camouflage.

The truck growled to life and rolled out.

It took just over an hour to reach the Border Patrol checkpoint in Hebbronville where green-uniformed guards waved them through without another look.

Flaco grinned to himself.

The magnetic signs on the truck's doors read: *TexOil, Inc. Health & Safety*.

35

Chapter 35 – The Cabin

GZD South Texas Cabin, Victoria, Texas, USA

The road was dry and cracked, pitted with caliche and old tire ruts.

Mason felt every bump in his stride. His shoulder throbbed where Rage had nearly chopped his arm off years ago. The shrapnel wounds from the refinery burned along his ribs.

He gritted his teeth and kept pace.

The GZD South Texas team ran in a tight line along the gravel road. Cole followed Mason in stone silence, the pace hardly raising his heart rate. Salgado followed him, head on a swivel, scanning fence lines and culverts while Benito huffed at the rear. Caleb had peeled off after the first mile, claiming an upset stomach and muttering something about powdered eggs.

About halfway through their daily route, they rounded a slow bend and passed a white pickup parked just off the shoulder. The truck idled quietly, hazard lights pulsing. Signs on the doors read *South Texas Electric Cooperative*.

Mason kept his eyes glued to the truck as they approached.

When they passed, he counted three men sitting inside. The driver, slouched behind the wheel, wore black sunglasses and a reflective vest. His clean white hardhat sat tilted back, exposing a face full of faded jailhouse tattoos that crept from under his collar and curled around his throat.

The men jogged past without turning their heads.

Once they were a hundred feet up the road, Salgado spoke up.

"Did y'all see what I saw?"

"Sure did," Mason said.

"Do you think it's them?" Salgado asked.

"Could be," Mason called back.

"Shit, how could they find us?" Benito shouted from the back of the line. "That man could just be a utility worker. A lot of fools look like that around here."

"Could be," Mason yelled back, never breaking stride. "Not gonna risk it."

He picked up the pace, and the men raced the last mile back to the cabin.

Mason hit the front porch at full tilt, slammed open the front door, and looked around quickly.

"Caleb!" he yelled.

"Yo! What's up?" Caleb yelled as he walked out from the kitchen into the living area, concern on his face.

"Get ready. Looks like a truck full of trouble just down the road. Get a drone up and track that vehicle. White truck. Two miles east, up the road."

Just then, his phone buzzed. It was Lisa.

As Cole, Salgado, and Benito filled the room, huffing and dripping sweat from their run, Mason turned to face them.

"You three, get kitted up and cover that road out front. Roger?" he asked.

"Roger that!" the men said back.

Each dashed to their bunk area to don bulletproof plate carriers, radios, and weapons.

Mason stared at the phone still vibrating in his hand. He cleared his throat, took a deep breath, and answered.

"Morning, beautiful," he said as calmly as possible.

"Morning, hero," she said. "How's Texas today?"

"Same as always. Hot and smells like cows. So, pretty much like home."

She laughed, and started talking about baby Ryan teething, and how the backyard had flooded during a recent rainstorm.

Mason listened as he wandered toward the front window.

He tipped open the blinds and peeked outside.

The same white utility truck sat idling out front now, hazard lights still blinking. It was parked near the cattle guard about fifty yards from the porch. Two men stood outside the vehicle, both in vests and hardhats, one crouched by the rear tire, appearing to check something.

Mason's smile faded. His voice dropped.

"Hang on a sec, babe."

He covered the mic and called down the hallway.

"Benito!"

Benito stepped from the back bedroom hall still in shorts and a T-shirt but now wearing a tactical vest and carrying an AR-15.

"Yeah?"

"The truck we passed earlier? It's right out front now."

Benito's expression hardened. The click of the ACOG lens cover flipping up was soft but solid.

Mason returned to the phone.

"Sorry, baby, what were you saying?"

Lisa didn't seem to notice the shift.

"Nothing important. I was just saying, I'm waiting on the garage door repair man because I can't even get my car out of the garage right now. You okay?"

"I'm good," he said, eyes fixed on the window. "Just some utility workers out front."

Benito stepped up beside him, scanning through the optic.

"Same decals. South Texas Electric. But I can't get a good read. The driver's the same guy. Face tats. I only see two now. Where's the third?"

Before Mason could answer, Cole walked up holding his scoped sniper rifle across his chest. He glanced out the window, eyebrows knitted.

"If they're linemen, why aren't they in a bucket truck?" he asked. "That's just a regular pickup."

Mason frowned.

"Where's the third guy?"

They all stared.

There was no sign of the third man.

Lisa's voice broke in.

"Mason? You still there?"

He exhaled slowly, jaw tight.

"Babe, I gotta go."

"Why? What's wrong?"

He hesitated.

"Just something I need to check on."

He hung up before she could ask more.

Just as he did, one of the utility workers opened the back door of the truck, reached in, and pulled out a belt fed light machine gun.

"Gun! Gun! Gun!" Benito yelled.

But before the machine gunner could open fire—a rifle crack split the morning.

The front window blew inward, showering the living room with glass. A heavy bullet smacked the wall to Mason's left.

He ducked.

"Sniper front!"

Outside, fifty feet up the road of the utility truck, Flaco worked the bolt on his rifle smoothly. He was lying in the shallow ditch, the barrel laid through the tall grass just under a strand of barbed wire. His breathing was slow. Measured. He chambered another round.

Inside, Cole whipped his rifle up, used the muzzle to smash out a windowpane, and took aim.

Beside the truck, Joker rested the M249 SAW across the bedrail. Holding the machinegun's pistol grip in one hand while supporting a belt of ammunition with the other, he spread his feet, then pulled the trigger.

The machine gun roared.

Tracer rounds tore across the porch, stitching orange lines through the air.

Wood exploded.

The front door disintegrated.

Bullets chewed through the cabin like it was made of cardboard.

Inside, walls shredded.

A ceiling beam groaned as rounds blasted it apart.

Cole never flinched. Before Joker could finish the belt of ammo, he fired.

Joker's head exploded in red mist, and his limp body tumbled to the ground.

Mason peeked through a hole in the front door.

"Yeah, that's definitely them," Benito said. He was lying prone on the floor.

"Salgado! You good!" yelled back into the house.

There was no answer.

"Salgado!" he repeated louder.

"Yeah! I'm good!" Salgado's voice carried from the back bedroom.

"Caleb?" Mason called.

"Holy shit!" Caleb's voice carried from the kitchen. "Yeah, I'm good, but holy shit!"

The cabin's front was Swiss cheese, and gypsum dust filled the air.

"Do I take the other one?" Cole asked, his crosshairs placed on the driver's forehead. The driver seemed to panic as he lurched back and forth.

Before Mason could answer, a buzzing sound drifted through the bullet holes.

It sounded like a metal wasp.

Mason froze, listening.

Not a wasp.

"Caleb, is our drone up?" Mason yelled.

"What? How can I launch a drone when I'm getting my nuts shot off?" Caleb yelled back.

The buzzing got louder as it passed over the cabin.

Outside, twenty feet above the roof, a quadcopter drone hovered. A cylindrical canister hung beneath it.

The canister began to smoke. Just a little at first, then sparks began dripping from the bottom. Within seconds, a waterfall of sparks and flames poured from the can onto the roof below.

The metallic incendiary splashed onto the cabin's thin metal roof, which stood no chance. At over four-thousand degrees, the molten composition ate through and into the wooden structure below.

Inside, Mason heard clicking on the roof, like rain or hail. He looked up at the plaster ceiling a few feet above his head. Here and there, dark spots started to form on the white plaster. The spots spread, first brown, then black as they grew larger. Each one looked like a burn spot eating through a newspaper, spreading like a puddle of destruction.

Cole and Benito followed Mason's eyes.

Plaster fell from one of the spots, revealing bright orange sparks in the wood above as it began to ignite. The sweet smell of burning chemicals filled the cabin.

"Thermite!" Mason yelled.

Outside, the drone pitched.

The canister ignited before it fully released.

The sound was violent, a sudden, howling *whoosh*, like a forge kicked open. A white-hot spear of molten metal poured down.

The tin roof peeled open like a can of beans under the intense heat.

Thermite punched through, spraying liquid fire across the ceiling in sheets. Pine rafters caught instantly. Fire raced along the roofline, hissing and popping, molten droplets falling like burning rain.

The air turned unbreathable in seconds.

"Get low and move! Out the back," Mason shouted, coughing as smoke filled his lungs.

Benito was already flat on his stomach, boots scraping as he belly-crawled toward the back of the house.

Glass detonated above them. Another gift from the sniper.

Cole stood by the window aiming through his scope, hunting for the sniper.

Mason sucked in a burning breath. "Cole! Move it! Back door's our only—"

Crack!

Suddenly, the smack of a rifle bullet against wood followed by the boom of a rifle carried from the back of the cabin.

Salgado called out in pain.

Salgado had just opened the back door when a round hit him. The impact spun him sideways. He slammed into the doorframe and dropped hard, blood already pouring down his back, soaking his shirt.

"Ah, fuck," he gasped.

Caleb's voice snapped sharp.

"Contact rear!"

Another crack echoed from the tree line.

Caleb was the first to Salgado, so he dragged him by the vest back into the kitchen.

Heat pressed in from above.

Caleb looked up. Black spots were forming on the kitchen ceiling.

"They've got us pinned," Caleb called out.

Mason, Cole, and Benito joined Caleb and the wounded Salgado in the kitchen.

Behind them in the living room, fire crawled down the walls now, licking doorframes.

"This place is coming down," Mason said.

Black smoke roiled down from the ceiling like smog. The air tasted like burnt copper and plastic. Every breath was a fight.

Mason crouched beside the pantry, AR-15 tight in his grip, boots slipping on the scorched linoleum. Flames spidered across the rafters above while the metal roof creaked and snapped as it peeled apart.

Caleb finished dragging Salgado behind the center island, then reached for his medical pack. Blood streamed from Salgado's shoulder in pulses. His teeth clenched, and his eyes fluttered.

"They've got us pinned," Caleb repeated. "Shooters front and rear. Thermite from above. Whole cabin's about to come down."

Mason watched the drywall blister like boiling skin.

Benito lay prone beside the back door, carbine up, breath fast but steady.

Cole crouched near the hallway, smoke curling around his head like steam off a warhorse.

Mason's voice came low, hard.

"We breach the side wall. East side. Right there."

Cole looked up.

"Better hurry."

"Benito, breach it," Mason ordered.

"Ay, Salgado!" Benito yelled. "Where's the breaching charges?"

In pain and barely coherent, Salgado groaned, "Trunk. Bedroom."

Benito was already moving, scrambling down the hall as low as he could. The ceiling was burning everywhere.

Salgado's room was the closest, so he reached the trunk in seconds. Benito opened the metal case, reached in, and pulled out a linear charge.

With the explosive in hand, he dashed back to the kitchen and slapped it against the wall beside the fridge.

Sweat poured down his face.

Mason turned to Caleb. "Get ready to move him."

"I can move," Salgado groaned.

Cole adjusted the sling on his .338.

"Remember the snipers."

A crash shook the house as the ceiling collapsed in the living room. Fire burst through the entryway in a snarling whoosh, licking the hallway carpet.

Mason barked, "Get ready to pop smoke."

Caleb reached into his rig, pulled two M83 TA smoke grenades, thumbed the pins, and waited.

"Charge is set," Benito said.

"Three... Two...Breaching! Breaching! Breaching!"

Benito hit the trigger.

The wall shattered outward in a thunderclap of dust, splinters, and heat. The house shook and groaned.

Caleb lobbed the smoke grenades through the hole in the wall and into the yard. Thick gray smoke blossomed, blanketing the east side of the cabin.

As a team, they moved.

Mason burst through first, his rifle sweeping. The world outside was a blur of grass, dust, and searing heat.

Behind him, Cole was already crawling through the smoke, his .338 dragging behind him, belly pressed to the dirt like a serpent stalking prey. His jaw clenched, eyes locked on the front ditch.

He spotted something.

A flash of reflection.

He stopped crawling and checked the wind.

Flaco's scope lens caught a glint of sunlight through the smoke.

Cole braced for a prone shot.

He counted breaths.

One. Two. Three.

Flaco's head shifted, a clear silhouette.

Cole fired.

Boom!

The shot hit like a freight train. Flaco's skull snapped back, red mist flashing against the grass behind him. His body went slack, face first in the mud.

Cole exhaled.

"Front sniper down," he called out.

Across the driveway, Mason was already moving.

He led the team through the smoke, weaving toward an old barn fifty yards from the cabin. The smoke grenades still hissed behind them.

Bullets snapped past.

"Machine gun! Cover!"

At the front of the white utility truck, Tigre had picked up Joker's M249. He braced it on the hood and started hammering rounds through the smoke.

Orange tracers ripped over their heads, chewing up the brush.

"Keep moving!" Mason barked. "Bound and cover!"

Benito dropped to a knee, fired three quick bursts toward the truck.

Tigre ducked but resumed firing.

Meanwhile, in the woods behind the cabin, Rage lay completely still. His Ghillie suit was covered with mesquite twigs so he blended with the landscape. His rifle sat steady on a bipod, optic trained on the smoke. Through the lens, he watched Mason move, a silhouette flickering in the haze.

He adjusted his aim. Crosshairs centered on Mason's chest.

Clouds of smoke drifted, concealing the men as they moved.

Rage took a deep breath.

Held it.

Mason paused in the open.

Rage lined up the reticle—

Then Mason dropped low, vanishing behind a cattle trough as tracers raced past him.

Rage breathed.

Down by the truck, Tigre cursed, brass raining around his boots. The engine block soaked up most of the return fire, but a few rounds had cracked the windshield.

He replaced the belt, slapped the feed tray closed, yanked the charging handle, and lit up the yard again.

At the barn, Caleb shouldered his rifle and leaned around a corner, trying to get a clean shot on Tigre. His drones were ash, burned in the kitchen fire.

He squeezed off two shots. One pinged the hood, the second snapped by Tigre's head.

Mason flanked right, dove behind an old tractor, then raised his rifle and fired.

One round hit the truck's door. Another hit the mirror.

Tigre flinched. Looked over his shoulder. Flaco was slumped in the ditch, his brains splattered across the road.

He dropped the SAW, jumped into the truck, and slouching low in the seat, fired it up.

The truck peeled out, kicking dust. Tigre floored it, fishtailing down the gravel road.

In the back woods, Rage began cautiously crawling back from the cabin.
His eyes lingered on the smoke drifting from the ruined cabin.
Then, little by little, he vanished into the scrub brush.

36

Chapter 36 – Survivors

Citizens Medical Center, Victoria, Texas, USA

The hospital room was quiet except for the steady rhythm of the monitor.

A soft beep. Pause. Another beep.

Salgado lay propped up in the bed, one arm free, the other immobilized and wrapped tight through the shoulder and across his chest. Fresh bandages showed beneath the hospital gown, clean white already tinted faint pink at the edges.

Mason stood just inside the doorway for a moment before stepping in.

"You look like shit," Salgado said.

Mason pulled a chair over and sat beside the bed.

"And feel even worse," he said.

Salgado gave a small nod. "Good. Means I ain't the only one."

Mason leaned forward, forearms resting on his thighs.

"How you holding up?"

Salgado glanced down at the wrap on his shoulder, then back up.

"Missed everything important," he said. "Still got an arm."

"Yeah," Mason said. "You got lucky."

Salgado studied his face for a second.

"That what we're calling it?"

Mason chuckled.

"We stayed in the fight long enough to get out," he said. "That's what matters."

Salgado shifted slightly in the bed. The movement pulled at the bandage and he winced, jaw tightening.

"Doc says no range of motion for a while," he said. "Gonna feel like hell."

"You'll deal with it," Mason said.

Salgado gave a faint breath through his nose.

"You always this motivating?"

"Only when it counts."

The monitor kept its steady cadence beside them.

Salgado's eyes drifted toward the ceiling for a moment, then back to Mason.

"What happened after?" he asked. "I heard some of it...not all."

"Cole dropped the sniper," he said. "Driver grabbed the gun, tried to hold us. We pushed out the east side, smoked the yard, made the barn, and broke contact."

Salgado nodded once, absorbing it.

"And the cabin?"

"Gone."

A small silence settled between them.

Salgado let out a slow breath.

"Damn. There was some good gear in there."

"All replaceable."

Salgado turned his head just enough to look at him more directly.

"How'd they find us? Trackers?" he asked.

Mason met his eyes.

"We swept the trucks. Nothing," he said.

Salgado held the look.

"It's sure as hell not random."

"No."

"And a daytime assault? Who does that?"

Mason's lips tightened.

"Risky, but not always dumb. They know we have NVGs and train for night ops. If the enemy has better night vision than you, daylight assault can help level the playing field. Plus, nobody expects it. We got lucky we made them on our run. Otherwise, we'd all be French fries."

Salgado nodded.

"We made them, but they made us first. That means nobody at GZD is safe."

Mason nodded.

"Don't worry about that. We already reported to Denver. They're taking steps company-wide to keep everyone safe."

The monitor beeped on.

Salgado studied him for another second.

"You sure you're good, bro?" he asked.

"I'm not the one in the bed," Mason replied.

Salgado laughed.

"Dude, you're impossible. That's not what I asked."

Mason leaned back in the chair, exhaling through his nose.

"I'm good, brother," he said. "I'm good."

The sliding doors whispered open and shut as people moved in and out of the emergency entrance. Late afternoon light washed the concrete in a dull gray, the air thick with heat and the faint smell of antiseptic drifting out from inside.

Mason stood just off to the side of the entrance, one hand resting on his hip, the other hanging loose. His shirt had been swapped out, but dried blood still marked the seam of his sleeve. Dust clung to his boots.

Cole leaned against a concrete column a few yards away, arms folded, eyes moving between the parking lot and the road. Benito sat in the driver's seat of the Suburban parked at the curb, ready to go. Caleb stood near the doors, pacing once, then stopping, then pacing again.

A black Tahoe rolled into the lot and parked behind the Suburban.

The driver's door opened, and Kim Wright stepped out, jacket off, badge clipped at her belt, eyes as focused as a red-tailed hawk's.

She walked straight toward him.

"How is your man?" she asked.

"Stable," Mason said. "Through-and-through. Missed the spine."

Kim nodded once, absorbing it.

"Good," she said. "That could've gone a lot worse."

"It almost did."

She glanced past him toward the doors, then back.

"The rest of your team?"

"Here," Mason said. "Shaken up. Smoke inhalation. No other hits."

"You're lucky," she said.

Mason nodded, his lips tight.

Kim studied his face for a second longer.

"Walk with me," she said.

They moved a few steps away from the entrance, toward the edge of the lot, out of earshot.

Kim stopped and turned to face him.

"What happened out there?" she asked.

"Ambush," Mason said. "Utility truck staged on the road. Three men. One sniper in the ditch, one driving, and one with a SAW. Full auto, the real deal. Another sniper covering the rear. Then a drone overhead with thermite."

Kim's eyes narrowed slightly.

"Thermite?"

"Yeah," Mason said. "A metal powder that burns hot enough to melt steel. Once lit, nothing puts it out. It'll burn underwater. The Ukrainians started dropping it on Russian frontlines a few years ago. They call them 'dragon drones'."

Kim held that for a moment.

"That lines up," she said.

"With what?"

"We pulled something off the drone wreckage," she said. "Not cartel work."

Mason glanced at her.

"What do you mean?"

"Build style. Flight control mods. Wiring. It all points to a Ukrainian unit called the Azov Battalion. They were accused of human rights violations, but now they're part of the Ukrainian military."

Mason looked out across the lot, thinking.

"So, they've got themselves a specialist," he said.

Kim nodded. "That's what it looks like."

Mason exhaled slowly.

"Damn."

Kim waited.

"Machine gun out front to pin us," Mason went on. "Sniper up the road keeps our heads down. Then the drone hits the roof, but not to kill us."

Kim's eyes narrowed.

"To flush you out?" she asked.

Mason nodded.

"Out the back. That's where the real shooter was."

His jaw tightened.

"Salgado got hit the second he cracked the door," he continued. "They were herding us. And if Rage is running this cartel op, who else do you think he'd let take that shot?"

"Only himself," Kim concluded.

"Right. No way he hands off a chance at getting me to someone else," Mason said.

"So, you think it was Rage covering the back?" Kim asked.

Mason nodded.

"I think that was the plan. He was back there waiting, expecting us to come through the back door."

"But you didn't."

"Salgado took the hit for that mistake. After that, we blew the wall."

Kim looked down at the pavement, then back up.

"What happens next time, when they're expecting that?"

Mason stared across the parking lot, his jaw working.

"Next time, luck won't cut it."

37

Chapter 37 – Permission

Zacatecas, Zacatecas State, Mexico

Rage stepped into the Bishop's study.

The cartel boss sat behind his desk, a book open in front of him. He didn't look up.

"El Mano. You are back from Texas," he said.

Rage closed the door behind him.

"It was them," he said. "Green Zone. Mason was there."

The Bishop turned a page.

"And?"

Rage stepped closer.

"They survived," he said. "Barely."

The Bishop looked up.

Rage held his gaze.

"I can take him out," he said. "Pull Green Zone out of Texas."

The Bishop watched him.

"You're certain."

"I've hunted this man for years. I already have it set up," Rage said. "Mason will come home. When he does, I'll be waiting."

A small pause.

"Colorado?"

The Bishop leaned back slightly.

"Yes," Rage replied. "There, I finish it."

The Bishop studied him.

"This is about more than business."

"It is business," Rage said. "Family business. Mine and yours."

Silence stretched.

Then—

"Go," the Bishop said. "Do it."

He lifted a hand.

"But not yet."

Rage's eyes narrowed.

"There's the other matter here at home," the Bishop said. "It won't take long."

Rage gave a faint smile.

"It never does."

The Bishop closed his book.

"Handle that first. Then you have my blessing for Colorado."

38

Chapter 38 – Lines Crossed

Historic Centre, Zacatecas, Mexico

The streets of the old Zacatecas colonial district glowed warmly in the evening light.

Families moved through the plaza beneath strings of lanterns. A guitarist played near the fountain. The smell of grilled corn drifted from the restaurants lining the square.

Octavio walked beside his wife Valeria, while their daughter, Luisa, walked behind with her face glued to her smartphone screen and their young son, Diego, held his father's hand.

Their bodyguards, Ramón and Roberto, followed a few paces behind, scanning the crowd.

Valeria was pointing out a dress in a shop window when the sound of engines rolled down the narrow street.

Two black Range Rovers turned the corner.

Pedestrians stepped aside as the SUVs crept forward like predators stalking into a pasture.

Octavio felt the change in the air immediately. His grip tightened on Diego's hand.

The vehicles stopped beside the curb, and the doors opened.

Three sicarios stepped out, scanning the street with calm, practiced eyes.

Ramón and Roberto backed away.

Then Rage climbed out of the lead Range Rover dressed in black jeans and T-shirt, the metal fingers of his prosthetic hand gleaming faintly in the lantern light.

"Octavio!" he called cheerfully, but the smile on his face didn't reach his eyes.

He walked toward him like a man strolling into a bar.

"Octavio," he repeated warmly. "Enjoying the evening?"

Octavio's brows lowered.

"El Mano," he said flatly. "I thought you were away handling business."

Rage glanced briefly at Valeria and the children.

"I came back to handle some other...business," he replied. "Your family is beautiful."

Valeria's arm slid protectively around their daughter's shoulders.

"Come ride with me," Rage said.

Octavio didn't move.

Rage gestured toward the Range Rovers.

"We need to talk."

Ramón stepped forward slightly.

"Jefe—"

Rage cut him off with a glance.

"Relax."

His smile never changed.

"Your boss is coming with me. You two can take the family home."

The plaza had grown very still.

Octavio looked from Rage to the sicarios around the vehicles.

Then to his own bodyguards.

Finally, Octavio turned to Valeria.

"It's fine," he said quietly.

She searched his face, fear flickering in her eyes.

"We'll take them home, jefe," Ramón said.

Octavio nodded.

He bent and kissed his daughter on the forehead.

"Go with Ramón."

Then he squeezed Valeria's hand once.

"I'll be right behind you."

She started to speak, but after a stern look from Octavio, let it go.

Ramón and Roberto gestured, and Valeria led the children away, casting a worried look over her shoulder.

Octavio could hear his son asking why he wasn't coming with them.

He turned back to Rage.

A sicario opened the passenger door of the Range Rover, and Octavio got in.

The door shut and the convoy rolled forward into the narrow street.

Inside the vehicle, Rage leaned back comfortably in the leather seat.

For a moment he said nothing. Then he sighed.

"You know," he said casually, "I owe you an apology."

Octavio stared straight ahead.

"For what?"

Rage smiled.

"For stepping on your operation."

Octavio turned slowly.

"What did you do?"

Rage tapped the metal fingers of his prosthetic hand against the console.

"The Bishop approved something new."

Octavio waited.

Rage's grin widened.

"An attack on Green Zone Defense. At their home in Denver."

The words hung in the air.

Octavio's cheeks started to turn red.

"This operation is mine," Octavio growled. "You went around me."

Rage chuckled.

"Yours? And here I thought it was the Bishop's."

Octavio stared at him.

"You're making a mistake," he said quietly. "We already have our hands full in Texas. We don't need a two-front war."

Rage looked at him with open amusement.

"Hey, man," Rage exclaimed, "you should be thanking me. While I get Green Zone off your ass, you can finally do what you were told—get TexOil to pay up."

"Who is going to attack Green Zone Defense? They're not mall cops. They are a private army. All our assets we have are already busy."

"Don't you worry about that," Rage replied. "My men are already in place."

Octavio exhaled.

"Of course, they are," he snapped. "You've probably been planning this all along. GZD killed your brother. You want revenge. Now you've convinced the Bishop to allow this—this—*distraction.*"

Rage suddenly went cold. His body relaxed. His eyes lowered.

"You're going to want to be real careful what you say next," he said.

Octavio stared back but said nothing.

The Range Rover turned onto the road leading toward Octavio's neighborhood.

Streetlights flashed across Rage's face.

The convoy rolled to a stop outside Octavio's home.

He stepped out onto the street.

Before closing the door, he leaned down and stared Rage in the eyes.

His voice was calm.

"Don't ever come near my family again."

Rage smiled.

He slammed the door, and the convoy rolled away into the night.

Octavio stood in the quiet street watching the taillights disappear.

He walked into his home.

Valeria was there in the living room holding the kids tightly, staring at him, her face pale.

A tear ran down her cheek.

He walked to her and placed his hand on her head.

He could feel her trembling.

Later that night, Octavio sat in the quiet of his home office holding an encrypted phone.

He stared at it for a long time.

Upstairs, Valeria packed their luggage in a rush.

With a deep sigh, his fingers moved across the screen.

He typed a message quickly.

Rage plans an attack on Mason in Denver. He will not stop.

He pressed send.

For a moment the silence in the room felt suffocating.

A moment later, Octavio stepped off the last stair and into the living room.

Ramón stood near the front window, hands folded in front of him. Roberto leaned against the wall by the kitchen entrance. Both men straightened when they saw him.

"Señor," Ramón said.

Octavio nodded once.

"My wife is upset," he said. "The children, too. We're going to have a quiet night. Just family."

Neither man moved.

Roberto glanced at Ramón.

"You can go," he said. "Take the night."

Ramón's brow tightened slightly.

"*Jefe*...we're assigned to stay."

"Not tonight," Octavio said. "I'm not going anywhere. Neither is my family. We need privacy."

Silence stretched.

Roberto pushed off the wall.

"If that's your order," he said.

"It is."

Ramón studied Octavio for another second, then gave a small nod.

"Of course," he said. "We understand."

Another glance passed between them.

Octavio held their eyes until it broke.

"Have a good night," Ramón added.

"You, too," Octavio said.

They turned and walked out without another word.

The front door closed softly behind them.

Octavio stood there a moment longer, listening.

Then he darted into the house.

He found Valeria in the living room.

"Grab the bags and call your man," he said. "We leave now."

Valeria's eyes widened.

"Should I bring the gun you gave me?" she asked.

Octavio paused.

"No. We can't bring it on the plane."

Twenty minutes later Octavio, Valeria, and the children were loaded into a Ford Explorer driven by an airport fixer named Jorge.

As they rolled through the dark streets toward the airport, Octavio consoled his wife with a hand on her knee, but he couldn't help but check over his shoulder every few minutes.

His wife Valeria clutched their daughter's hand while their young son leaned against the window, half asleep.

The city lights glowed faintly ahead.

"You have the passports?" Jorge asked.

"Yes."

"And the money?"

"Yes."

Jorge nodded.

"You don't have any weapons, do you?"

Octavio's eyes flicked toward him.

"No."

"Not even a pistol?"

"No."

Jorge forced a smile.

"It's just so security doesn't stop us," he said. "Private terminal, but sometimes they get curious."

Octavio said nothing.

The airport appeared ahead.

Rows of lights, hangars, and private jets resting like silver birds in the dark.

"We're almost there," Jorge said as he navigated the airport roads.

He steered toward a side entrance to the private terminal, then kept driving.

Octavio noticed.

"Why didn't you stop at the terminal?"

Jorge smiled.

"Don't worry. My guy inside doesn't like when I park right by the door. Makes it too obvious. I'm going to let you out over here. It looks cooler. No worries."

The SUV slowed as they rounded a line of parked cars.

Then he saw them.

Two black Suburbans parked near the gate.

Several men were standing beside them.

His stomach dropped when he recognized two of them.

Roberto and Ramón.

His own bodyguards.

"What is this—" he started to say.

Valeria looked up.

It was too late.

The Explorer stopped in front of the men.

The door opened.

"You need to come with us," Ramón said calmly.

"Where?" Octavio asked.

"The Bishop wants to see you."

Valeria's grip tightened on his arm.

Octavio forced a smile.

"Of course."

He stepped out of the vehicle.

The night air felt cold.

Roberto opened the back door.

"Your family, too."

Valeria's voice trembled.

"Octavio—"

"It's fine," he said quietly.

He squeezed her hand.

The sicarios guided the family toward a waiting Suburban.

Ramón opened the back door.

Octavio looked over to Valeria.

"Stay calm," he whispered.

They loaded into the vehicle.

"Where are we going now?" his daughter asked.

"Nowhere, my love," Valeria said. "Just a quick meeting with daddy's boss."

Ramón and Roberto climbed in the front seats and the doors slammed.

They started to drive.

Octavio looked at Valeria.

"Just know that I have always loved you," he whispered.

Tears fell down her face as she leaned her forehead into his shoulder.

"I love you, too," she said.

With that, Octavio moved.

He gripped the necklace bearing the obsidian cross Valeria had given him and yanked. The fine chain broke easily.

Razor-sharp cross in hand, Octavio lunged over the seat.

The obsidian edge flashed.

It opened Ramón's throat in a single brutal slash.

Blood sprayed across the door.

The Suburban swerved and slammed into a parked car.

"Run!" Octavio shouted.

He ripped open the rear door.

"Take her!"

Valeria grabbed Luisa's hand and bolted from the vehicle and across the pavement.

Octavio scooped up Diego and ran after them as Roberto yelled from the passenger seat.

Gunfire erupted behind them.

Bullets cracked across the asphalt.

They were twenty yards from the fence.

Fifteen.

Ten—

Then a van screeched to a halt beside them.

The side door flew open.

Sicarios poured out carrying rifles and pistols.

Two of them grabbed his wife and their little girl.

Valeria screamed.

Octavio raced forward, their son in his arms—

A rifle butt slammed into his chest, knocking the wind from him.

He collapsed to the asphalt, Diego clinging to his neck, crying.

The men dragged Valeria and Luisa into the van, hands covering their mouths.

The sicario who had struck Octavio waved the muzzle of his rifle for Octavio to get up.

He looked up at his wife, then down at their son.

The cartel soldier kicked him in the ribs.

"Move it!" he barked.

Finally, little by little, Octavio rose from the ground.

He set Diego down on his feet and held his hand.

The boy was crying.

Valeria and Luisa were huddled together, trembling in fear.

The sicario racked a round into his rifle.

Head down, Octavio stepped forward and climbed into the van with his family. The sicarios kept their guns trained on him the whole time.

The van door slammed shut.

The engine started.

There was no light inside the van.

They drove away in darkness.

39

Chapter 39 – Mother

Historic Centre, Zacatecas, Mexico

Rage returned to his mansion that night.

The gates closed behind the Suburban with a low mechanical hum.

The driver stopped at the front steps.

Rage stepped out without a word and entered alone.

Inside, the air was thick with the scents of perfume and wine.

A champagne bottle sweated onto the marble beneath a crucifix. A woman's heel lay near the stairs.

He moved through the house slowly.

The lower level was empty.

He climbed the stairs.

Her door stood partially open.

He pushed it in.

The room was dim. Curtains drawn. The ceiling fan turned in a slow, lazy circle.

She lay on the bed, one arm hanging off the side, fingers brushing the floor. Her lips were blue.

A mirror lay shattered nearby.

White powder dusted the hardwood.

Rage stepped closer.

Touched her shoulder.

Cold.

He checked her neck.

Nothing.

Behind him, a toilet flushed.

Rage didn't turn.

A young man stumbled out of the bathroom, shirtless, wiping his nose.

He froze.

"Hey— I didn't— she just—"

Rage drew his 1911 smoothly and pointed it at the boy.

He crooked a finger.

"Come here."

The boy didn't move.

He stood there in the doorway, chest heaving, eyes flicking between the gun and the woman on the bed.

"I didn't know," he said. "I swear to God, I didn't know she'd—"

The muzzle stayed fixed, steady as a nail driven into wood.

The boy swallowed.

"She told me she was fine. She always says that. I thought—" He shook his head, words tripping. "It was just coke. She had it already. I didn't bring anything."

Rage watched him.

"I can fix this," he pleaded. "I know people. I can— I can get money. Whatever you need."

The ceiling fan turned overhead, slow and uneven, clicking faintly with each rotation.

Rage's gaze drifted past the boy for a moment, settling on the vanity. A line of powder still cut across the glass. Lipstick rolled on its side, uncapped, staining the marble like a bloody wound.

"How long?" Rage asked.

The boy blinked. "What?"

"How long have you been here?"

"Just—just tonight," he said quickly. "She called me. Said she didn't want to be alone."

Rage studied him another second.

Young. Early twenties. Soft in the face.

The boy's voice dropped.

"I didn't hurt her. I promise."

Rage stepped closer.

The boy stiffened as the gun came with him, the barrel hovering inches from his face now.

Rage's grip tightened around the pistol.

Then—

"I know," he said.

The boy's brow furrowed.

"You... know?"

Rage held his eyes.

The boy suddenly got excited.

"Yeah. Yeah, exactly. You know how she is—"

Rage pressed the muzzle to his forehead.

The boy froze again, breath catching halfway in his chest.

For a moment, neither of them moved.

Then Rage stepped back.

"Turn around."

The boy hesitated, then he started crying.

"*Por favor, señor*... Please...."

Rage whispered.

"Run."

The boy froze.

"What?"

Rage didn't blink.

"Run."

The boy turned his head and stared at him another second.

Then he turned and bolted.

He clipped the doorframe, caught himself, kept going. His feet slammed down the hallway. Down the stairs, a stumble, a hand dragging along the wall to stay upright. Then the front door opened hard, banged against the stop, and the night swallowed him.

Rage stood where he was, listening until the sound was gone.

He holstered the pistol.

The room settled back into stillness.

He turned to the bed.

Up close, her face looked smaller. The sharpness gone. Whatever had animated her—rage, hunger, need—had burned out, leaving something almost fragile behind.

He brushed her hair back from her face. Closed her eyes with his thumb and forefinger.

The ceiling fan clicked overhead.

Footsteps approached in the hallway.

A bodyguard filled the doorway, taking in the scene in a single sweep—the bed, the powder, the stillness.

"What happened?" he asked. "Should we stop the boy?"

Rage didn't look at him.

"No."

The guard shifted, uncertain.

"He saw everything."

"She's been trying to die for fifty years," Rage said. "No point blaming him."

"Ambulance?"

"No."

Rage stood.

"Call the funeral home."

"*Sí, jefe.*"

The guard turned to go.

"Wait."

He stopped.

"Call Arturo in Colorado," Rage said. "Tell him Los Tejanos are taking over. He picks them up, brings them to the house, then he's done."

"*Sí, jefe.*"

The guard disappeared down the hall.

Rage looked back down at his mother's corpse.

"It was always you who abandoned me," he said.

40

Chapter 40 – Fall Back

Motel 6, Victoria, Texas, USA

The room at the Motel 6 in Victoria buzzed with low, constant tension.

Maps were taped across the walls showing county grids, refinery layouts, and satellite overlays marked with grease pencil. Radios hissed and cracked on the table. Laptops cast cold light over tired faces. Empty water bottles and ammo mags sat side by side in the crowded room.

Kim Wright stood in the center, jacket open, sleeves pushed up, a phone still in her hand.

"That's right," she said. "It said, 'Mason in Denver'."

No one spoke.

Mason didn't move. His eyes stayed on the map in front of him, but he wasn't seeing it anymore.

Benito shifted his weight.

Caleb leaned forward over the table, one hand braced against it.

"How old is the message?" he asked.

"A few hours," Kim answered. "We think it's the same source that alerted us to the refinery attack."

Cole straightened.

"Then they're already moving," he said.

"That's our assessment," said Kim.

Mason finally looked up.

"And it used the name 'Rage'?" he asked.

Kim held his gaze.

"Yes."

Silence again.

Benito let out a slow breath through his nose.

"As in a feeling," he said, "or as in—"

"As in the person," Kim cut in.

Mason's jaw tightened.

"There's only one," he said.

Kim nodded.

"That we know of."

Caleb looked between them.

"You're telling us the cartel hired a ghost from our past and pointed him at Mason's house?"

"They don't just hire locals anymore," Kim replied. "They subcontract globally. North Koreans, Eastern Europeans, outlaw bikers. Anyone who can produce results."

"And this one produces results," Caleb said.

Kim didn't disagree.

"There were rumors," she said. "One-handed North American operating in South America. Colombia, Peru, Guatemala. No confirmation. No photos. Just... 'results'."

"How far out?" Cole asked.

Kim didn't hesitate.

"Soon."

"That's not a timeline," Caleb said.

"It's the only one we have," Kim replied. "If the message is recent, assume he's already inbound or staging."

Benito shook his head.

"Denver's a long way from here," he said. "That's not a quick move unless—"

"Unless he's already in the States," Cole finished.

Kim nodded once.

"That's our concern."

Mason stepped back from the table.

"We're leaving," he said. "Pack it up."

Benito looked at Mason.

"You want local law to cover your house?" he asked.

Mason nodded.

"Yes. Call your guys at Jefferson County."

Kim stepped forward.

"I can get Denver PD spun up," she said. "FBI field office, too."

Mason met her eyes.

"You know they won't stop him."

Kim didn't argue.

"They'll slow him down."

Mason nodded once.

"Do it."

"Air or ground?" Cole asked.

"Air," Mason said decisively. "Caleb, get the office to book the soonest flight."

"Don't bother," Kim said. "I've got a plane waiting. Pack it up. Let's go."

41

Chapter 41 – Switchblade

Zacatecas, Zacatecas State, Mexico

Rain hammered the hacienda roof in steady sheets. Water spilled from the tiles in thin waterfalls that pooled across the courtyard below.

Inside, the air smelled of smoke and mezcal.

The Bishop stood near the fire, one hand resting on the stone mantle, watching the flames.

Behind him, boots crossed tile.

Reza Farhadi entered.

He wore a dark overcoat, water beading on the fabric and running off in thin lines as he stepped inside. His eyes moved across the room, taking measure of everything.

Two bodyguards stood along the far wall.

The Bishop didn't turn.

"You are late," he said.

Farhadi stepped closer to the fire.

"The storm delayed the road," he replied, "but not the outcome."

The Bishop reached into the flames with a pair of tongs and shifted the burning stack.

"Outcomes are always delayed," the Bishop said. "That is the nature of men."

Farhadi watched the fire.

"It is the nature of weak men," he said.

The Bishop smiled faintly.

He set the tongs aside and turned.

"You have seen the reports," he said.

Farhadi nodded once.

"Of the failures, yes," Farhadi replied.

The Bishop stepped away from the fire, folding his hands loosely in front of him.

"True, TexOil has proven to be stubborn so far," he said. "But that was expected. We are targeting a *gringo* company in their own land. They feel strong."

Farhadi's eyes shifted to a table near the wall.

He moved to the table.

"When the enemy feels strong, they dismiss small nuisances," Farhadi said. "Your men must strive harder."

Rain filled the silence between them.

The Bishop walked to a cabinet, opened it, and removed two glasses. He poured mezcal and set one on the table beside the maps.

Outside, a faint sound grew behind the rain.

Distant.

Rhythmic.

Thudding.

Rotor blades.

Farhadi heard it first.

His head turned slightly toward the window.

The Bishop followed a moment later.

The sound was still far out. But closing.

"Your people?" Farhadi asked.

The Bishop shook his head.

"No."

The two bodyguards at the wall moved.

One crossed to a laptop, snapping it shut.

The other moved toward a concealed door near the rear of the room, pulling it open to reveal a narrow passage beyond.

The rotor noise grew louder.

Farhadi looked to the Bishop.

"I must leave you, my friend. I cannot be captured here," he said.

"Yes, go!" the Bishop said.

"Come with me," Farhadi said.

The Bishop shook his head.

"I will not run in my own land, from my own home. Let them come."

The rotors were deafening now.

"May God protect you," Farhadi said, and he ducked into the passage.

The storm rolled over the hills like an artillery barrage.

Rain hammered the compound, turning dirt to slurry and rooftops to waterfalls. Lightning flashed beyond the ridgeline, white and distant followed by thunder, low and heavy.

Pierce lay prone on a scrub-covered rise two hundred meters out, eye glued to the night vision scope atop his Sig Sauer M7 rifle.

His men spread out as the Little Birds that had delivered them lifted back into the sky.

Below him, the hacienda spread across the slope.

There was movement everywhere. Lights flashed as men ran and armed silhouettes crossed doorways.

An operator dressed in black dropped a launch tube at his side and flipped the latches.

"No waiting on a Hellfire this time," he said.

Then he opened the case.

Inside, a Switchblade 300 loitering munition sat folded tight, wings tucked, waiting.

He keyed the controller on his wrist, his thumb moving through the startup sequence. A faint electric whine came alive inside the mortar-like tube.

He tilted the tube skyward.

"Send it," said Pierce.

A muted thump and the drone punched out into the night.

Its wings snapped open in the air, then it climbed fast into the storm. The sound vanished almost immediately, swallowed by the wind and rain.

On Pierce's wrist-mounted screen, the camera steadied as the kamikaze-style drone settled into orbit above the hacienda.

He tracked the movement with his thumb, dragging the view across the compound. Heat signatures flared white against gray showing men moving, posted along the walls, a few clustered near the main building.

Pierce watched the feed closely, memorizing positions and counting bodies.

He looked up at the dark compound beyond the wall, then back to the screen.

"Let's go," he said into his headset.

Pierce rose to a crouch.

Black shapes rose from the earth around him. His men, shadows in the rain.

They crossed the two-hundred meters of open ground quickly, boots cutting through mud and standing water as the rain blurred the world.

A cartel guard rounded the corner of the courtyard wall. He spotted the team of CIA tactical operators bearing down, started to yell, then—

Pop! Pop!

Two rounds of subsonic .45 ACP fired from a suppressed Kriss Vector dropped him.

They were close enough to hear men shouting in panicked Spanish within the walled estate.

At the exterior wall, the team stacked up.

Two operators peeled off and dashed forward to set a charge low against a service door. Rain streamed down their sleeves as they worked.

A muted *THUMP.*

The wooden door split inward.

"Go!"

They flowed through the breach, rifles up, lights cutting tight cones through dust and mist.

The room was a storage space packed tightly with crates of ammunition and plastic-wrapped bales of narcotics stacked nearly to the ceiling.

A cartel sentry stood from a chair, confusion forming on his face.

Two suppressed shots.

He dropped where he stood.

"Clear."

Gunfire cracked from the east side of the compound.

"Bravo, contact!" came across comms.

Pierce didn't break stride.

"Keep pushing. Don't stall," he said out loud.

They exited into the courtyard.

Rain poured in sheets, bouncing off stone. Muzzle flashed through the storm as sicarios spilled from a side hall, firing blindly.

Rifles popped in controlled double-taps.

POP! POP!

One down. Two.

Another spun into the fountain, blood turning the water pink.

Pierce's Rattlesnakes moved like machinery—bounding, covering, cutting angles. No wasted rounds. No shouting.

Within seconds, the courtyard belonged to them.

"Alpha, status?"

"West secure. No movement. Bravo's engaged but moving."

Pierce keyed his mic. "Collapse on the main house. Find the target."

Above them, the Switchblade banked.

A cluster of heat signatures broke from a rear outbuilding. Six men, moving fast, rifles up, trying to flank Bravo element.

"Alpha, eyes on rear movement," the drone operator said.

Pierce glanced at the feed.

"Charlie, send it."

"Roger that."

From a support-by-fire position on an incline overlooking the hacienda, an MK48 light machinegun opened fire, the muzzle flash and tracers lighting up the night.

Joining him, an operator opened up with a Milkor M32 six-shot 40mm grenade launcher. In quick succession, he launched all six high explosive rounds from the massive revolver toward the attacking cartel foot soldiers.

The cartel flankers dropped in rapid succession as tracers and shrapnel mowed them down.

Pierce turned back to the hacienda.

"Move."

They rushed to a side door into the main structure.

"Stack up."

Charge set.

Detonation.

The door blew inward.

"Go, go!"

They flooded the entry hall, rifles snapping to targets. Sicarios fired from behind overturned furniture, shouting over each other, rounds tearing into plaster.

Pierce advanced through it.

Two shots. One body down.

A man rushed from the stairs with a machete. He was cut down before closing half the distance.

Another tried to retreat through a side door. He was dropped on the threshold.

The team pushed deeper, step by step, overwhelming resistance with speed and precision.

Up the stairs.

Left.

Right.

Rooms cleared in seconds.

Bodies everywhere.

"Master suite," Pierce said.

He took point.

The door burst open under his boot and four operators flowed into the room.

Inside, kneeling before a blazing fireplace—

The Bishop.

Papers, tapes, and hard drives burned and melted in the fire pit.

The Bishop stood up when they burst in.

The operators spread out, their weapons trained.

The cartel boss reached for a gold 1911 pistol on a side table.

He picked it up, let it hang by his side.

Pierce kept his rifle trained on him.

"Drop it," he said.

The Bishop's eyes never blinked.

"*Muerto o vivo*," Pierce said. "Dead or alive. *¿Entiendes?*"

The Bishop started to raise the pistol.

Pierce's eyes narrowed.

The Bishop faltered.

His arm sagged.

The pistol clattered to the floor.

"On your face. Hands out," Pierce ordered.

The Bishop complied.

Operators moved in fast. They wrenched his arms back and zip-tied him.

"Bishop secured," Pierce radioed. Then, "Bag him. Put out the fire and bag the trash."

An operator jerked the Bishop to his feet and slipped a black bag over his head while two others reached in with their rifle butts and dragged the burning evidence out of the fireplace, scattering it across the floor to extinguish the flames. They quickly gathered the larger bits and pieces and bagged them.

They moved through the house, tearing it apart with disciplined speed.

Office. Bedrooms. They knocked on walls in search of hidden compartments.

One of the operators called out, "Got something."

Pierce entered.

Maps spread across a table. South Texas marked in red grease pencil. Oil infrastructure circled. Notes mostly in Spanish—but one in Farsi.

Another man held up a phone.

"Satellite comms."

Pierce looked at the documents.

"Take everything," he said.

They finished clearing the house.

Pierce keyed his mic.

"Bishop secured. No sign of the Persian."

Outside, the storm was breaking. Rain softened to a steady fall. Bodies lay scattered across the compound, cooling in the mud.

Pierce led his men through the courtyard toward the exfil point, an open patch of dirt just outside the wall.

Two operators led the Bishop by the arms, the black bag over his head dripping with rain.

They could hear helicopter blades faintly in the distance.

"Bird inbound," an operator said to Pierce.

"Get ready to move," Pierce said. "Put the Bishop in the first chopper—"

Suddenly—

"Contact! North side! Multiple vehicles!"

Headlights burst through the darkness beyond the compound as engines roared, tires slipping in the mud.

Pierce's jaw tightened.

"Cavalry's late."

The first truck slammed through the front gate, splintering the wood and metal. The second and third followed close behind, their momentum carrying them deep into the courtyard before they slid to a stop.

Doors flew open. Sicarios poured out of the beds and cabs, rifles up as they fired on the move. Muzzle flashes strobed across the courtyard, cutting through the drizzle in violent bursts of orange light.

"Contact front!" someone shouted.

The men from Bravo squad trotted into the rally point.

"Where's he at?" Bravo leader asked Pierce.

Pierce gestured with his chin toward the Bishop kneeling with a bag over his head.

"Hell yeah," Bravo leader said cheerfully.

Rounds snapped overhead and cracked into the dirt around the landing zone, sending small fountains of debris into the air.

Bravo leader dropped behind a low berm and brought his rifle up.

"Return fire!"

The Rattlesnakes answered immediately, their response controlled and precise. Short bursts and double taps cut into the advancing line, dropping two men near the gate and another as he tried to take cover behind a truck.

The Mk 48 opened up beside them, its deep, sustained roar punching through the storm as tracers stitched across the vehicles and the men using them for cover.

The attackers kept coming.

They pushed through their casualties, using the trucks as moving cover, firing in volume as they closed the distance toward the LZ.

A gunman climbed into the bed of the lead truck and braced himself against the cab, firing aggressively into the Rattlesnakes' position.

The rounds struck closer now, snapping just overhead and slamming into the berm in front of Pierce, forcing the team lower.

The distance was shrinking.

Too fast.

"Taking heavy!" someone called out.

An operator to Pierce's left recoiled as a round struck his plate carrier, the impact knocking him backward into the mud.

"I'm good!" he grunted, rolling back into position and bringing his rifle up again.

Pierce lifted his wrist and brought up the drone feed.

The thermal image snapped into focus.

White shapes flooded through the breach, stacking near the gate and pressing forward in a tight cluster. More heat signatures lingered just beyond the opening.

Pierce dragged his finger across the screen, isolating the densest group of shooters near the gate. He held it there for a moment, watching as more bodies crowded into the same choke point.

Pierce let them take another step forward.

Then another.

"Not today," he said.

He tapped the screen, confirming target.

High overhead, the Switchblade loitering munition rolled into a steep descent, its nose dropping as it locked onto the cluster of heat signatures at the gate.

Pierce kept his eyes on the feed.

The drone fell fast through the rain—

Then struck like a snake bite.

The explosion hit hard, punching through the group at the breach. Bodies lifted and slammed back against the gate and vehicles as fragmentation tore through the group. The lead truck shuddered as the blast ripped across its front end, and the gunman in the bed disappeared in the detonation.

For a brief moment, the incoming fire faltered.

Men hesitated. Some stepped back.

Pierce rose from behind the berm.

"Push fire! Push fire!"

His team came up with him, rifles snapping back onto target as they pressed the advantage. Two more sicarios dropped near the gate, and another turned and ran as the momentum shifted against them.

A few survivors dragged wounded back.

Within moments, the courtyard fell quiet again.

Only rain and smoke remained.

The team held their positions, scanning, breathing hard but controlled.

"LZ is green," Pierce radioed. "Let's roll."

42

Chapter 42 – Dragon

Denver, Colorado, USA

Cold air rushed past the open side door of a helicopter as it lifted off the dark landing strip.

Inside, Sergi sat across from Rage, a hard case between them, his hands resting on its handle.

Rage stared out into the night.

Below them, the ground fell away. Lights scattered across the distance.

"Never been here before," Sergi said.

Rage stared out at the city with hate in his eyes.

Sergi tapped the case.

"Don't worry. We've got him this time."

Rage stared. One hand rested on his knee.

The steel fist caught a faint glint of light as the helicopter banked.

Rage lifted a cell phone and punched a number.

Oso took the call.

"They're setting up," he said into the phone.

He was standing inside the front window of a house, one finger lifting the edge of a blind as he peeked.

Snow drifted down outside, soft and steady, settling over the roofs and lawns of the subdivision.

The home was clean, new, and empty of furniture. Instead, the floor was covered in sleeping bags, food wrappers, and piles of gear. AR-15s and AK-47s leaned in corners. Stacks of magazines lined the walls next to empty ammo boxes.

Oso watched as headlights turned.

Black SUVs. Marked police units followed behind. They parked at the house across the street. Doors opened. Men stepped out. They all wore vests and carried rifles.

He released the blind.

"Cops. Everybody," he explained into the phone.

Behind him, Chino sat at the dining table, a laptop open, cables running into two hard cases on the floor. One lid sat open revealing a drone, its rotors folded tight inside. The faint glow of a spectrum display reflected in his glasses. A series of metal canisters with wires coming out were lined up before him.

"We're going to bomb the po-po today," he said and smiled. He leaned down to snort a line of cocaine before he resumed wiring the explosive devices to the drones.

Tigre stood in the hallway, AR-15 already in his hands, checking the chamber once again out of habit.

Two more Tejanos members joined them. Both were young men who looked fresh out of jail. They sat on the floor casting each other concerned looks.

"*How many?*" Rage asked through the phone.

Oso lifted the blind again.

More vehicles.

"A lot. They're locking it down," Oso said. "Sheriff's. Feds, too."

"*I'm coming,*" Rage said.

Oso straightened.

"How long?"

"*Not long,*" Rage replied. "*Don't do anything until I get there.*"

The call ended.

Oso peeked through the blinds again.

Outside, more vehicles rolled in at the far end of the block.

Tigre moved to the window, taking Oso's place, lifting the blind just enough to see.

"Damn, *carnal*," he said. "This shit is getting wild."

Oso walked to the table and picked up a glass pipe coated in burned drug residue. He lit a small torch and held the flame under the bowl. Then he took a hit of ice—nearly pure crystal meth.

He blew the smoke out, filling the room with a sweet chemical smell.

"Don't sweat it," he said. "El Mano is almost here. We're going to fuck these pussies up for killing the homies."

"Damn right," Tigre growled. "Fuck these Green Zone punks."

Then he walked over to hit the meth pipe.

Outside, the snow fell, blanketing the ground, muting every sound as if the entire neighborhood were holding its breath.

Across the street, Mason's house crawled with men.

Snow fell in a slow, steady curtain, softening the edges of the neighborhood and swallowing sound until the world felt padded and distant. By late evening, a thin white layer had settled across the rooftops and lawns, turning the street into something quiet and almost peaceful.

Stripped of comfort, the two-story home was turning into a fortress.

Furniture had been pushed back to the walls, rugs rolled up, and lamps unplugged. What had been a home was now a defensive position, every room measured, every angle considered.

Rifles rested where family photos had been. Magazines were stacked on the kitchen counter. The air carried the metallic scent of oil and gunmetal, the low murmur of radios, the muted clack of bolts being checked and rechecked.

Outside, the perimeter was set.

Jefferson County Sheriff's cruisers and FBI vehicles blocked the approaches into the subdivision, angled across the roadways at key choke points. Engines idled low, exhaust drifting in pale clouds that blended with the falling snow.

Light bars were dark, the officers relying on night vision and ambient glow for visibility.

In the kitchen, Lisa sat with the baby in her arms, wrapped tightly against the cold. Her face was pale but steady, her eyes tracking Mason as he stepped in.

"They're ready," Kim said gently. She was standing by the back door wearing a bulletproof vest.

Mason nodded.

Lisa stepped closer, adjusting the blanket around the child, then reached up and took Mason's face in her hand. She held it there for a moment.

"Be safe," she said quietly. "It's just a house."

"I will," he answered. "But this ends now."

She nodded.

Outside, a Suburban waited, engine running, two armed agents waiting outside.

The door opened, and Lisa climbed in without looking back. The vehicle pulled away a moment later, taillights fading into the snow-muted dark.

Bud watched the door after it closed, then let out a soft whine.

"They'll be okay, buddy. Now, let's get to work."

Mason moved through the house inspecting positions.

He came across an FBI SWAT agent sitting in a chair behind a dresser he had positioned in front of a living room window overlooking the front yard, his M4 carbine aimed outside.

"Make sure you can cover the right-side approach. If they come from that side, it'll be on you to hold them until the others can redirect," Mason said.

The officer nodded and shifted his chair a few inches over, opening up the angle.

Mason continued his inspection with Bud at his side.

At the back of the house, Benito held position near the door that opened onto the yard. He sat angled in a chair, rifle across his lap, a blanket thrown over his shoulders against the cold seeping through the walls. The blinds were cracked just enough to give him a view of the dark backyard where the snow was collecting in patches.

"All quiet," Benito said as Mason approached.

"The back is the side I don't like the most," Mason replied. "Too many approaches."

Benito smirked faintly.

"Then they'll come from the front."

Mason chuckled.

"Yeah, probably."

Upstairs, "Keep that lane clear," he said, gesturing through the living room toward the front windows. "If they come up the street, I don't want a single blind spot."

A sheriff's deputy with a rifle nodded.

Cole had already settled into his sniper's hide.

Ryan's nursery had been blacked out completely with every light source removed or covered. The curtains were pinned tight, leaving only a narrow slit toward the street. Cole sat behind his rifle, mounted steady, his eye pressed to the optic. Through thermal, the world below was stripped to heat and movement—engine blocks glowing, breath plumes drifting, the faint signatures of men outside holding their posts.

"Front is clear," he said without looking up. "No movement beyond perimeter."

"Copy," Mason replied.

In the game room, Caleb worked over his equipment.

His backpack jammer sat on a reinforced table near the window, a compact but aggressive-looking unit bristling with antennas. Indicator lights pulsed in a slow, steady rhythm. Cables ran to battery backups.

Caleb adjusted a dial, watching the spectrum readout scroll.

"Range is holding," he said to a SWAT sergeant standing nearby. "Half mile, give or take. If anything comes in on a signal, we'll see it and hear it. Just listen for a beep and watch this LED. If it goes from green to flashing red, that's a drone inbound."

Mason stepped in, eyes on the rig.

"You good?"

Caleb nodded.

"Yes. I've got three drones staged outside. One inside the garage door, two under the covered patio outside."

"Stay on it," Mason said. "If they use drones, that's our first problem."

"Won't be our last," Caleb replied.

Mason stepped to a window overlooking the front.

Across the street, the rent house sat dark.

No lights. No movement. Just another quiet home under a layer of snow.

At his side, Bud stood still, ears forward, body tense.

A low growl rumbled in the dog's chest, barely audible.

Mason glanced down at him.

"What is it, boy?"

"Bud onto something?" Caleb asked.

"Hard to say," Mason replied.

"Crazy to think we're back here finishing what was started all those years ago," Caleb said.

"That's right. Finishing," Mason replied.

Caleb turned toward Mason.

"The thing is—"

Boom!

An explosion rocked the neighborhood.

Mason froze, listening.

Down the street, a police cruiser disappeared in a bloom of white and orange light.

The explosion lifted the vehicle off its suspension and slammed it sideways into the curb, metal folding, windows bursting outward in a spray of glittering shards. A half-second later, the siren screamed to life, wild and continuous, its pitch warping through damaged speakers.

"Contact!" someone shouted over the radio.

Then came a rifle crack.

One of the deputies in the backyard jerked, stumbled, and dropped, his silhouette collapsing into the snow.

Another shot followed almost immediately, punching through the windshield of another police unit.

"Sniper! Sniper!" a voice yelled over comms. "West side—west side!"

"Explosion at the front—vehicle hit—"

"Taking fire—unknown direction—"

"Units down at perimeter—"

The voices overlapped, stepping on each other.

Mason grabbed his shotgun and dashed from the room.

Upstairs, Cole shifted behind his rifle, scanning through thermal, but the snow and distance blurred the edges of everything beyond the immediate street.

"I've got heat signatures moving near the downed unit," he said, voice controlled. "But no clear shooter. No muzzle flash."

Another rifle crack split the night.

A round snapped through a side mirror outside, sending it spinning into the snow. Someone shouted, dragging a wounded officer behind the engine block of a cruiser.

"Still taking fire!" the radio barked.

In the game room, Caleb stared at the jammer.

The steady green light flickered—once, twice—then shifted to a rapid pulse of red.

"Oh, shit," he muttered, leaning in.

Mason looked over. "What is it?"

Caleb's fingers moved across the controls, pulling up a spectrum readout that jittered wildly across the display.

"Multiple signals," he said. "They're not holding on one frequency—they're jumping. Fast."

"Can you lock it?"

Caleb shook his head, already adjusting gain and sweep ranges.

"Trying, but the signal, it's— it's dirty. It's like they're—"

The hum reached them then.

Faint at first, barely audible beneath the distant siren and the hiss of falling snow.

Mason picked up a Mossberg 590A1 pump shotgun and looped a bandolier of red 12-gauge shells across his chest.

Outside, the neighborhood still looked the same—snow-covered lawns, dark houses, the soft glow of streetlights diffused through the storm.

Another shot cracked.

Another voice shouted.

And beneath it all, just at the edge of hearing, the mechanical buzz grew louder.

The hum rose above the sirens and rifle cracks, drawing eyes upward.

A dark shape settled over the roofline, steady against the falling snow. Rotors held it in place, the machine hovering with a cold, deliberate precision.

"Caleb," Mason said. "Fix it."

"I'm trying," Caleb said through gritted teeth as he tapped at buttons.

Overhead, the cylinder beneath the drone sparked.

Then it opened.

A stream of white-hot fire poured down onto the roof, thick and blinding, splashing across shingles and vents in a molten cascade. The impact flashed brightly enough to wash the yard in harsh light. Snow hissed to steam. Then the roof caught at once, flame racing along the pitch, finding the seams, biting into the wood.

"Contact overhead!" someone shouted.

Heat pressed down through the ceiling in seconds. The smell of burning insulation and tar filled the house, sharp and choking. Smoke rolled along the upper corners of the rooms, dark and fast, gathering into a low ceiling that dropped with every breath.

Upstairs, Cole shifted behind the rifle as the glow from the roofline bled through the edges of the window frame.

Movement flickered across his scope—figures repositioning, bodies shifting in the open.

The rifle cracked.

One of the agents moving between cover outside snapped backward, collapsing near the front walkway. Another round followed, striking sparks off the hood of a cruiser as a second man dove for cover.

"Sniper still active!" a voice called over comms.

Glass shattered along the side of the house. A round punched through the window and buried itself in drywall, spraying dust across the room. Another followed, tighter, angling through the opening toward the interior.

The fire above them spread with a hungry speed, flame pushing through the attic space and finding new paths downward. A dull crack echoed overhead as rafters gave way, sending a tremor through the ceiling.

Mason moved into the center of the room, eyes tracking the smoke as it thickened.

"Time's up," he said into his mic. "We're not holding this."

Another burst of rounds snapped through the front of the house, stitching across the window frames, forcing the men near the living room to pull back from their positions.

"Rear's covered," Benito called from the back. "No eyes on the sniper. I can't hold it from here."

Mason looked around one last time.

"Everybody move!" he shouted. "Front exit—now!"

Chairs scraped. Boots pounded against the floor. Men grabbed rifles and slung gear as they broke from their positions, moving through the smoke-choked rooms toward the front of the house.

Above them, the roof burned hot and bright, flame cutting through the night as the drone lifted away into the dark.

The front door burst open and cold air rushed in, cutting through the smoke as the first men pushed out into the night.

Snow crunched under boots. Breath plumed white in the glow of burning light behind them. The yard and street beyond flickered between shadow and orange as the roof fire climbed.

Mason came through the doorway with Caleb at his shoulder, shotgun in one hand, eyes already sweeping the street.

"I can't get it...." Caleb was saying as he tapped angrily at the screen.

Once he was outside, he looked up at the dragon drone sitting over Mason's home raining white sparks down.

He reached for the short-barreled shotgun slung over his back, but Mason grabbed his arm.

"No," he said, "it'll crash into a house."

Caleb looked at the drone, then Mason.

"Shit!" he yelled and lowered the shotgun.

As the mix of FBI, sheriff's department, and GZD operators spread out across the yard, Bud's body went rigid. Ears forward. Teeth bared.

A deep bark tore out of him, sharp and violent. He lunged sideways, pulling toward the house across the street.

Mason felt the leash snap tight in his hand.

"Easy—" he started, then followed the line.

The rent house.

A shift behind the front window.

Something shifted behind the glass.

The outline of a figure behind the blinds.

Then a muzzle easing into position.

Mason's voice cut through the chaos.

"Front's hot! House across the street!"

The first men pivoted instantly. They dropped hard behind what cover they could find—engine blocks, trees, the edge of the driveway.

Just then—the window across the street erupted.

Muzzle flashes punched through the blinds in a tight, controlled burst, rounds tearing across the space where the team had been moving a second earlier. Glass shattered outward, spraying into the snow as bullets chewed into the front steps and doorframe.

"Contact front!" someone shouted.

"Multiple shooters!"

Mason moved, dragging Bud back and dropping behind the front corner of the house. He brought the shotgun up and fired toward the window, buckshot punching through what remained of the glass and into the dark interior beyond.

Beside him, rifles answered—short, disciplined bursts that stitched across the facade of the rent house. Sparks jumped from the frame. Wood splintered. The blinds shredded under the impact.

Across the street, the shooters adjusted, firing again from deeper inside, rounds snapping past low over the snow, searching for angles.

Above them, the roof collapsed, red sparks bursting into the snow.

Mason dropped lower, teeth clenched.

The fight across the street held for a few seconds, rifles cracking in tight rhythm as Mason's team pinned the windows of the rent house.

Then the street to the right exploded.

43

Chapter 43 – Collapse

Mason's home, Golden, Colorado, USA

Across the street, Oso leaned into the shattered front window, AR-15 braced against the frame.

He watched as Mason's front door blew open.

Figures spilled out into the snow moving low and fast.

"Now!" Oso barked.

He opened fire.

The rifle bucked against his shoulder, rounds snapping across the yard. Glass and splinters kicked from the doorframe as the first men hit the steps.

Beside him, Tigre stepped into the gap and opened up. Brass clattered across the hardwood floor as the muzzle blasts blew the miniblinds apart.

"Get their ass!" Tigre shouted.

Rounds stitched the front of the house, chewing into siding, forcing the men outside to break and dive for cover.

One of the younger Tejanos—Rafa—leaned too far, firing fast and sloppy. His shots walked high, kicking sparks off the roofline instead of cutting the yard.

"Lower," Oso snapped. "Shoot at them or the ground. Make them stay down."

Behind them there was a sharp metallic click.

Luis stood near the dining table, staring at his rifle.

"Fuck—fuck—"

He yanked the charging handle again and again.

"Clear it!" Tigre shouted without looking back.

"I'm trying!"

The rifle jammed halfway open. Luis smacked it, his hands shaking.

At the table, Chino sat hunched over a controller, eyes locked on the screen.

The faint whine of the FPV drone threaded through the room as it slipped out the open back door and cut around the side of the house.

"Got one up," he said.

He leaned with the controller, like he was riding the drone.

"I see them. They're pinned down on the front corner… hold on…"

Oso kept firing.

"They're not breaking," Tigre said as he reloaded.

"Keep bustin'," Oso replied.

His phone buzzed.

He pulled it free with his support hand, never taking his eye off the fight.

"Yeah?"

Rage's voice came through.

"Time for you to move."

"Yeah," Oso said back.

The line went dead.

Oso stepped back from the window.

"Move!" he barked. "Out the back."

Tigre broke contact immediately, grabbing fresh mags as he moved.

Rafa hesitated, then followed.

Behind them, Luis finally forced the jammed round loose. It clattered to the floor.

He stared at it, then at the door, then hurried after the others.

At the table, Chino didn't look up.

"Give me ten seconds," he said. "I'm bringing it around."

Oso glanced at the screen to see the drone skimming across the snow-covered landscape, cutting toward the front yard from a new angle.

"Let's go!" he said.

Then he moved.

Figures poured out from the rent house's back door moving fast and low, their rifles swinging in all directions.

They cut across the yard, vaulted a waist-high fence, and dropped into the next property without breaking stride. Snow kicked up under their boots, dark shapes flowing through white background.

"Movement!" someone yelled. "Right side—multiple!"

They split as they moved—two cutting along the fence line, another pair angling toward a backyard gate, the rest pressing forward through open grass and narrow side yards. Muzzles flashed as they advanced, short bursts snapping toward the police vehicles and the front of Mason's house.

Rounds slammed into the cruiser nearest the driveway, sparks jumping from the engine block as a deputy huddled behind it returned fire. Another man dragged him back by his vest, both of them slipping in the snow as they fought for position.

From above and behind, the sniper spoke again.

A single crack.

One of the agents shifting between vehicles jerked and dropped, his rifle skidding across the pavement.

Another round struck the edge of the retaining wall, stone chipping outward in a sharp burst.

"He's still got us pinned!" a voice called.

Mason shifted tighter to the corner of the house, tracking the movement across the yards. The attackers kept coming, using fences and parked vehicles as steppingstones, closing distance with each bound.

Then the hum returned.

Higher this time.

An FPV drone skimmed low over the street, cutting between the houses with a fast, erratic motion. It dipped toward the front yard, a small charge dropping and bouncing once before detonating in a sharp blast that kicked snow and dirt into the air.

"Drone!" Caleb shouted from behind cover. "Multiple still up!"

Another streaked overhead.

The burning roof threw wild light across everything, turning the snow into a shifting field of orange and black. Shadows jumped and twisted. Muzzle flashes strobed in rapid bursts, each one carving sharp lines through the storm. Rifle blasts echoed down the streets.

Mason moved along the wall, keeping low, eyes tracking each angle as it opened and closed.

"I'm breaking off," Mason said into the radio. "Pursuing my target."

"Good hunting," Caleb radioed back.

Caleb was hunched behind a stone wall near the driveway, the jammer unit pulled in tight beside him, antennas angled toward the street. The display jittered with overlapping signals, bands sliding and snapping past each other in fast, uneven jumps.

Rounds cracked overhead. Snow kicked up along the edge of the wall. He didn't look up.

"Come on," he muttered, fingers moving across the controls.

Another drone cut low across the yard, banking hard between the vehicles before climbing again, its path jagged, aggressive. A second followed higher, circling with tighter control, holding position as if waiting for a window.

Caleb watched the pattern.

One of them didn't match.

Its signal skipped—not clean, not tight. A slight hesitation in the hop sequence. A fraction late on the shift.

"There you are," he said under his breath.

He adjusted gain and narrowed the sweep, trimming everything else away until the one signal stood out against the noise. It flickered on the edge of the display, unstable, slipping in and out of alignment.

He locked onto it.

The drone jerked in the air.

Outside, the machine dipped unexpectedly, correcting a second later with a sharp climb.

He pushed the signal harder, forcing interference into the control band.

The drone shuddered again—nose dropping, then snapping back up. It yawed left, overcorrected, then steadied just enough to stay airborne.

Across the link, someone fought him.

The response came quick—tightening control, pulling the drone back into line. The signal shifted again, hopping faster, trying to shake him loose.

Caleb stayed on it, riding the change, matching the rhythm as it jumped.

"Not tonight," he said.

He drove the signal deeper, pushing through the noise, forcing the connection to hold.

The drone's path broke again.

This time it didn't recover clean.

It drifted sideways, then snapped forward in a hard surge, caught between two commands, its motors whining under the strain.

Caleb leaned closer to the screen, hands steady now.

"Come on," he said quietly.

Caleb tightened his grip on the controls, eyes locked on the feed. The signal steadied under his hands, the jitter smoothing out as the competing input fell away.

"I've got it," he breathed.

He pushed forward.

The drone dropped hard, nose dipping as it broke from its hover and accelerated low across the street. It skimmed over the tops of the vehicles, cutting through drifting smoke and falling snow, then cleared the far curb and drove west.

"Where's it going?" a nearby deputy asked.

Caleb watched the drone disappear.

"Return to sender."

He tapped the controller until the drone's front-mounted camera feed appeared.

The feed bounced once, then stabilized, the camera snapping into a forward view of the open field beyond the houses. Snow lay thin across the ground, broken by dark patches of dirt and scrub.

The drone zoomed through the night, back to its owner.

A few seconds later, an image appeared of a figure standing near a make-shift control station, cases and antennas half-shielded by a fold-out panel. He was leaning over a controller, then turned to look up.

The drone came in fast.

The man stepped back, hand lifting as if to shield his face.

Caleb drove the nose down.

The frame filled with Sergi's bald head.

He looked into the camera, realization hitting him too late.

Caleb tapped a button.

Then white light.

The detonation punched outward in a tight, violent bloom, throwing dirt, gear, and tissue into the air.

The feed cut to static.

Caleb pulled his hands back from the controls.

"One drone operator's down," he said into the mic.

Just then, another FPV drone zipped overhead.

"At least one more to go," he said.

Benito dropped hard behind the engine block of a cruiser, the metal ringing as rounds punched into the door above him.

"Stay low!" he shouted.

Snow kicked up in bursts across the yard as rounds snapped past, tearing through shrubs and chewing into the siding behind them. The house across the street flashed with muzzle bursts.

Benito leaned out just enough to fire two quick shots then ducked back as bullet fragments exploded off the hood inches from his face.

"Front window, left side!" an agent yelled from somewhere behind him.

"I see it!"

He popped up again, this time longer. Fired three rounds into the window frame. The muzzle inside pulled back.

To his right, a sheriff's deputy fumbled a reload, hands slick with blood.

"Easy," Benito said. "Slow it down."

Another burst ripped across the cruiser. The windshield shattered inward, spraying glass across the dash.

Benito risked another look.

Movement across the street. Shadows pulling away, then snapping back out to fire.

A round cracked past, close enough he felt the heat on his cheek.

He dropped again, breathing hard now.

"We're pinned," the deputy said.

Benito didn't answer.

Every time someone tried to shift, fire followed.

Every angle was covered.

They were stuck.

Across the yard, Mason was down behind the corner of the house, working his own angle. Caleb was beside him, shouting something over the noise, still fighting that jammer.

Another burst erupted from the rent house.

Then the fire from the house stuttered.

Then stopped.

Benito leaned out—

"Hold—" he started—

—and caught it.

A flicker. To the side.

"They're moving," he said.

"What?" the deputy asked.

"They're breaking right!"

Benito stood and fired four rounds across the rent house windows.

There was no response.

"Push it!" Benito barked. "Push it now!"

To his left, two agents rose together, firing in controlled bursts at the rent house.

"They're breaking contact front!" someone called.

Benito didn't wait.

"Move!" he shouted, already up and moving.

He sprinted to the next piece of cover—a retaining wall near the driveway—boots slipping on the snow as rounds snapped past him.

He dropped in, rolled, and came up firing.

"They're not holding it!" the deputy yelled, scrambling up behind him.

"Because they're shifting," Benito said.

Benito keyed his mic.

"Push the house," he sent.

Across the yard, five deputies and agents rose from the snow and moved to cover behind vehicles.

"Jefferson County, cover us!" one man yelled. "SWAT, bound forward,"

"Roger!" came the response.

Two deputies opened fire on the house, shifting fire to put rounds through each window as three FBI SWAT operators charged across the street.

On the other side, they dove into whatever cover they could find—car in a neighboring driveway, a decorative boulder, the street curb.

From their new positions, they fired into the house sending wood splinters flying.

No return fire came.

"Hold your positions," Benito sent.

He watched, waited.

The house was silent.

"SWAT, get ready to take the house," Benito called. "Jefferson County, get ready to cover them, but hold your fire."

Officers reloaded with practiced skill, the click of metal filling the street as magazines were slammed home.

"Move on three," Benito said. "One...Two...Three!"

All three SWAT team members charged across the yard.

The first officer to the front door kicked it on the run, shattering the door jamb.

They burst inside.

"FBI! FBI! Drop your weapons!" they shouted over each other.

They swept the living room, then the downstairs rooms.

Moments later, sheriff's deputies poured in through the front door.

"Cover the rear!"

"Check under the beds!"

"Watch that corner!"

Once the officers had checked the entire house, the lead radioed Benito.

"The house is empty," he said.

The crack of rifles carried across the street, sharp against the snow.

Mason pressed against the corner of the house, breathing steady, eyes moving across the street and back toward the yards behind the line of homes. The angle of the shots settled into place—where they struck, where they missed, how they cut across movement.

He'd let Bud off his leash, but the dog stayed close.

Mason leaned out a fraction, just enough to see past the edge of the wall.

He was watching a house directly behind his and about two-hundred yards across an open field.

Second story. Front side. A narrow window looking down into the yard.

A flash.

Mason pulled back as a round snapped past the corner, chewing into the siding inches from where his head had been.

"Sniper," he said into the mic. "Two-story house, red brick, white trim, two-hundred yards west."

On the roof of Mason's garage, Cole adjusted, shifting the rifle to the new angle. He was laying prone, a white bed sheet over him to blend with the snow.

"I've got it," Cole replied.

His rifle cracked.

Across the field, the window shattered inward, glass spraying into the dark. The thermal image flickered as something inside the room moved fast, dropping out of the line.

Another shot came back almost instantly.

The round punched through the wall near Mason's position, sending splinters across his shoulder as he pulled tighter into cover.

"Still there," he said.

"Roger that," Cole replied flatly.

The next shot came from another window. The shot cut across the yard toward one of the FBI vehicles, forcing two men down behind the engine block.

Cole fired again, tracking the shift, sending a round through the new angle.

"He's moving room to room," Cole said.

"Stay on him," Mason replied.

Another round snapped back in response, tight and fast, forcing Mason down again.

"He really likes you," Cole quipped.

Mason gritted his teeth.

"Oh yeah. If it's who I think it is, we're old buddies."

"You'll have to tell me all about it when this is over," Cole replied.

Mason backed around the corner, out of the line of fire.

"You bet. Can you keep him busy for a minute?"

Cole fired again, then waited to judge the response.

"Yeah," he said, never taking his eye from the scope.

"I'm moving," Mason said.

Then he ran.

44

Chapter 44 – The Chase

Golden, Colorado, USA

Mason cut across backyards, opening gates and climbing fences as he moved house to house.

Rounds still cracked in the distance behind him, but they were thinning.

He hit the back of the target house and crept to the door.

From the front, he heard gunshots, then an engine revving followed by tires squealing as some unseen vehicle raced away.

He listened.

Nothing.

He stepped back once and drove his shoulder into it.

The door blew inward.

Mason entered fast, shotgun up.

He moved through the dining room, then the kitchen.

The living room came into view.

An older couple sat on the couch, wrists bound, duct tape wrapped tight around their mouths. Their eyes were wide and faces pale.

No shooters.

No movement.

Mason moved to them cautiously, then lowered the muzzle.

He ripped the tape from the woman's mouth.

She gasped.

"He—he took our car!" she said immediately. "He just left—he—"

"What make and color?" Mason cut in.

"A—a—Cadillac. Blue!"

Mason drew the Randall knife and sliced the man's bindings with two quick cuts.

"You can cut her loose," Mason said, already turning.

"Hey! What—" the man started to say.

But Mason was back through the door at a run, shotgun in hand.

Bud was there with him as they ran to the front of the house and the street.

The dog sprinted ahead, then stopped halfway across the yard, turned, and barked sharply at Mason. Then he took off again.

Mason frowned, then saw.

A Golden Police Department Ford Explorer sat in the middle of the road as a roadblock just two houses down.

Mason ran after Bud.

The Explorer sat angled across the street, engine still running.

Bud reached it first, then veered around the front.

Mason came around after him—

—and saw the officer.

Young. Down in the street. Still. Blood frozen around him.

Mason didn't slow.

He pulled the door open and slid behind the wheel.

Bud launched into the passenger seat in one motion.

Mason slammed it into gear.

"Only one way out of this neighborhood," he said.

Then he floored it.

The SUV tore down the street, taillights streaking red through the falling snow.

Mason pushed the cruiser hard, engine whining as he closed the distance. Tires hissed over the slick pavement, the rear end stepping loose on a turn before he corrected and drove through it.

The neighborhood blurred past—dark houses, parked cars, fences flashing by in quick succession. The glow of the burning house faded behind them, replaced by the dim wash of streetlights and the pale reflection of snow.

Ahead, he caught sight of the blue Cadillac CT4 just as it cut a hard right.

Mason followed, swinging wide through the turn, the SUV sliding before catching. Bud braced against the seat, his eyes forward.

"Hold on, buddy," Mason said.

The road narrowed as they pushed toward the edge of the subdivision. Houses thinned. Fences gave way to open stretches of ground and patches of scrub dusted in white.

The Cadillac accelerated.

Mason gritted his teeth.

Then—

A flash burst from the driver's side window.

A round slammed into Mason's windshield, spiderwebbing the glass just left of center. He ducked instinctively, one hand tightening on the wheel as the truck drifted toward the shoulder.

Another flash.

Another crack.

The second round punched into the hood, metal snapping upward as the impact hit.

Mason leaned into the wheel, bringing the truck back in line, pushing forward through the fire.

He reached across, grabbed the shotgun from the passenger side, and braced it against the window frame. The truck rocked as he lined it up, closing the gap just enough.

He fired.

The blast roared inside the cab, the recoil driving back into his shoulder as the shot tore downrange toward the blue Cadillac. Pellets sparked off the rear quarter panel, scattering across the metal.

The Cadillac swerved, correcting as it hit a patch of ice.

They broke free of the last row of houses.

But instead of heading straight out of the subdivision and onto the highway, the Cadillac made a screeching turn to the right onto a rough service path, a narrow stretch of packed dirt and snow running along a drainage line at the edge of the development. Low brush and scattered rocks lined both sides.

The Cadillac hit it fast. Its rear tires fishtailed, sliding wide before the driver brought it back under control.

Mason followed without slowing.

The Explorer bounced hard as it left the pavement, suspension jolting over the uneven ground. The wheel kicked in his hands, but he held it, driving straight at the Cadillac as it struggled for traction ahead.

Another flash from the driver's window.

The shot went wide.

Mason closed the last few yards.

He didn't slow.

The truck surged forward and slammed into the rear of the Cadillac.

Metal crushed on impact. The sedan's back end snapped sideways, tires losing grip as it spun across the narrow path. It slid broadside, struck a low embankment, and rolled onto its side in a violent crash of steel and glass.

Mason braked hard, the cruiser skidding to a stop at an angle.

The engine idled rough.

Snow fell around them in a quiet drift as the wreck settled.

The Cadillac lay on its side, engine ticking, a thin plume of steam rising into the falling snow.

Mason shoved the police Explorer's door open and stepped out, boots sinking into the uneven ground. The cold hit hard, cutting through sweat and smoke.

He brought the shotgun up as he moved forward, angling around the front of his truck.

Bud jumped down beside him, landing light, then pacing tight at his flank.

The Cadillac shifted.

A boot struck the shattered window from inside. Glass gave way, and a dark figure forced through the opening, dropping hard into the snow.

"Hey!" Mason yelled down the barrel of his shotgun. "Hands!"

Slowly, the figure turned, and the two men faced each other.

He held out his hands.

"The trouble is, Travis—I only have this one."

Standing just fifteen feet from Rage, Mason braced.

"Rage!" he yelled. "Do it!"

Rage smiled.

"Do what?" he asked. "This?"

In an instant, a burst of flame flared from his steel hand, straight at Mason.

Mason fired at the same instant then dove out of the way.

The flames singed his hair and he could taste the fuel-gel in the air.

The shotgun roared, the blast tearing across the space between them. Rage twisted with the shot, the pellets grazing past as he moved offline.

Mason pumped and fired again, hitting his nemesis fully in the chest.

The blast drove Rage back a step, forcing him to shift his footing on the slick ground.

Mason saw the plate carrier Rage wore under his jacket. He pumped a new shell into the breech and shifted aim.

Too late—

Rage drew a pistol and fired.

The round struck the Explorer behind Mason, metal ringing sharp.

Mason rolled and fired again.

The shotgun bucked.

Rage was already behind the Cadillac's engine block.

Mason rose to one knee and tried to raise the shotgun—but faltered.

He'd fallen on his bad arm, the old shoulder wound aggravated by the very man who'd given it to him. Now, he couldn't raise the shotgun.

"Shit!" Mason cursed.

Bud ran back and forth, barking and growling toward Rage who was turning to fire again from behind the car.

Mason dropped the shotgun, drew his pistol, and dumped the magazine at Rage.

Rage ducked as rounds skipped off the hood and shattered the windshield.

The empty click snapped under Mason's finger as the mag ran dry.

Rage heard it.

He leaped from behind the car and surged forward, closing the distance with sudden speed, his pistol driving up toward Mason's center.

Mason dropped the pistol just in time to catch Rage's wrist as the shot broke, the round tearing off into the sky.

The two of them slammed together, boots sliding in the snow as momentum carried them.

The pistol fired again—wild, off angle—then jammed as the slide caught half out of battery under their struggle.

Mason drove his hurt shoulder into Rage's chest, forcing him back a step, eating the pain, then another. Rage twisted with it, turning his body, trying to free his arm.

The pistol dropped between them.

Both men broke for it.

Mason kicked it away, sending it skidding across the frozen ground.

Rage came up from the motion with his left arm swinging in a tight hook.

The metal fist slammed into Mason's side, driving the air from his lungs and forcing him off balance. Pain flared through his ribs as he staggered a step, boots slipping.

Rage pressed in.

Fast. Controlled. Relentless.

A strike to the head. Mason slipped it. Another to the body. Mason caught it on his forearm, the impact jarring up through his shoulder.

They circled in close, breath heavy, feet searching for traction in the churned snow.

Bud barked once, sharp, stepping forward, then stopping as Mason shifted his stance.

Mason reset his footing and drove back in.

He threw a short, tight punch into Rage's ribs. He felt it land. Rage answered with a quick strike that snapped Mason's head to the side.

They broke apart for a fraction of a second.

Both men reached to their belts at the same time.

Steel flashed into their hands.

Mason's Randall Model 1 fighting knife came free in a smooth pull, the blade catching what little light there was. Across from him, Rage brought up his own blade, a big Bowie.

Snow drifted between them.

"For your brother?" Mason asked.

Rage spit blood into the snow.

"Fuck my brother," he growled—then he lunged.

Meanwhile, back in the neighborhood, snow drifted across the side yard in thin sheets, catching in the dead grass and along the low fence line.

Benito moved through it in short bounds, rifle up, breath steady.

"Left side," he said. "Stay off the street."

Two agents peeled with him, spacing out along the fence, using the dark between houses as cover.

He slowed near the corner of the lot, raising a fist.

The team froze.

Ahead, beyond the next house, a narrow gap opened toward the drainage line. A broken fence. Fresh footprints cut through the snow.

"This way," the agent whispered.

Benito nodded.

"Two go right, hold the flank," he said. "We take the center."

The agents split without another word.

Benito stepped forward.

Slow now.

Measured.

The world tightened. Doorways, fence breaks, shadows between structures.

He eased to the corner of a house and pie'd it.

Slowly.

Nothing.

Then—

Movement.

Low. Fast. Crossing the gap.

Benito snapped the rifle up.

"Contact!"

The first burst cracked through the quiet.

Rounds chewed into the fence post as Tigre dove past the opening, disappearing into the dark on the far side.

Benito dropped behind the corner as rounds snapped past, splintering wood and kicking snow into the air.

"Right side, hold!" he barked into the mic.

Another burst tore across the gap.

Benito leaned out, fired twice, and pulled back.

"They're trying to wrap!" one of the agents called.

He shifted position, sliding along the wall.

"On me," he said.

He moved.

Two steps.

Three—

A shape filled the opening.

Oso.

Big. Solid. Rifle already up.

They saw each other at the same instant.

Both fired.

Muzzles flashed lighting the space between them, rounds snapping past at close range.

Benito dropped hard to a knee, firing at an upward angle.

Oso shifted left, using the fence line for partial cover, then leaned out and fired again.

Benito ducked but slowed his breathing.

Watched the rhythm.

Counted it.

One—

Two—

Oso leaned again.

Benito was already there.

He came up just ahead of the movement and fired.

A round hit Oso center mass.

He staggered but didn't fall as his body armor absorbed the blast.

Oso drove forward anyway, trying to close the distance, bringing his rifle up for another shot.

Benito tracked him.

Two more shots.

The first struck Oso's shoulder, turning him.

The second hit clean in the side of the gang leader's tattooed head.

The rifle dropped from his hands.

For a second, he stayed upright.

Then blood gushed down his side, and his knees gave.

He went down hard into the snow.

The world went quiet in that narrow space.

Benito held his sight picture a moment longer.

Waiting.

Nothing.

He stepped forward carefully, rifle still up.

Oso lay on his side, blood already darkening the snow beneath him.

Still.

Benito exhaled once.

Behind him, boots crunched as the others closed in.

"Clear," one of them said.

He looked once more at Oso, then turned back toward the fight.

Across the open ground, gunfire still cracked.

But it was thinning.

"Follow the others," Benito said.

They moved.

In the open field next to the wrecked Cadillac, Mason and Rage circled each other, blades flashing.

Rage moved first, fast and low, the blade cutting a tight arc toward Mason's ribs.

Mason turned with it, catching the strike on the flat of his Randall. Steel rang sharp in the cold air. The force of it drove through his arm, pain flaring up into his shoulder where the old injury lived.

Rage stayed inside the contact.

A second strike came quick, reversing direction, snapping up toward Mason's throat. Mason leaned back, the blade grazing across the front of his vest.

Then Mason lunged in.

Their bodies slammed together, boots sliding in the churned mix of snow and dirt. Rage twisted with the impact, turning his hips, trying to create space for another cut.

Mason kept it tight.

Short movements. Close control.

He hammered an elbow into Rage's chest, felt the resistance, then brought the Randall back up, driving for the midline.

Rage slipped it.

The blade cut past him, slicing through fabric instead of flesh. He answered with a fast, hooking strike that caught Mason along the side, the edge biting through layers and opening skin beneath.

Heat spread under the cold.

Mason didn't flinch.

He stepped again, boots slipping, catching himself, pressing forward through the uneven footing. The ground shifted under them, dirt and snow mixing into a slick surface that gave way with every step.

Rage circled with it, light on his feet, changing angles, the knife moving constantly, probing, testing for openings.

Another strike came low.

Mason blocked late.

The impact jarred his arm, the damaged shoulder flaring hard, forcing a hitch in his movement. Rage saw it and pressed, driving in with a flurry of short, controlled cuts that forced Mason back a half-step at a time.

Steel flashed between them.

Contact. Break. Contact again.

Mason's back foot slipped.

For a moment his balance went.

Rage drove in to finish it.

Mason caught his sleeve.

He closed both hands on Rage's knife arm, dragging it offline.

Rage staggered forward, off balance, and Mason used the momentum against him. Leaning back, Mason slammed his forehead hard into Rage's face.

The impact shattered Rage's nose but it knocked both men off their feet.

Rage twisted hard, trying to free his arm, his nose scattering blood across the snowy ground.

Mason drove forward, using weight, forcing him down a step, then another.

But the ground dropped slightly under Mason's heel, throwing his balance off just enough.

He lost his grip, and they broke apart.

Both reset in the same instant.

Blades up.

Breath heavy.

Snow falling between them.

Rage lunged again, faster now, driving Mason back with a series of tight, snapping strikes.

One caught Mason across the forearm.

Another glanced off his side.

Mason took it and stepped through.

He let the next strike come.

Turned into it.

He caught Rage's wrist with his left hand, locking it for a fraction of a second—long enough.

The Randall drove forward.

Straight. All the way.

The polished blade punched through cloth and into flesh, burying deep under the ribs.

Rage's body jolted with the impact.

Mason drove it further, closing the distance until they were chest to chest, the knife seated hard.

Rage's breath came out in a rough burst against him.

For a moment, they held there.

Then Mason twisted the knife hard.

Rage cried out, staggered, then dropped to his knees in the snow.

Mason stepped back, breathing heavily, blood dripping bright red from his blade.

The snow kept falling.

Sirens and gunshots carried across the distance.

Mason stood watching the man.

Rage stayed there on his knees, staring into the distance, his mouth trembling.

The cold wind blew across the field, and in the distance, the Rocky Mountains bore witness.

Rage's breath caught and he coughed up blood. A pool was forming in the snow-speckled ground at his knees.

"Finally," he whispered.

Then Rage fell face first into the dirt.

The body lay still in the snow, dark spreading beneath it. Steam rose in thin wisps from the warm blood leaking out.

Mason's chest rose and fell. The Randall hung at his side, its blade dark, catching the distant glow.

Bud moved in beside him.

The dog's sides heaved with quick breaths. He stood close, eyes fixed on the body.

Mason reached down and rested a hand briefly against his neck.

Bud leaned into it for a second, then straightened again.

They turned.

Behind them, the horizon burned.

The neighborhood glowed in uneven orange light where the fire had taken hold, flames pushing up through rooftops and licking into the night. Smoke rolled low and thick, drifting across the streets and into the open ground where they stood.

Voices echoed faintly in the distance, sirens, the occasional crackle of gunfire.

Snow gathered on his shoulders.

On Bud's fur.

On the ground around them.

On Rage's corpse.

He stood there a moment longer, then lowered the knife and let his arm fall still at his side.

45

Chapter 45 – Debrief

Denver, Colorado, USA

The snow stopped sometime before dawn.

Gray slush covered the street, churned with ash and debris. Boot prints cut across it in every direction, layered over tire tracks and frozen runoff from fire hoses. Spent casings lay scattered along the pavement and into the yards, dulled by moisture and half-buried in the slush. Shards of glass caught the early light.

Mason's house stood black and open.

The roof had collapsed inward. Sections of framing jutted at angles where walls had burned through. Smoke drifted up in thin lines from the interior.

Fire hoses lay coiled along the curb. Sheets of ice spread across the asphalt where water had frozen. Red and blue lights flashed across it in broken reflections.

Neighbors gathered along the sidewalks in coats and blankets. Some watched. Some turned away.

Police units blocked the street. Unmarked SUVs sat angled along the curb. Yellow tape stretched across the approaches.

Mason stood near the curb.

A blanket hung loose from his shoulders. His clothes were stiff with sweat, blood, and melted snow. Soot marked his hands and forearms.

Bud pressed against his leg.

Down the block, Caleb sat on the open tailgate of an FBI truck. One arm rested in a sling while a medic tightened a wrap at his shoulder.

"...next time I'll just let them win," Caleb said.

"Try not to move it," the medic replied.

"I'll add it to the list."

Cole stood near a SWAT vehicle, speaking with a supervisor. His rifle leaned against the bumper. His eyes moved across the street, then back again.

Benito leaned against the front of an ambulance, one hand pressed against the bandage under his jacket.

Kim approached from the command vehicles, a folder in her hand. Her breath showed in the cold as she stopped beside Mason.

"It's confirmed," she said.

Mason kept his eyes on the house.

"The funding trail runs through shell companies tied to Tehran. Money was moved through the Virgin Islands and then Panama into Mexico. Enough to cover equipment, training, and logistics."

She held out the folder.

Mason took it and opened it.

Satellite images. Compounds cut into dry ground. Vehicles staged in rows. Heat signatures. Men moving in formation.

He turned a page. Stopped. Closed the folder.

"It's not just about cocaine anymore. The bad guys are pushing into multiple sectors," Kim said. "Energy, shipping, technology."

Mason handed the folder back.

"Where's the Iranian?" he asked.

"Gone," Kim said. "Last seen in Mexico."

Mason nodded once.

A black SUV pulled up near the command post.

Two men stepped out. One in a dark overcoat. The other moved like military, eyes scanning, posture set.

They walked toward Mason and Kim.

"Mr. Mason," the man in the coat said.

Mason turned to face him.

"I'm with the Agency."

Mason nodded.

"We'll need formal statements," she said. "Debriefs, timelines."

Mason nodded.

"You'll also need to make arrangements. We can help."

He looked at his burned-out house.

"I will."

Kim watched him.

"Get out of this cold. Get some rest. Let these people handle it. Okay? We'll talk soon."

He nodded, and Kim stepped back toward the command vehicles.

Mason let the blanket fall from his shoulders into the slush.

He stepped over the curb and walked toward the house.

Bud stayed close at his side.

The crime scene tape sagged. Mason lifted it and passed beneath.

Inside, the air held the smell of burned wood and melted plastic.

Everything was soaked from the fire hoses and covered in black soot.

The front entry stood open. The door was gone. The frame was blackened along the edges.

Ash shifted under his boots as he stepped inside.

The floor dipped where sections had collapsed. Insulation and drywall lay scattered, soaked and freezing.

He paused, then moved forward.

The outline of the living room showed through the damage. The kitchen beyond it. The stairs partially collapsed.

A section of ceiling lay across the center of the room. The remains of furniture stood in dark, twisted shapes.

Mason moved through it, taking it all in.

Bud followed, head low, silent.

He stepped into the hallway.

Studs showed through where walls had burned away. Wiring hung loose.

He moved into the nursery.

The window had blown out. Snow had drifted in along the floor.

A small shape lay near the far wall.

Mason crossed to it and crouched.

A toy. Half-melted. The surface bubbled where the heat had taken it.

He picked it up, turned it once in his hand, then set it back down where it had been.

He stood and looked once around the room.

Then turned and walked back out.

Outside, the sun had risen above the horizon. Light spread across the street, cutting through the smoke.

Mason stepped back onto the curb.

Bud settled at his leg.

A vehicle door closed behind him.

Mason looked.

Pierce walked toward him.

No coat. Just a light jacket. His eyes moved once across the house, then settled on Mason.

"I heard," Pierce said.

Mason nodded.

"You usually do."

Pierce stopped beside him.

They stood facing the house.

"You and your people held up," Pierce said.

"We did."

Pierce glanced down at Bud, then back at the house.

"Looks like he did, too."

"He always does."

Pierce nodded.

"You lose anything inside?" Pierce asked.

Mason kept his eyes forward.

"Nah. Everything that mattered is still here," he said.

Pierce didn't respond. He stood with him, looking at the structure.

"They came hard," Pierce said.

"Yes, they did."

"You handled it the way we would have."

A siren sounded somewhere in the distance, then faded.

"You built something worth breaking," he said.

Mason said nothing.

"That means you're doing something right," Pierce added.

Mason glanced at him once, then back at the house.

"That's all I am," Mason said. "A bad man trying to do something right."

Pierce chuckled and laid a hand on Mason's shoulder.

"That's all any of us are."

Chapter 46 – Ash and Iron Make Steel

March 2026

Houston, Texas, USA

Morning light drifted through the blinds in thin bars and laid across the hardwood floor.

Cardboard boxes sat stacked against the walls of the home, some open, some sealed with shipping tape. A lamp stood in the corner without a shade. The dining table had been assembled but not fully arranged. One chair was still turned upside down against the wall. In the living room, a rolled rug waited beside the couch. The place smelled faintly of fresh paint, cut cardboard, and coffee.

Mason stood in the nursery doorway with a screwdriver in his hand.

The crib frame was together. One rail still needed to be tightened. A mobile lay on the floor beside him, half unwrapped in plastic.

He crouched, set the screw into place, and tightened it down until the wood drew snug and square. He checked it once with both hands, gave it a harder shake, then rose.

Behind him, Lisa stepped into the hall carrying a box marked KITCHEN in black marker.

She wore jeans and a loose shirt with the sleeves pushed up. A strand of hair had slipped free near her face. She shifted the box against her hip and looked past him into the room.

"You get that side finished?" she asked.

Mason nodded.

She walked in and set the box down by the wall.

"We still need pictures," she said.

"We need a lot of stuff."

Lisa nodded.

The baby made a soft sound through the monitor from the next room. Not crying. Just moving in his sleep.

Both of them listened.

The sound stopped.

Lisa looked at Mason.

"This place still doesn't feel like ours yet."

He laid the screwdriver on the dresser.

"It will."

Lisa glanced toward the window. Outside, a live oak spread over the back fence. Sunlight touched the grass. Somewhere beyond their new subdivision, a truck downshifted on the feeder road and kept going.

She folded her arms loosely and looked back at him.

"I'm not talking about the boxes."

Mason met her eyes.

The room held quiet between them.

She looked past him for a moment, toward the hall, toward the rest of the house.

Mason stood still.

Sunlight moved another inch across the floor.

Lisa stepped closer and rested a hand on his forearm.

"I'm here," she said. "I chose this with you. I'm still choosing it. But I need you here too. Not just your body. You."

Mason looked at her hand where it rested on his arm. Then back at her.

"You have me."

She studied his face a moment longer, as if weighing the words against the man standing in front of her.

Then she nodded.

"All right."

He reached past her, picked up the mobile from the floor, and began unwrapping the plastic.

Lisa watched him for a moment.

He fitted the arm into the side of the crib and tightened the fastener.

Bud wandered into the doorway and stood there watching them. He looked from Mason to Lisa, then around the room, then turned and padded back down the hall.

Mason finished with the mobile and set it spinning once with his finger. Small shapes circled above the crib.

Lisa looked up at it and smiled faintly.

"That'll do," she said.

Mason nodded.

She picked up the empty box and started for the door, then paused and looked back at him.

"How long before you head out?"

"Half hour."

She took that in without reaction.

"You eat yet?"

"Coffee."

Lisa gave him a look.

He almost smiled.

"I'll eat at the office."

"At the office," she repeated.

He reached for his boots.

She left the room carrying the box.

Mason stood alone for a moment in the nursery.

The crib sat assembled beneath the window. The mobile turned slowly overhead, catching the light. On the dresser beside him lay a folded blanket, a baby monitor, and a framed photo still wrapped in paper.

He picked up the photo and peeled the paper back.

The glass caught the window light. Him, Lisa, and the baby. Taken before the move. Before the new house. Before the walls here had learned their names.

He set the frame on the dresser.

Then he turned and walked out.

The air outside was already thick with Gulf humidity.

Sunlight lay flat across the neighborhood streets. Lawns shone wet from sprinklers. The sky was pale and wide, the clouds high and thin. Mason backed the truck out of the driveway and turned toward the main road.

Houston spread around him in layers.

Subdivision. Feeder road. Warehouses. Concrete. Billboards. Utility corridors. Tank farms in the distance. Refineries lifting pipe and steel into the sky. Eighteen-wheelers moved in long strings along the highway, hauling pipe, equipment, fuel, and things more expensive than they looked.

He drove south and east, away from the subdivisions and toward the industrial edge.

The new Green Zone Defense headquarters sat outside the city in a strip of low commercial buildings near a rail spur and a pipe yard. The structure was two stories of brick and steel with a warehouse bay attached at one end. The sign over the entrance had been mounted clean and level.

GREEN ZONE DEFENSE – SOUTH

Pickup trucks and SUVs already lined the lot.

A box truck stood with its rear door open. Boxes and furniture were stacked near the entrance. Two movers carried office chairs wrapped in plastic.

Mason parked his truck and got out.

Warm breeze pushed across the lot carrying the smell of cut grass, diesel, and distant refinery stacks.

Caleb stood on a ladder near the corner of the building, one hand resting against the siding while he checked the angle on a mounted camera.

"It's a little low," Caleb muttered without turning. "I told them it was low."

Mason shut the truck door.

"How low?"

"Low enough that some asshole with bolt cutters and ambition could probably dead-space it if he knew what he was doing."

"Then move it."

"That's the plan."

Mason looked toward the roofline. Additional cameras were already mounted along the rear corners, their housings bright and clean. A spool of cable lay on the ground beside the ladder. Caleb climbed down, landed lightly, and rolled his shoulder once.

The sling was gone, but the arm still moved a little stiff.

"You eat?" Caleb asked.

"Not yet."

"There's breakfast tacos in the conference room."

"Cool," Mason said.

He walked toward the entrance.

Inside, the building sounded empty. Footsteps echoed off bare walls. A drill ran somewhere upstairs. The front office held a few desks, a printer, and stacked boxes of files waiting to be shelved. The walls were clean. The floors had been swept but still held streaks from boots and hand trucks.

A woman from the furniture company wheeled a dolly past him with a boxed credenza.

Mason stepped aside and continued deeper into the building.

The main operations room sat in the center of the first floor.

Folding tables had been set up in rows until the permanent furniture arrived. Laptops, radios, spare monitors, and bundled cables covered the surfaces. A large map of South Texas was already fixed to one wall. Another wall held aerial imagery of refinery corridors, pipeline routes, compressor stations, terminals, and offshore support yards linked by colored lines and grease-pencil circles. One corner had been set aside for equipment racks— body armor, helmets, med kits, spare batteries, comms gear.

Cole stood near the far wall with a tape measure in one hand and a grease pencil in the other.

Benito knelt by an open Pelican case, inventorying optics and spare parts.

Salgado stood near the rear exit with two facility diagrams spread on a folding table, comparing door swings and access control points.

They all looked up when Mason came in.

Cole capped the grease pencil.

"Morning."

Mason nodded.

"Morning."

Salgado pointed with a pen at the floor plan.

"The rear roll-up needs a secondary bar inside," he said. "And this side door needs steel around the frame. Right now, somebody could get through it with enough time and a Halligan."

"Do it," Mason said.

Salgado nodded and wrote it down.

Benito lifted a pair of binoculars from the case, checked the glass, and set them aside.

"Internet contractor was here an hour ago," Benito said. "Says we'll have Wi-Fi by tomorrow. Maybe."

"Maybe?"

Benito gave a slight shrug.

"His mouth said tomorrow. His face said maybe."

Caleb came in behind Mason.

"Typical," he said.

Cole turned back to the wall and marked another distance.

The room looked rough half-finished, but alive.

Mason walked to the conference table where a whiteboard had been propped against the wall. Across the top someone had written:

PRIORITIES

- *Facility hardening*
- *Local liaison contacts*
- *Regional site survey schedule*
- *Training block / weekly cadence*
- *Family security protocol*

He stood reading it.

Caleb moved to the taco box, opened it, and handed one over.

Mason took it.

"See?" Caleb said. "Leadership means accepting support."

They ate standing up.

Salgado folded the facility diagram and set it aside.

"We've got enough room out back for a range lane if we berm it right," he said. "Not rifle distance, but enough for pistol, movement, emergency drills."

Benito shut the Pelican case.

"And enough traffic around here that nobody will care if we're moving early."

Mason finished the taco and set the foil down.

He looked around the room again.

Temporary tables. Unpacked gear. Maps pinned to walls.

Satisfied, Mason turned to walk out.

"Follow me," he said.

They did.

Behind the headquarters, the lot opened into a long rectangle of cracked asphalt and packed gravel bordered by chain-link fence. Beyond it sat a drainage ditch, a service road, and a wide strip of industrial land dotted with storage tanks, stacked pipe, and utility poles. In the distance, refinery towers stood against the sky.

The morning had warmed fast. Humidity clung to their skin and sweat came easily.

A shipping container sat near the fence with its doors open. Weight plates, kettlebells, medicine balls, sandbags, and ropes had been stacked inside. Someone had leaned a tractor tire along one wall. A pallet of bottled water sat in the shade beside it.

Benito spread his arms as they stepped outside.

"Home sweet home."

Salgado walked the fence line, checking the gate chain with one hand.

Cole stood still for a moment and looked out across the neighboring parcels, tracing sightlines with his eyes.

Mason stepped into the center of the lot.

The asphalt held old oil stains and patches where the surface had split from heat and settling. A painted stripe from some previous tenant cut across the ground and vanished under gravel.

He looked at the team.

Caleb wore shorts and a shirt already darkening under the arms. Cole wore running shoes and a black tee. Salgado's calves were dusted from the gravel at the rear fence. Benito cracked his neck once and rolled his shoulders.

They looked back at Mason.

He looked from one man to the next.

Denver came back for a second. Explosions. Sand. Smoke.

Then his home in Golden. Fire. Gunshots. Rage dying in the field.

He stood in Houston now with the Gulf air on his skin and a new headquarters at his back.

His face was stone. He set his truck keys on the Conex ledge and stripped off his watch.

"We start now," he said.

No one answered.

"Road loop," he said. "Two miles. Then sprints."

Caleb took a deep breath.

"You know technically I'm not part of this team. I am going back to Denver—"

Mason cast him a look, and Caleb hushed.

Cole stretched his quads.

Salgado shut the shipping container doors and snapped a padlock through the hasp.

Mason looked at them one last time.

"From now on, all we do is train," he said.

Then he took off jogging.

The gate clanged open automatically. Gravel crunched underfoot. The team fell in behind him without a word.

They hit the service road together and turned south.

Mason took the lead.

His boots struck the pavement in a clean rhythm. Heat rose off the road in faint waves. The old injury in his right arm tightened as the stride settled in, the shoulder pulling first, then loosening by degrees as the blood moved.

He kept going.

Behind him, he heard the others spread into their natural places.

Cole closest. Silent. Measured.

Salgado breathing through his nose, efficient and controlled.

Benito heavier through the first stretch, then smoothing out.

Caleb somewhere back and left.

The refinery towers rose higher as they moved along the road, pipe racks and storage tanks catching the sun. A flatbed truck passed in the opposite lane and pushed a gust of hot diesel exhaust across them.

They ran past a fenced yard stacked with casing pipe, a welding shop with the doors open, and a drainage ditch full of green water and beer cans.

A gray pitbull barked behind a fence and threw itself against the chain link as they passed.

No one broke stride.

After half a mile, Caleb's voice came from behind.

"This is a terrible neighborhood for leisure fitness."

Benito answered between breaths.

"You're the boss. You could always stop."

"And let old age win? Never."

Mason said nothing.

He kept the pace.

They reached the end of the service road where it met a wider frontage road running parallel to the highway. Trucks roared past in both directions. The morning sun flashed from chrome and windshields. Mason touched the corner post at the turn and kept running east.

The team followed.

Sweat ran down his spine now. His shirt stuck between the shoulder blades.

The frontage road bent around a tract of undeveloped land where scrub and tall grass pushed up against a berm. Beyond it, a new warehouse shell was going up—red iron framing, cranes, lift trucks, men in hard hats moving like small figures under the structure.

Caleb grunted as he came through the pivot.

"You know what this office needs?"

Mason kept running.

"A coffee machine that can survive a hostile breach."

Benito laughed.

"Do you ever think about what you're going to say?" he asked.

"Nope," Caleb said. "All I think about is how much I love you guys."

Later that afternoon, Mason drove north out of the city. Traffic thinned as concrete gave way to two-lane blacktop lined with pine and oak.

The air shifted to less diesel exhaust and more cow manure and pine needles. Water sat in the ditches from a recent rain. The sky opened blue above the tree line.

He turned onto a narrow county road, his tires kicking up dust.

The mailbox came up on the right, leaning, the numbers faded. Gravel stretched back through the trees. The house sat at the end of the road.

One story. Weathered siding. The porch sagged a little. A metal chair sat by the door, the cushion sun-bleached and flattened. Wind chimes hung crooked and clinked softly.

An old white eighteen-wheeler was still parked off to the side. Rust streaked the seams and dust filmed the glass.

Mason shut off the engine and stepped out.

Gravel crunched under his boots.

He walked around to the back. The screen door creaked when he opened it. The main door gave with a shove.

Inside, the air was stale.

Cigarette smoke permeated the walls. Old coffee lingered. Something medicinal drifted beneath it. The curtains were half drawn, and dust particles drifted in the light.

The television murmured low.

His father sat in a recliner facing it.

The chair was worn into him. One armrest was darkened from years of use. An oxygen tank stood beside it, hose running up under his nose. The line shifted with each breath.

He looked smaller.

The old man kept his eyes on the screen a moment longer, then shifted them over.

"Took you long enough."

Mason stepped in.

"I came as soon as I got back."

"Houston ain't that far."

The old man looked him over.

"You look like hell."

"I feel great," Mason replied.

"Bullshit."

The oxygen line hissed softly.

On the TV, jets cut across a dark sky. Flashes on the horizon.

"—joint strikes conducted by United States and Israeli forces overnight targeting Iranian military infrastructure—"

Mason glanced at it.

His father followed.

"The war machine never slows down," he said.

"No, it doesn't."

He shifted in the chair, a tight movement.

"Doctors want me to quit smoking."

Mason looked at the ashtray.

Two cigarette butts. One still fresh.

"They've been saying that."

"Yeah. They say a lot of shit."

A cough hit him, short and sharp. It folded him forward. The oxygen line pulled tight.

Mason stepped in and caught the tank before it tipped.

The old man waved him off once it passed.

"I got it."

Mason let go.

His father leaned back, breathing through the tube.

The TV rolled to another angle, smoke, vehicles burning, a reporter talking over it.

Mason sat in the chair across from him.

It creaked under his weight.

"You still running that Green Zone outfit?" his father asked.

"Yeah."

"Private security?"

"More or less."

A small nod.

"Figures."

The old man watched the screen.

"You got a son now I heard."

"Yeah."

Another nod.

"Be a shame if I never meet him."

The oxygen tank clicked softly.

"Sure thing," Mason said.

They sat in silence for a while.

"You should've come sooner," his father said.

Mason held his eyes.

"I'm here now. Probably for good."

The old man looked at him a long moment.

Then nodded once.

"Yeah."

The TV filled the room.

Voices. Headlines. War somewhere else.

Outside, he wind chimes jingled on the porch.

Mason sat in the chair.

Across from him, his father rested back, breathing steadily through the line.

Light from the windows moved across the room as the afternoon wore on.

THE END

Afterword

Thank you so much for reading this book! It is my sincere pleasure to share my thoughts with you.

I hope you will take a moment to leave this book a review on Amazon. Reviews are crucial for new authors.

Also, please visit my website rexhollowaywriter.com to keep up with my latest plans and maybe read a blog post or two.

About the Author

Rex Holloway writes crime thrillers shaped by a life that has seen both darkness and redemption.

His Mason Series (*The Wolf and the Lion*, *Gladiator Farm*, *A Fire Devours*, and the upcoming *Jaguar Hunting*) plunges readers into a brutal world of outlaw bikers, crime syndicates, cartel violence, and elite security operators. Known for gritty realism and relentless pacing, Holloway's stories explore the thin line between justice and vengeance, loyalty and betrayal, survival and faith.

Before becoming an author and entrepreneur, Holloway lived a life far removed from the world of publishing. As a young man he became involved in gangs and the outlaw lifestyle that surrounds them. Those choices eventually led to prison, where he spent years in solitary confinement. It was during that time that he rebuilt his life through discipline, faith, and an unrelenting commitment to change.

After his release, Holloway went on to build successful businesses and begin writing the stories that had been forming in his mind for years. Today he writes stories about violence, consequence, and redemption for crime thriller readers who crave authenticity.

When he's not writing, he lifts weights, draws portraits, and spends time with his wife.

You can connect with me on:

🌐 https://rexhollowaywriter.com

Also by Rex Holloway

The Wolf and the Lion: Mason Origins Book One

In a gripping tale of crime, redemption, and the search for meaning, a disillusioned war veteran named Mason, working for a cannabis security company in Colorado, and a ruthless Canadian outlaw biker gang known as the Dead Wolves MC, entangled in a deadly conspiracy led by a cunning mastermind, ultimately confront their inner demons and the consequences of their choices as they collide in a violent and fateful showdown.

Galdiator Farm: Mason Origins Book Two

Zane, a young, fame-hungry influencer boxer is seduced into a Houston crime empire rooted in prison violence, while Mason, now sober, must rescue him from a world that feeds men to hogs and brokers death through sports and fentanyl.

Executive Powerbuilding

In a world engineered for comfort and excess, modern professionals have become biologically mismatched to their environment—trading strength, resilience, and mental clarity for convenience and decline. *Executive Powerbuilding* equips readers with a top-down system to reclaim control, combining decades of real-world training insight into simple, actionable strategies for building muscle, optimizing nutrition, and operating their body like a high-performance enterprise.

www.ingramcontent.com/pod-product-compliance
Lightning Source LLC
Chambersburg PA
CBHW070851160726
48004CB00003B/1014